«Out of
the Hive»

« Out of the Hive »

based on the television stories

OUT OF THE HIVE

and

ASSASSINS INC.

Paul Leonard

First published in Great Britain in 1996 by
Virgin Books
an imprint of Virgin Publishing Ltd
332 Ladbroke Grove
London W10 5AH

BUGS the television series is produced by
Carnival Films Ltd and broadcast in the UK by BBC1

Text copyright © Paul Leonard 1996
adapted from screenplays by Duncan Gould

Cover photographs © Carnival (Film & Theatre) Ltd, 1995

ISBN 0 753 50015 9

Typeset by Galleon Typesetting, Ipswich
Printed and bound in Great Britain by
BPC Paperbacks Ltd, Aylesbury

for Shelly

with thanks for the tea and sympathy

Acknowledgements

Thanks to Jim Mortimore (as usual) – humungous amounts of text editing, pertinent observations (some of them even printable), etc. Also Bob O'Brien, for reading it and enjoying it and making many useful suggestions, and to his mum Lyn for lasagne and apple pie (yum, yum).

My mother should get a mention for loan of telly, and the videos she would have loaned if she hadn't wiped them (you're forgiven).

Thanks also, of course, to all at BFW – Mark, Nick, Chris, Simon and George – for moral support and inter-writer chats, and all at Bristol SF Group for frenzied appreciation (OK, well, not *that* frenzied, but thanks for the mineral water, lads).

And finally – yes, this is the end – thanks to all at BT for a grand goodbye. Yes, I really am making my living out of this stuff now! Oh, to be a freelance . . .

« One »

Stupid decision.

Ballantyne looked at his watch, then out of the reinforced windscreen of the van.

Grey sky. Green grass. Black tarmac. The white target markings of the helipad. In the distance, the main road, cars moving. But nothing moved in the sky. Not so much as a starling, let alone a helicopter.

He wasn't going to turn up.

Stupid decision, to use a freelance pilot in a situation like this. Dent ought to have his head examined. What was wrong with using the Air Contingency people?

No doubt they were less cost-effective, thought Ballantyne sourly.

But a freelance! He could have been bribed. Anything. He could be working for anyone. He could have boasted to his mates in the pub last night, 'I'm on a top secret mission tomorrow.' No use observing radio silence then.

Dent. Idiot.

And SACROS . . .

Ballantyne glanced over his shoulder at the steel panelling that divided the driver's compartment from

1

the rear of the van, where SACROS was stowed, guarded by two White Line Security men. Why the van? he'd asked Dent. Why the trip to the helipad, more than twenty miles from the factory? And the man had waffled on about the possible security risk of an outside pilot knowing the location of both the factory and the Hive.

As if it wasn't a security risk for an outside pilot to know *either* location. As if it wasn't a security risk for Ballantyne to be sitting in a van in the middle of nowhere with two unarmed security men and the most dangerous piece of equipment invented since the last generation of nuclear missiles, waiting for a freelance pilot who might or might not turn up.

Ballantyne checked his watch again. Thirteen minutes late. He looked at the driver sitting next to him.

'Two more minutes,' he said. 'Then we go back to the factory.'

'Whatever you say.' The voice was muffled by the mouthpiece of the padded white helmet. The driver hadn't spoken much on the way out. He wasn't particularly young. Neither were the guards in the back. And of course they weren't armed with anything heavier than a truncheon.

No doubt White Line were 'cost effective', too.

Dent. Idiot. Stupid *old* idiot. But he was the boss, and there wasn't anything you could do about that.

'There,' said the driver suddenly. 'Is that it?'

Ballantyne jumped, unconsciously reached for the gun in its shoulder holster beneath his padded jacket. Then he saw the moving speck above the hills.

Yes. That had to be it.

'Go!' he said.

The engine started. The van began to move across the concrete apron. The dot grew, became the unmistakable shape of a helicopter. It was flying low – too low – skimming across the fields as if the pilot were trying to collect bugs from the grass.

Stupid, thought Ballantyne again. Not just a cheap pilot, a stupid pilot. Trying to impress.

The helicopter vanished overhead at the same moment as Ballantyne became aware of the roar of its engine and the clatter of blades. The sound was muffled by the van's armour plating but still loud enough.

The driver slewed the van around, stopped suddenly. More suddenly than Ballantyne would have liked. He thought of SACROS in the back.

'Be careful!' he said to the driver. 'We're supposed to be delivering SACROS, not smashing it up.'

He didn't like to think about what would happen if SACROS got damaged.

'All right.' The man was pulling on the handbrake, stopping the engine. 'I'll just stay here then.'

Ballantyne cursed under his breath, opened the door, and quickly jumped out.

Cold air whirled around him, full of grit and dust raised by the downwash of the chopper. The roar of the engine, the clatter of blades, were almost deafening. Ballantyne screwed up his eyes against the dust and hurried around the side of the van.

He saw the chopper landing, bang on target in the middle of the helipad, and gave a thumbs-up to the pilot. After all, he *had* arrived, even if he was fifteen minutes late. Even if he was a show-off. Even if his helicopter was painted in candy striped fluorescent blue and yellow, with the words ED'S HELIS sprayed in purple along the tail as a final touch.

Well, hope for the best.

Ballantyne looked around, saw nothing moving on the concrete apron. Satisfied, he thumped on the back door of the van. A hatch sprang open, revealing a cluster of flashing red and green lights mounted on a rectangular panel. Ballantyne leaned over the panel and pushed in some of the lights, a seemingly random zig-zag pattern.

The lights went out. Ballantyne waited.

When he heard the thud of the latches releasing, he opened the door from the outside. The younger of the two White Line guards handed SACROS down to him. He quickly checked the unit, the armoured casing with the yellow and black labels, the strobing orange warning lights mounted around the seal.

So far, so good.

Ballantyne gave a last glance around the helipad, checking for any sign of an unwanted onlooker. He saw a single bird, big and black, standing on the edge of the concrete where it joined the grass, staring at the chopper as if mesmerised.

Nothing else.

Good.

He hunched himself up against the grit and the noise, started walking towards the chopper. Then allowed his impatience to accelerate him into a run. The guards followed.

Ballantyne thought: a lot of use they'd be, unarmed, if there was anybody here who really wanted to take SACROS away from us.

The helicopter door swung open as he approached. 'Mr Ballantyne!' shouted the pilot, all broad grin and Australian accent, as if they were old buddies. He was wearing a leather flight jacket and a black balaclava helmet, pulled down so that any hairline he might have was invisible.

Definitely a cheap option.

Ballantyne couldn't help it. A fluorescent helicopter, and now this. He shouted. 'What kept you?'

'Yeah, right,' shouted the pilot, in the same irritatingly relaxed drawl. 'I know you Civil Servants are clock watchers but I can't beat a thirty knot head wind.' He glanced at SACROS, which Ballantyne had propped between his body and the frame of the chopper. 'Is that it?'

'Don't look so disappointed,' said Ballantyne dryly.

'I thought this one was high security,' complained the pilot.

'It is,' said Ballantyne. He wondered if the man really had boasted in the pub last night that he was going to be flying a Top Secret load. He looked capable of being just that stupid.

He met the pilot's eyes, spoke slowly, emphatically. 'If this falls into the wrong hands –'

'– it'll be the end of civilisation as we know it, yeah.'

Ballantyne grinned tightly. 'Maybe,' he said.

A welcome note of sobriety crept into the man's face, but he kept up the banter nonetheless. 'People are always so melodramatic.'

After that, thankfully, he shut up.

Ballantyne stowed SACROS behind the seat, then got in next to the pilot. The chopper throttled up and the ground fell away. Ballantyne had a glimpse of the two White Line men jumping back into the van, then the pick-up point was behind them and green fields were scudding beneath, too close for Ballantyne's liking. He noticed a purple stuffed dinosaur hanging from a hook on one of the cockpit struts, perilously near the controls. He watched it swaying, its big yellow eyes rolling and winking.

'So,' said the pilot suddenly. 'Now can you tell me where I'm meant to drop this thing?'

'The Hive,' replied Ballantyne, without explanation.

'The what?'

Ballantyne glanced at the man. 'Government listening agency.'

'Never heard of it.'

'You're not supposed to.' Ballantyne risked the ghost of a smile. 'It's secret.'

The pilot gave him an oh-yeah? glance and said, 'Well you'd better tell me where it is pretty soon. Unless you want to fly round in circles until we run out of fuel.'

OK, thought Ballantyne irritably. Love-thirty. He rather resented the fact that he'd let himself be drawn into the man's verbal games at all. Flying a piece of top security electronics across half the country was hardly the occasion for macho one-upmanship and office banter. But then, he supposed, this man did something pretty exciting every day and thought it was all part of the fun. He glanced at the Australian's relaxed profile and felt an obscure pang of envy.

A shadow moved behind the pilot, outside the canopy, and, as Ballantyne realised what it was, he felt something else: fear.

The helicopter was black, with a yellow stripe down the side. A white searchlight glared in its belly, bright even in the daylight. A door at the side was open, and there was a man crouching there, gesturing fiercely at the ground. Black flight jacket, black helmet, black glasses covering his eyes.

There was a machine pistol crooked against his shoulder, pointing straight at Ballantyne's head.

The pilot had seen it. 'I think your secret's out, sunshine.'

Even through the cold buzz of panic that was beginning to grip him, Ballantyne had to admire the pilot's unflappable humour. 'What do they want us to do?' Ballantyne asked, though the answer was obvious enough.

'I think they want us to land.'

The gunman was repeating his thumbs-down gesture. Ballantyne clenched his jaw, glanced at SACROS stowed behind him and, keeping his voice as firm as he could, he said, 'We can't.'

There was a sudden patter of sound which, after an instant's incomprehension, Ballantyne recognised as gunfire.

'Lose them,' he said, the panic rising in his voice.

The pilot glanced at him. Didn't nod. But Ballantyne knew the man had got the message when his stomach sank down into his boots, and the black helicopter seemed to fall out of the sky. Their own chopper swerved violently. For a moment, it was all Ballantyne could do to hold on to his seat. He managed to check on SACROS, saw it safe in its restraining clasps. Grey sky whirled to his left, brown land to his right. Then they were flying upright again, brown moorland below, following the course of a clear grey stream. Far too fast, far too low, sheep fleeing in panic.

The black helicopter was still behind them. And ahead was the sheer concrete wall of a dam.

Ballantyne felt the panic rise again. His stomach lurched as the chopper soared over the top of the dam and out over the lake behind it, but he didn't need to look round to see that it hadn't been good enough. The gunman was still in the doorway. Ballantyne could see the muzzle flashes as the gun fired, the black-gloved hand gesturing them down. Below, the lake was gone, replaced by woodland.

'Boy, I really think they want us to land,' commented the pilot.

'Why can't we lose them?' Ballantyne made no attempt to conceal the frustration in his voice.

The pilot didn't take his eyes off the trees below as he said, 'I'm trying, but I'm afraid they've got a little more horsepower than we have.' Even he was beginning to sound worried. Oddly, this had the effect of making Ballantyne feel better. At least the man was human.

Trees lurched below as the chopper swung to one side then the other. Standard, basic, evasive tactics. Ballantyne found himself wondering if the man was Air Force trained.

'Where the hell are they?' shouted the pilot suddenly.

He sounded as panicky as Ballantyne had a moment ago, and Ballantyne realised it was his turn to be reassuring. He looked round, saw the twin yellow nose lights of the enemy, the searchlight below them, the whole cluster almost hidden by the tail of their own machine. 'All right,' he said, 'they're behind us. Seven o'clock high.'

The pilot calmed instantly. 'OK. I'll just –'

Suddenly, there was a railway line below them. Again, they were very low. Ballantyne looked at the embankment, the branches of the trees reaching dangerously near to the rotor blades, and realised that the pilot had found a way of keeping the opposition at bay. Extra horsepower meant bigger rotors. They were out of it.

But not for long. The embankments vanished, were replaced by an iron, arched bridge. The black chopper was on the other side. They flew along close to the arches, making the best of the cover.

The gunman fired, again and again. Bullets ricocheted off the metal. But Ballantyne noticed that as soon as this happened, the gunman adjusted his aim, firing under the bridge.

'I don't think they're trying to hit us,' he said. 'They're deliberately aiming low.'

'They're after your device. They're trying to force us down, but in one piece. They don't want to destroy it.' The pilot said the last sentence slowly and clearly, as if for his own reassurance.

Never mind your neck, thought Ballantyne. There's more at stake than that.

'They mustn't get their hands on it,' he said.

This time, to his surprise, the firmness in his voice wasn't at all forced.

The pilot glanced at him, looked ahead for a moment, then said, 'Hang on to your hat, Mr Ballantyne.'

The chopper swooped. Ballantyne saw the open water of the estuary, the two bridges, road and rail, crossing it. The water got closer, the masts of yachts bobbed about ahead of them. The helicopter bounced and swerved, dodging the masts. Ballantyne saw the black chopper racing ahead, unable to follow them through the obstacles.

But again, they couldn't stay in cover for long. The water got closer still, and Ballantyne realised that they were going to go under the bridges. He held his breath.

Iron overhead. Concrete, frighteningly close.

Then open water.

'They still there?' asked the pilot after a moment.

'Yeah. They're coming up now,' said Ballantyne. A burst of gunfire underscored his words.

'Damn.'

Ballantyne wondered if that single swear word meant that they'd run out of options. The cliffs and rocks of the upper estuary approached. There was another patter of gunfire.

Ballantyne reached for the gun under his coat, then hesitated. He would have to open the door to fire. He might fall out. SACROS might fall out. The helicopter might lose stability. Anything could happen.

He looked at the cliffs, approaching fast now – the grey shingle of a beach, waves breaking – then shook his head suddenly. He had no time to look at the scenery, he had to do something.

'Want to return fire?' asked the pilot suddenly, glancing across at him. 'I've found that useful in the past.' He indicated a small hole in the canopy. It was

9

barely big enough for the barrel of the gun, but Ballantyne knew that it was going to have to do. He pushed the gun through and aimed as best he could.

It wasn't like a firing range. The targets there were cardboard, man-shaped, and didn't move. This one jigged about wildly and, worse, he couldn't aim the gun properly. The bullet went wild, and the recoil would have knocked him out of his seat if the restraining straps hadn't held him. He squinted and tried again. This time he couldn't even guess where the bullet had gone.

Another patter of automatic fire came back in response. Ballantyne was sure he could hear the bullets whistling under the fuselage. He cursed.

A shadow ahead.

He looked, saw a huge, tooth-shaped rock rearing out of the water.

'Watch out for that rock!' he yelled, but it was too late, surely too late. He could see tufts of grass growing on the grey stone, a patch of brown lichen.

Stupid decision, he thought. Cheap pilot. And now I'm going to die.

Then there was only water ahead, the grey beach below.

'What rock?' said the pilot scornfully.

Ballantyne looked behind, saw the jagged mass of stone receding.

Not such a cheap pilot.

Beaches, cliffs, water, whirled around Ballantyne. He considered using the gun again, then thought better of it.

'Very sneaky, they're forcing us up the mountain.' The pilot gestured ahead to the wooded slope rising above the estuary, the jagged grey scarp at the top.

'So?'

'So we get caught between a rock and a hard place.

Until we run out of fuel. Then we have to land.'

Ballantyne swore, looked at the gun again. Four more bullets in the clip, another clip of six in his coat. He would have to hit them, somehow. Disable them. Otherwise –

'Fly level,' he said to the pilot. 'I have to get a good shot at them.'

'I'll do my best. But we are going to be flying up a slope you know.'

Ballantyne readied the gun, tried to get a bead on the moving target. 'You know your little joke about the end of civilisation?' he said.

'Yeah, what?'

Ballantyne squeezed off a shot. It missed.

'Well, I'd start taking it seriously if I were you.'

From the ground, from the road by the beach next to the modern flats and the old, whitewashed cottage, the chase didn't look like a chase. It could have been two chopper pilots practising low altitude aerobatics. Unusual, irritating, noisy, but hardly dangerous.

Unless you knew better.

The woman in the royal blue coat, standing by the big off-road car in the lane outside the cottage, did know better. She enjoyed knowing better. She had known better than everyone, all her life. She knew better, for instance, than the man sitting in the passenger seat of the car, with his beefy, nervous self-importance and his red tie. She knew a lot better than any of the people in the helicopters. Especially, she knew better than Ballantyne, which pleased her. From what she'd heard about him – timid, pompous, limited – she was pleased that he was up there in the sky, probably terrified, effectively helpless.

And all because of me, she thought. Because I made it happen.

11

Her lips tightened with excitement as the choppers raced overhead. She didn't attempt to hide her excitement from the man in the car. That, too, was part of the game.

'It's working!' she said. 'We have them cornered!' She got into the car as she spoke, moving quickly.

'When do I get paid?' he asked. Voice dull, unexcited, even now. Only thinking about the money, the facts, the results.

Another Civil Servant. Another bee from the Hive.

Never mind. He had his uses. 'When we get our hands on the goods,' she told him briskly, because that was what he expected to hear. Then she started the engine and began following the road to where she knew the helicopter carrying SACROS would have to land.

'Watch out for the downwash.'

The black helicopter was above them. The chopper tilted to one side; for the first time Ballantyne saw the pilot having to struggle to keep control.

He pushed the gun through the ventilation port again. He'd reloaded: six bullets left.

'Ballantyne, listen,' called the pilot. 'Aim for the rear rotor.'

As the black chopper sank past them again, Ballantyne tried. He fired three times, wincing at the recoil. Each time the target seemed to bounce out of the way.

He shook his head. 'Can't hit it.'

A gloved hand touched his arm. 'Here, allow me.'

Before Ballantyne could think of an objection, the pilot had taken the gun. There was another hole in the canopy on his side of the chopper. The man pointed the gun through it, aimed, fired once.

A tiny plume of smoke appeared above the tail rotor of the black helicopter.

'And they say video games aren't any good for

you!' exclaimed the pilot in triumph, twirling the gun in his hand as if he was taking part in a Wild West shoot-out.

The plume of smoke grew rapidly. The black chopper started to spin, then to fall. Ballantyne realised with a shock that people were going to die. He watched the craft spinning lower and lower towards the canopy of trees, willed the occupants to somehow get out.

'There's no way you can use a parachute in that situation,' said the pilot, as if he had read Ballantyne's mind. His voice was more solemn now.

The black helicopter hit the trees and was immediately engulfed in a ball of orange flame. Their own machine lurched as the blast from the explosion tipped it sideways.

Ballantyne stared and stared, infinitely glad that he hadn't been the one to fire the killing shot.

And aware that, on his report, he would have to tell them that he had. He wondered what the consequences of that would be.

They'd probably let him quit target practice for a while, he thought sourly.

He looked over his shoulder and checked on SACROS. Still there.

Still dangerous.

The chopper lifted, curling back towards the estuary.

'Right then, Mr Bee-llantyne,' said the pilot, his antipodean cheerfulness already restored. 'Let's buzz off back to your Hive.'

The woman in the royal blue coat watched the smoke rising above the bare, autumn branches of the trees. Quickly, she suppressed feelings of panic and disappointment. They were, she knew, entirely natural. But unnecessary. There was nothing in the crashed helicopter that would allow anyone to trace her, unless any of the crew had survived. And that seemed very unlikely.

It had been bad luck, she decided. It happened. Ballantyne must have got in a lucky shot. Still, the fact remained that she knew better than Ballantyne, knew better than Cottrell, knew better than Dent, knew better than all the bees in the Hive. The situation was recoverable. It had to be.

She took three deep breaths of the musty woodland air then got back into the car, her face calm.

The man in the passenger seat was frightened. She could smell his sweat.

'What do we do now?' he said.

'I don't know,' she said quickly. There was no point in pretending she could come up with an alternative plan instantly. She knew she would have to think. Besides, uncertainty would keep this man on his toes.

'We'll have to forget it,' he urged. The smell of his fear was stronger. The woman felt contempt, irritation. Didn't he possess any control over his feelings?

'Don't be stupid,' she said. She started the engine, turned the car round and drove back down the dirt track. The trees closed overhead, a tangle of bare autumn branches.

When they reached the main road she stopped.

'I'm leaving you here,' she said. 'I'll contact you tomorrow.' She smiled at him: her best smile, her mysterious-foreigner smile. 'Don't worry, Mr Moore. You'll get your money. We'll get SACROS, whatever it takes.'

14

« Two »

The Hive communications room was half dark, as if light was rationed by government order. Most of what light there was came from the small, low windows, the ones that you couldn't open. There was equipment. Benches of it. Cables, consoles, laptops. Moving dots, words on LCDs. A faint clatter of morse. A vast panel of TV screens along one wall, able to show between them every TV programme transmitted in the world, official or unofficial.

It was a room in which secret deals should be done, thought Nick Beckett. In which the fate of the world should be decided.

Instead of which, we listen to it being decided by other people. Military communiqués, diplomatic assessments, politicians' secret memos. Oh, and news programmes of course.

And what do we do about them? File reports, make occasional recommendations. Do photocopies, chat about the football, drink coffee.

Waste time.

He leaned on the bench and stared at the latest LCD screen, the one in the steel case with the word SACROS glimmering on it. There was a keyboard attached, and a trackerball, and a black, spider-legged device that Beckett recognised as a 3D joystick. The metal surface beyond the screen had several rows of scart and super-scart sockets, plus two faint ribbons of many-coloured light: optical interfaces. It even had a tiny golfball magneto whirling in the corner, so that it could sense the electrical fields around it and compensate for them internally.

Someone had packed a lot of power into a pretty small box, thought Beckett. As if that would make any difference. Another toy, a dangerous toy. One they wouldn't be using for anything serious unless World War Three started, and then not without a directive signed in triplicate.

'Beckett, make yourself useful and plug the links in.'

Dent's voice jolted Beckett out of his reverie. The Hive chief was standing by the low windows, his slight figure almost in silhouette, the lines on his face made prominent by the sideways light. Beside him stood the heavyweight figure of Moore, the security manager. Both seemed content to watch as Beckett and his boss, the ops controller John Cottrell, set up the equipment.

Cottrell was already hovering over the SACROS keyboard. Beckett had always thought his boss a cold fish: too calm, too collected, too polished, with his high, domed forehead, his staring blue eyes, his neatly trimmed beard. But today he seemed unusually excited, his hands dabbing down to the controls and then back again without touching them, as if he could hardly wait to get started.

Beckett nodded to Dent, fetched the slack ends of the cables which would connect SACROS to the trans-mission system, checked the numerical tags against

16

the scart sockets on SACROS and began plugging them in. He knew he was a humble operative, a nobody in this situation, only in on the show at all because Dent wouldn't mucky his hands touching a piece of real live cabling and Cottrell had wanted an assistant. Beckett only wished he'd read his brief, so that he knew more about what the equipment was supposed to do.

All he knew so far was that three people had died because of it. And he'd heard that in the tea room.

'What exactly does it do, Mr Dent?' he asked.

Dent always insisted on the 'Mr'. No one admitted to knowing his first name.

'It's a vital new piece of equipment for the nation's defence, Beckett,' said Dent, proving to Beckett's satisfaction that he hadn't read his brief either. 'And we're lucky to have it here in one piece,' he added pointedly.

Dent's pompousness was, as usual, too much for Beckett's patience. 'From what I heard,' he said, 'luck had nothing to do with it. It was all down to some chopper pilot.'

Dent appeared to take no notice of the remark, though Beckett had no doubt that it would have the usual effect on his promotion prospects. 'What worries me,' said the chief, 'is how they knew about this at all. Moore, haven't your security people come up with anything?'

Moore shrugged and shook his head. 'Nothing so far. Ballantyne's gone to take a look at the crashed chopper but –' he shook his head '– I doubt it'll tell us anything.'

'Maybe not, but keep me informed.' He turned to Cottrell. 'Now, let's get on with this, eh? You'd better try one of the news channels. We don't want to mess with anything serious.'

Cottrell reached forward for the input control panel and pushed a selector switch. A newscaster appeared on one of the TV screens, the small globe-net logo of MPTV in the bottom right hand corner.

'– a setback in the efforts to bring peace to a troubled area. On the scene, our reporter Bob Gaden reports now live by satellite.'

The screen split and a field-weary reporter appeared in front of a burned out building.

'Bob, you've been in the capital since the ill-fated elections two days ago. Just how bad is this latest setback to the peace process?'

'Well, Dick –'

As the reporter began speaking, his picture now filling the screen, Beckett saw Dent nod to Cottrell. The man reached forward to SACROS, eager as a dog fetching a stick.

'– talks with the rebels have broken down completely. Heavy shelling from the surrounding –'

The screen blanked for a couple of seconds, then returned to the newscaster in the studio, who looked off screen, a little startled, then said, 'Umm, we seem to have temporarily lost Bob. We'll re-establish that satellite link –'

'If we let him,' broke in Cottrell. Dent and Moore grinned. Beckett watched them, enjoying their moment of total power, and managed a tight smile.

'– Gaden in just a moment when we've lost that little gremlin.'

'A gremlin called SACROS,' said Dent proudly. 'She jams satellites. Calls them up and won't let go!'

Sounds like an advertising jingle, thought Beckett sourly. And, just like a jingle, it means nothing. He wondered if Dent had ever worked in advertising. Probably not. So perhaps he was just a frustrated jingle writer.

Aloud, Beckett said: 'SACROS? Why SACROS? It sounds like some Greek island.'

'Satellite And Communication Remote Override System,' said Dent, proving that he had after all read his brief, at least to the extent of memorising the nomenclature.

'I'll stick to SACROS.' With difficulty, Beckett suppressed a grin. He often wished there was someone he could grin with in the Hive, someone to share the jokes that inevitably came to mind working with old pedants like Dent and cold fish like Cottrell. The only one round here who seemed to be less than seventy in the head was Ballantyne, and Beckett didn't often get a chance to see him outside the tea room. He wondered if Cottrell would give him permission to help Ballantyne with the investigation, but killed the idea as soon as he thought of it. No chance. Photocopy this, please, Beckett. Check this person's file for me. Less an operative, more a glorified clerk.

Well, at least it was a job. And the low-level lighting was supposed to be good for your eyes.

Cottrell was fiddling with SACROS again, allowing MPTV to re-establish their link. On the screen, Bob Gaden and the ruined building appeared in an inset behind the newscaster, who was talking about something else.

'Ah, we seem to have found Bob.'

This time, Beckett noticed, only Cottrell seemed to enjoy the joke. While he grinned at the screen, Dent said calmly, 'Well, that seems to work OK.'

'Nice machine,' said Beckett thoughtfully. He felt, rather than saw, Cottrell glance at him. 'Powerful weapon,' he added, thinking it was time an element of seriousness was injected into the conversation. 'We rely so much on satellite communications.' He was going to say more, but Cottrell interrupted him.

'Absolutely. Anything and everything that goes via satellite becomes vulnerable.' Beckett glanced at his boss, sensing an unusual current of emotion. The man's voice was almost shaking. 'At the flick of a switch,' he was saying, 'we could disable a country's telephones, defences, financial transactions.' He took a step towards SACROS, stroked the plastic cover of the machine. 'With this, you could bring half the world to a halt.'

Ballantyne stirred his coffee slowly and wondered who he could trust. He looked around the empty station café. Clean white walls stared back, white tables and chairs, the white digital display of the machine that had served him. There was no sound, not even music, only the faint rumble of traffic soaking through the ceiling from above. Outside the half-shuttered windows the platform was grey, deserted, a commuter station mid-morning.

Ballantyne was glad of the quiet, of the empty tables. He needed time and space to think. If he was right –

He had to be right. No other explanation was possible.

Or was it?

He reviewed the facts again. The witness, the woman in the royal blue coat. The car. The casual check on the registration number, just in case.

The *address*.

She could be his girlfriend. She could be using him as cover, operating independently.

Maybe. But it didn't look that way.

The only way to find out was to check. And the only way to check was to get someone in the Hive – someone who wasn't officially on the case – to make a few behind-the-scenes enquiries.

Ballantyne didn't like it. This wasn't the way the

Hive operated. It wasn't the way he was trained. Like the chopper pilot had said, he was a Civil Servant. A Civil Servant who carried a gun, maybe, but a Civil Servant nonetheless. A by-the-book man.

Now, who had called him that?

Beckett.

Of course. Beckett. Beckett, who was anything but a by-the-book man. Bright shirts, brighter ties. Protest marches, court martials. A rebel, a man in the wrong job.

And the one best placed to check the facts, too.

Ballantyne stood up, leaving his coffee, staring around the café in search of a phone. He had his mobile, but a call box would be better. Less traceable; at least, not traceable to him personally.

The blank white walls stared back. The coffee machine flickered its digital prices at him. But there was no phone.

He saw the covered bridge outside, a smooth white tube arching over the tracks, and remembered that there was a phone box mounted halfway across. He almost ran out through the doors, across the platform and up the ramp. More digital displays flickered at him from the slanting walls: arrival times, departure times, connecting services. Video advertisements moved silently on their poster screens, splashes of colour on the walls. Ballantyne saw a sports car, an ice cream, a chocolate bar.

The model eating the chocolate winked as he passed. SensorGraphics, they called it.

The phone box was vacant. The whole bridge was empty, caught in the mid-morning calm. A train slid below with a low, electric hum. Ballantyne dialled, pausing for a second halfway through to remember Beckett's extension number, then listened to the phone ring.

And ring.

And ring.

Come on, *be there*, thought Ballantyne. I can't risk leaving a message on the machine.

The phone was picked up. 'Beckett.'

Ballantyne closed his eyes with relief, but didn't speak. Instead, he listened to the background at the other end of the line, making sure as far as he could that Beckett was alone.

'Hello? Hello?' A pause. Beckett didn't speak to anyone. The background was silent. Good. 'Who's there?'

Ballantyne decided to risk it. 'Beckett, it's me.'

'Ballantyne,' said the voice at the other end.

Ballantyne cursed inwardly. If anyone was with Beckett, they knew who he was now.

Nothing to do but go for it.

He spoke quickly: 'There was a woman involved in the attack on the chopper. I found her car. I put a tracker on it.' He paused, wondering what to say next. Wondering if he had already said too much. Finally he said, 'I think we should meet. Away from the Hive.'

'Away from here? Why?' Beckett sounded only puzzled.

Good. Very good.

Now for the tricky bit.

'I think it was an inside job. Someone in the Hive set it up.'

There. It was out. Now Beckett might tell Cottrell, might tell anyone.

Anything could happen.

But with luck . . .

'Excuse me, will you be long?'

The woman's voice made Ballantyne jump. He frowned, half turned.

Didn't think.

'I'm sorry, I'll just be a couple of seconds –'

The bullet punched him in the chest at the same instant as he saw the royal blue coat, the pale face framed by dark hair, the gun.

He stared, startled by pain, recognising the coat, the face.

Recognising too late.

Through the mist of shock and pain, he thought: with luck, it's only a flesh wound. With luck, I can surprise her, get the gun off her, bring her in.

But his legs crumpled, the breath choked off in his throat. The pain stabbed through him, the pain of his heart rupturing, stopping. He closed his eyes and then there was only pain, a white tunnel of pain, immeasurable, irreversible.

Ballantyne's luck had run out.

Beckett stared at the phone handset for a moment, but he knew the line was dead.

And Ballantyne?

That sound, that faint metallic cough he'd heard before the line cut off, had seemed appallingly familiar.

Beckett put the phone down, looked around the cluttered surface of his desk. The larger objects – computer, printer, lamp – emerged from a sea of paper, cabling and minor pieces of electrical hardware.

Somewhere in all that was the DAT recorder that was connected to the phone. He'd set it up to record all his conversations automatically. The sound would be on the tape.

If he could find it.

He pushed some paper aside: the report he'd been photocopying for Cottrell when the phone went. He lifted up the paper feed of the printer. No. He pushed aside a heap of computer data, old CD ROMs and the newer optical discs, found another heap of paper.

He cursed under his breath. They'd told him in the Army to always keep a tidy desk, and he'd never learned then. It was at times like this that he wished he had.

He tried following the cable from the phone by eye. It seemed to be heading for the back.

At last he saw the little machine. He'd pushed it behind the computer monitor when he last cleared the desk. He hauled it out, bringing a spaghetti of cabling with it, and set it down on top of Cottrell's report. He rewound the tape to the mark, watched the LCD indicators jump and flicker.

Replay. Now. What had he heard?

He listened to the playback, listened to Ballantyne's careful, by-the-book voice saying that he thought it was an inside job.

Heard the metallic cough again, a thud of impact, and something that might have been a grunt of pain.

This time he was sure.

Beckett got up from his desk, looked around the half-darkened office. He had to get help. Ballantyne had been shot, was probably dead or dying. He thought about trying to get the number Ballantyne had called from, but knew it would be useless. Ballantyne would certainly have been taking precautions against that very thing, precisely because he feared he might be tracked down from inside the Hive.

He picked up the phone and dialled Cottrell's extension.

Cottrell's voice answered, but it was the machine: 'Sorry, but I'm engaged on another call at the moment . . .'

Beckett slammed the phone down, hesitated, then got the tape out of the DAT and put it in his pocket. He almost ran from his office and along the short length of corridor to Cottrell's. He didn't bother to knock.

Cottrell was just putting the phone down. His desk was immaculately tidy: computer, printer, lamp, and a brand new DAT machine, neatly arranged. In tray, out tray, a single pink folder in front of him.

'Sir, can I have a word with you?'

Cottrell looked up, frowned distractedly. 'Is it urgent, Beckett?' I'm –'

'Yes sir. Ballantyne's been shot.'

'Shot?' Cottrell stared at him. 'How do you know?'

'He was on the phone to me when it happened. I've got it on this tape. Listen.'

Cottrell took the tape, put it in the DAT machine, rewound it to the mark and played it back. Beckett went around the desk, crouched beside him, listened again.

Ballantyne's voice said: 'Someone in the Hive set it up.'

Pause. Click.

Beckett glanced at Cottrell. The man's face remained unmoved. 'Could be anything,' he said.

Beckett stood up, but carefully kept his voice as calm as Cottrell's. He didn't want to be accused of hysteria. The situation was too important for that.

'Ballantyne's been shot, sir,' he said. 'That's a gun with a silencer. I'm sure of it.'

Cottrell shook his head slowly. 'Beckett, it's been over ten years since a Hive operative has been shot in action.'

Beckett met Cottrell's eyes. They were calm, clear, cold.

Cold fish.

'So?' asked Beckett.

Cottrell looked away. 'I'm sure Ballantyne is perfectly all right.'

25

Beckett stared at his boss for a moment, hardly able to believe what he'd heard. He thought about making a protest, then thought better of it. Ballantyne's taped words came back to him: 'Someone in the Hive set it up.'

Cottrell? It didn't seem possible. He'd been so pleased with SACROS, so obviously excited when he'd got his hands on it.

Beckett bit his lip, took the tape out of the machine, turned to walk out of the office. He needed to think. He needed to get away from that immaculate desk, from those cold eyes.

Cottrell spoke from behind him: 'If you're that worried, I'll have a word with Dent about it. OK?'

Beckett turned, stared again. He opened his mouth to say: we need to do something now, at once, Ballantyne could be dying. But Cottrell got there first.

'Oh, I'll have that tape filed.' He was getting up from his desk as he spoke. He walked across the office after Beckett and held out his hand.

Beckett held out the tape, an automatic response. Cottrell took it, smiled slightly. Beckett stared at it in the man's hand, the evidence. The proof.

His only evidence. His only proof.

I should take it back, he thought. But he knew he couldn't.

'Thank you, Beckett,' said Cottrell softly.

Elena was wearing her royal blue coat again. She liked her coat in this cold weather, and she saw no reason not to wear it. There was no risk. She could see the Hive, across the narrow water of the old city dock, twin towers of steel rising high above the pale stone frontages of the converted warehouses. She could almost see inside it, see all the Civil Servants in there buzzing like bees.

Programmed, yes. Insects. And, now that Ballantyne was dead, there wasn't anyone there who was programmed to sting her.

So Elena could wear what she liked.

She glanced at her watch: four minutes past twelve. He would be here in sixty seconds exactly, like the good Civil Servant he was. She was sure of it.

Elena waited, not bothering to count the seconds, just standing looking into the water. She saw his reflection first, the familiar beefy figure in his long coat and red tie, then looked up, followed him with her eyes as he hurried along the chained-off walkway on the other side of the water. Elena smiled and walked towards the end of the bridge where he would have to cross. She passed the concrete archway, the little café closed because the owners were on holiday, and arrived at the spot first.

A moment and he was beside her, angry and afraid as usual. He was wearing aftershave, but she could still smell his sweat. He began talking straight away, which she'd known he would, of course.

'So what is it you want? Why the sudden meeting here?'

Elena made a cursory check around her before replying. There were people, but in her experience ordinary people never really heard anything. And there was no one who looked as if they were there specifically to listen.

Good.

'We've decided we must take SACROS out of the Hive itself,' she said. She felt the man's hand grip her arm. She'd known he would be surprised, of course. She always knew these things. She let him stop her, let him turn her to face him, then started speaking before he could. 'We need you to supply us with the access codes.'

'Take it from the Hive?' He said it too loud, then glanced around, obviously worried in case he'd been overheard. He went on more quietly: 'That's crazy! It's impossible!'

Elena couldn't repress a smile. Yes, that was what he had to say. He was like a bee, buzzing with aggression. *Can't take the honey, can't take the honey.*

Oh, yes we can.

'Easier than you think,' she said, still smiling, knowing that he was far too stupid, far too desperate, to guess why it would be easy. 'Anyway, all you need worry about is getting us the codes.'

'Look –' he began, still buzzing aggression.

'You need money, don't you?' She spoke clearly, with emphasis, not caring who heard. 'A lot of money? Well, do as we ask.'

She watched the man's face change as she spoke, watched his expression become uncertain, and she knew then that he would obey. What was it they called those chemicals that controlled the insects? Pheromones? People like this were even easier, thought Elena. She felt a moment's pity, that anyone so stupid, so limited, should nonetheless live in the guise of a human being.

Then she turned and walked away.

Cottrell stood at the main entrance to the Hive, watching. He didn't have a camera with him, he didn't have a pen mike or a DAT. He didn't have anything.

He didn't need anything. He just needed to see.

There. Moore was coming back, his heavy figure hurrying across the main road that separated the Hive from the docks.

Cottrell had watched him go out. Now he was watching him come back.

And now he knew. That was enough. He didn't need a recording.

He walked back through the entrance, his expression unreadable. But his heart was beating faster. Because he knew.

This time it was going to work.

« Three »

Stupid customer. Boring day.

Ros Henderson stared into the bulging, idiot eyes of the man standing in front of her and repeated the instructions for the third time.

'You wait until you're about fifty metres away. No further than that, OK? Then you take the pen mike out of your pocket, point it at the target.' She demonstrated, aiming the gizmo in her hand at a point somewhere in the middle of the customer's chest. 'And then turn on the transmitter.'

The man nodded, but Ros knew from two lots of very recent experience that nothing had actually gone in, and that he was going to ask her to explain it all over again when she'd finished. What had he said he wanted it for anyway? Bird watching? Snail watching? It had to be something like that. No one else would wear an anorak in that particular shade of green.

She looked around the office in desperation, hoping for a distraction. Any distraction. The roof caving in, an invasion by five-legged aliens, the beginning of World War Three. Anything. All she saw was the room she used as a front office for her company, Gizmos. Two other customers were sitting on the plump white couch, headsets on, happily listening to the feed from a RaSearch portable radar unit. The rest of the furnishings in the room – chairs, coffee table, glass display stands – were all pressed into service as temporary holders for various pieces of electronic and optical equipment, and were wound about with cabling like black and yellow creepers. Most of the stuff was switched off, though the occasional beep or chitter indicated that some of it wasn't.

Sadly, nothing seemed to require Ros's immediate attention. She turned back to her customer.

'If you want to record, you press the record button on the machine.' The man's eyes followed her hand downwards, but Ros's very recent experience again told her that this was no more than a gesture. He wasn't listening. There wasn't anything but cabbage between his ears.

And they'd all been like that, all of them since nine this morning. Bird watchers. Snail watchers. Train spotters. Whatever. She wondered why she let them all in.

And people thought that electronic gizmos meant spy stuff, glamour, excitement.

Well, sometimes. And sometimes not. Mostly just explaining things very slowly, and a very untidy front room.

As Ros turned on the recorder for the customer, the phone rang. She had never been more relieved to hear a phone. It was wonderful. It meant she didn't have to keep on explaining a pen mike recorder to a cabbage-brained idiot. It meant, with luck, a new customer. Something exciting perhaps. Someone trying to bug the Defence Minister's private database, or download plutonium delivery schedules.

You never knew your luck.

'Excuse me a moment,' she said smoothly to cabbage-brain, and pulled up the aerial on the phone. 'Hello, Gizmos.' Her professional voice, but the exasperation was creeping in there. Had it been that bad today?

'Who's that?' A man's voice, quick, worried.

'Ros. Who's that?'

A pause. Background noises: echoes, crowd sounds, the rumble of a train. A railway station, then. And a public phone, not a mobile; she could tell by the sound of the line. Probably a CommEx box. They tended to lose the high end more than the others.

The man was talking again, more hesitant now. 'Look, umm, I need something enhancing and it's, uhh, well, rather sensitive.'

Ros grinned. 'Sounds intriguing.'

'I want the guy I dealt with before. Terry.'

Don't we all, thought Ros. 'Well, Terry's gone. I'm the guy now.'

'Uhh, forget it, I'll –'

Ros was used to this. Very used to it. What had it been about Terry? Was it the smell of cider on his breath, or had he actually known more about electronics than she did? She interrupted quickly, before the caller could hang up. 'Oh, come on. You want something doing, I can do it. No questions asked.' She turned, suddenly remembering her other two customers still listening to the RaSearch on the couch. They'd wanted to see the visual output version as well. 'What's the originating format?' she asked into the phone, as she pulled the RaSearch screen unit out of a heap of old circuit boards. She set it down on the coffee table in front of the couple and flipped the saucer-sized dish into position. It began to rotate slowly. Meanwhile there had been no response on the phone, so Ros began reeling off possibilities, 'Minidisc,

CD, optical disc, DAT...' As she was talking she flicked a switch on the RaSearch. An orange and blue LCD display powered up, dots slowly delineating the walls of the office as the unit scanned the space around it. Ros nodded and smiled at her customers: yes, this is how you do it. The younger man, Japanese by the look of him, nodded and smiled back. Unlike cabbage-brain, he looked as if he had actually understood something.

'DAT,' said the man on the phone suddenly, after a fairly long pause. Obviously he'd thought about it, and decided to go for it.

OK. Time for the sales pitch. 'Oh, no problem then. I can get that on audio file, pull up the signal.' She stood by the window, gazed through the half closed blinds into the grey daylight outside. 'So clear you could hear a pin drop, and know where to find it.'

An alarm went off behind her. Oops. Must have left that bug detector wired up to the RaSearch. Ros rushed back to the coffee table, where the bewildered Japanese and his friend were gesturing at the unit as if it were a magic talisman that needed a special spell to turn it off.

Ros turned it off at the switch, heard something from the man on the phone.

'What was that?'

'Meet me there.'

'Meet you where?'

The man repeated an address. Ros picked up the nearest gizmo that was any good at recording anything, tapped a button and keyed the address in one-handed.

'Right,' she said. 'I'll be there.' She pointed the gizmo, which had an infra-red link, at the nearest computer, accessed the gas company's customer data-base, read the name which was returned to her

'. . . Nick Beckett.' She stuffed the gizmo into her pocket.

'Can I rely on you?' The man – Nick Beckett, she reminded herself, she had a name for him now – sounded suddenly anxious. He hadn't even realised that she'd got his name without asking him for it. Ros had a gut feeling, then, at that moment, that this might be serious. More than just another job.

Good.

'I'm reliable,' she said simply.

'Five o'clock,' said the man.

'See you then.'

She smiled as she switched off the phone and pushed in the aerial. Whatever the hell was happening to Nick Beckett, it sounded interesting. He sounded interesting.

With luck, it might not be a boring day after all.

Beckett glanced up and down the corridor outside the records room and frowned.

This could be a stupid decision, he thought. But I have to do it.

He slid the pass card into the slot, punched in the five-digit code. Not his pass card, of course. Nor his five-digit code. No.

He knew better than that.

He glanced up and down the corridor once more. All clear. He pushed open the door.

Inside, the records room was small, silent, blue-lit. The security camera was above the door. Beckett reached inside his jacket, pulled out the mirror. Simple, but effective. Clip it to the lens of the camera, tilt it at the right angle, and all the security people would see was the ceiling.

But Beckett knew it would be detected pretty quickly. He'd given himself twenty seconds to find the tape and get out, before someone from security came down to investigate. As soon as the mirror was in place, he tapped the button on his watch that would start counting down those seconds.

Then he glanced around the room, at the neatly ordered cabinets with their drawers and slots for pass cards. Cottrell would have filed the DAT in sequence order, which meant – Beckett examined the tallest cabinet briefly – BHQ54328.

Right. Now for the difficult bit.

Beckett took the card wallet from his jacket, pulled out the first of the cards. Scavenged cards. Dead cards from security. Cottrell's 'just destroy these, would you?' cards. Beckett was glad he'd kept them now.

He slid a card in, the one he'd selected as being most likely to have general access. The control unit made a faint buzz and a red light lit under the key slot. The drawer wouldn't budge. Beckett swore under his breath, fumbled a second general access card out of the wallet. He pushed it in.

The same derogatory buzz. Another red light.

Three fails and the security lock would close. No way in after that.

Beckett glanced at his watch. Five seconds left. He pulled out a third card, any card, this one had to *go*.

A faint chime. A green light. The welcome click of a lock release.

Beckett let out the breath he'd been holding from the moment he'd clipped the mirror on the camera, then pulled open the drawer. The DAT was there, the word BECKETT written in Cottrell's own neat block capitals on the label. Beckett pulled it out just as the alarm beeped on his watch.

Time to go.

He pushed the cards and the DAT into his jacket, ducked under the camera, reached up and pulled the mirror away from the lens. Then he left, tape in hand, shutting the door quietly behind him.

Around the corner he almost ran into Alan Moore, the security chief, walking fast and looking worried.

'Problem, Al?' he said, as casually as he could.

Moore stopped and looked round. 'Fault in the records room,' he said. 'Probably nothing.'

Beckett nodded and went on. But his heart was beating, if possible, faster than before. If Moore was looking into it himself, instead of sending one of the guards, then he must know it was serious. Must have some sort of security man's hunch.

But Moore wouldn't find anything. And with the camera disabled, there was no way the security chief could know that he, Beckett, had just come from the records room.

Not for sure.

But when he half-glanced over his shoulder, he saw that Moore had stopped, and was looking back at him, frowning.

Alan Moore stared at the open drawer, at the gap where the missing tape should be.

Who the hell had taken that? And why?

He remembered Beckett passing him in the corridor, the studied casualness of his manner. Yes, it was him all right. But why on earth would Beckett go to that much trouble to take a DAT out without logging it?

Unless he was trying to hide whatever he was doing from someone inside the Hive.

Moore winced at the thought. If Beckett knew that someone in the Hive was suspect . . .

He might know who.

Moore realised that he was going to have to act quickly. He checked the log number of the tape, slammed the drawer shut, then set off at a run.

* * *

36

Easy does it, thought Ros, as she tapped the access code into the keyboard. Easy as pie. Easy as one, two, three.

Her reflection stared back at her from the computer screen, grinning slightly. Dark skin, dark eyes, dark hair in frizzy waves falling below her shoulders. She liked that new style, she decided. It suited her image.

The screen blinked, and the words LINK ENABLED appeared in the top left hand corner.

She tapped the ENTER key, and watched as the words changed to ENTER PASSCODE. The yellow and blue logo of BHQ – the Hive – appeared on the right of the screen.

Ros's grin broadened as she tapped in the familiar passcode, then the command line: LOCATE BECKETT, NICK.

Probably Nicholas on their records, thought Ros suddenly. But the computer didn't seem to have a problem with that. A photo ID appeared. Dark hair, squarish face, clean shaven. Green eyes. An appalling taste in ties.

Ros began to read the confidential information on Beckett's file, frowning slightly as she did so.

But, after a while, her frown turned back into a grin.

Elena's lover was worried again. Ballantyne's killing had been a mistake, he was telling her. People in the Hive had guessed what was happening. He wasn't safe any more.

She let him talk for a while, holding the phone a little way away from her ear and settling herself in comfort on the pink chair by her bed. She kept herself amused by making faces at a neighbour's cat that was sitting on the windowsill, washing itself. Eventually, when she sensed her lover was winding down, she interrupted him.

'Darling! You know, you almost sound like one of those bees yourself when you're in this mood. Don't worry so much. All we need to do is fix up this – this Beckett. Moore will help you.'

'Moore?' So edgy, so astounded. So predictable. 'You think I should tell Moore? Are you sure we can trust him that much?'

'He needs the money. And he's worried too, about the same man. That Nick Beckett. He phoned me about it.' Elena smiled to the cat on the windowsill, then to herself, to her own dark eyes in the mirror across the room from the phone. 'We can trust him for today. And tomorrow, who knows? But if there is a problem, I will take care of it.'

A pause. She could feel his mind working. So dear, so familiar, so inferior. 'Yes. I'll tell him, then. But how do we "fix up" Beckett?'

Elena told him how. It was so simple. You just had to play pretend. Like children. Her fingers played with the pink pom-pom tassels on the bedspread as she talked, weaving them into patterns, cat's cradles.

Her lover liked the plan. He even had an idea which would make it a little bit better. Which was good, because now he wouldn't feel inferior. Elena didn't like him to feel inferior, even if he was. It had – repercussions.

He ended confidently: 'Well, that's arranged then. Moore and I will take care of Beckett.'

'And you won't even get your hands dirty,' said Elena.

'No, darling. Look, Moore's waiting and he's pretty rattled. I'd better go.'

Elena smiled. 'Goodbye darling,' she said softly, and blew a kiss into the phone before she hung up.

It was all arranged. Even neater than before.

Moore takes care of Beckett, she thought, and I take

care of Moore. We all take care of each other. Which is how it should be.

The flats were redbrick, modern-looking. Narrow towers, steep black roofs, large windows. Alan Moore guessed that they'd been built within the last ten years. Difficult to break in to.

Good job he didn't need to.

He reached into the pocket of his overcoat, drew out the passkey. His hands, clumsy in the gloves, almost lost their grip on it as he approached the glass doors that led to the lobby of the building.

He looked at the reinforcing strips in the glass, just visible in the grey November light. Pushed the card into the slot, tapped in the code he'd been given. The entry light glowed green, the locks clicked.

Moore pushed the door open, looked around the lobby to see if anyone was watching.

Nothing. Only a ceiling camera, probably vidlinked. He stared at the camera for a moment, then realised he was acting guiltily.

Authorised, he thought. I'm authorised to do this. It doesn't matter whether I'm seen on the tapes, as long as they don't see what I do when I get inside. And they won't see that.

Elena really did have friends in high places, after all. I'm authorised. I'm covered.

He pressed the button that called the lift, and was relieved when the doors slid open at once.

The lift was plush. Black carpet, mirror on the wall so that you could straighten your tie. Moore looked at his tie. It was straight enough.

He pressed the button for the second floor. As the lift accelerated, he checked the inside pocket of the over-coat, felt a corner of hard plastic through the leather of his glove.

All ready.

The door opened, and Moore snatched his hand away. There might be a camera in the corridor.

There wasn't. More black carpet, bright, soft lighting, a rubber plant. A small arrow pointed left, FLATS 2–6. That way then. Moore moved swiftly, checking the cream coloured doors, until he came to number 3.

He swiped the passkey through the lock, waited. No keypad here.

The lock clicked. Moore pushed the door open.

Cream coloured inside, too. A round, wood-framed mirror on the wall. Moore glanced in it, reflexively checked his tie again.

Now to find a good place to plant the evidence. Moore looked in the lounge, saw a TV with a wallscreen, a video, a hi-fi, a computer. A stack of audio CDs. Ornaments on shelves.

No. Too obvious.

He tried a door, saw a bedroom. Black furnishings, grey counterpane on the bed.

No. Definitely not.

A study: a second computer, more modern than the first. An optical link card tied in with some loose cabling. A videophone.

Drawers, with alarmed locks. A coffee cup. A DAT machine cabled to the phone and the computer.

Yes. Perfect.

Moore reached inside his coat and pulled out the plastic bag containing the five tapes. He pulled open the top of the bag, resting it on the desk to do so. Then he simply poured the tapes on to the desk top, adding them to the mixture of optical discs, pens, highlighters and paperclips already lying there.

'Authorised,' he muttered.

Then left the room, closing the door quietly behind him.

* * *

The only light in the office came from the computer screen. Hive colours: yellow and blue. Beckett leaned over the keyboard, typing awkwardly, one-handed, the other hand straightening his coat.

He'd only thought of this at the last minute, just as he was about to leave.

He typed the access code. The database number. Then: LOCATE: HENDERSON, ROS.

The computer beeped, the photo ID downloaded. A young woman, dark skin, dark eyes, dark hair, in frizzy waves falling below her shoulders. She gazed out at him rather stonily, as if she hadn't wanted to be photographed.

Well, lots of people didn't. For various reasons.

Beckett glanced at the clock, buttoned his coat, then read Ros's specs: name, date of birth, address and contact number, and, most important, surveillance category.

It read: 'Not currently targeted.'

'Good start,' muttered Beckett. He touched the 'biog' icon on the screen, waited the fraction of a second it took the outgoing data to get clearance, then read:

> Highly motivated, above average IQ. Independently researches and develops clandestine surveillance equipment for supply to freelance market. Attempt to recruit for Hive work failed, but has contacts with some operatives on an ad hoc basis. Two reports on file.

One of the reports was written by Ballantyne. Beckett called it up, read it, began to smile.

The phone rang. Beckett scowled and picked it up, gave his name.

'Dent here, Beckett.'

'Hello sir.' Beckett was still reading: 'Illegal misdirection of Minister's –'

'I've been told you're worried about Ballantyne.

41

Can you brief me?'

'– cheap Japanese hotel. Illegal telephone tapping, apparently in order to –'

'Yes – uhh – when?' said Beckett, hoping he would
have time to finish the reports first. They looked as if
they were interesting reading.

'Five minutes, in the conference room. Oh, and
Beckett, I'll need Ballantyne's file. Could you pop into
my office and bring it down to me?'

Beckett struggled to get his attention away from the
screen. This was important. Shame it was now, when
he had to meet Ros in half an hour, but . . .

But Ballantyne might be dead.

'Sure,' he said briskly. 'I'll see you in a minute.'

He put the phone down, touched the 'save' icon on
the computer screen, and hurried to Dent's office.

Alan Moore waited, his coat over his arm.

He hadn't had time to go to the monitor room after
driving back across the city. Besides, it would look
better if he 'just happened to be passing.' And 'on my
way out', when in fact he was on his way back.

Familiar tricks. Almost like a legitimate operation.

And it is a legitimate operation, he thought. As far as
I'm concerned. I've had an order from a superior. I'm
duly authorised.

Wait for Beckett to go in, he'd been told. Wait a
minute or so. Then go in after him.

Movement along the corridor: Beckett. I'd never fail
to recognise that tie.

Moore stayed where he was, in the half-light, waiting. He watched Beckett go into Dent's office, waited a
little longer.

Then he started down the corridor, walking softly.

* * *

42

Odd, thought Beckett.

He scanned the desk top again, just to be sure. None of the files there were Ballantyne's – none at all were the buff-coloured files used by personnel. Beckett checked the computer, just in case Mr Dent had meant an electronic file, but the machine was shut down for the day, the screen showing the BHQ symbol, the optical drive empty.

Beckett glanced around the office, at the glittering LEDs on the traffic monitors in the corner, the plush leather chair, the thick pile carpet. Nothing had been left lying about.

Then he noticed the green 'unlocked' light winking on the filing cabinet.

'Careless, Mr Dent,' muttered Beckett, grinning to himself. It was nice to know that the boss could make mistakes too.

He went to the cabinet, pulled open the drawer marked A–D and rifled through the paper files. Ballantyne's had to be here somewhere.

The door thudded open behind him. Beckett glanced up and saw Moore standing in the doorway. He nodded at the man and looked down again.

'Can I help, Mr Beckett?' The voice dripped irony.

'No, I'm just getting a file for Mr Dent.'

The lack of response made him pause and look up.

' 'Course you are, sir,' said Moore in a flat voice.

Beckett frowned. 'He rang me and asked me to meet him in the conference room. He wanted me to bring Ballantyne's file. He said it was in his office.'

Moore shook his head. 'Mr Dent,' he said, with slow emphasis, 'isn't in the building this afternoon.' A pause. 'I think you'd better come with me.'

« Four »

The Managing Director's office was a palace of glass.

Transparent desks, transparent chairs. Glass walls, rendered opaque and secure by patterns of diffracted light. Engraved glass screens in several colours: turquoise, topaz, amethyst. A huge wall screen, glass fronted, showed the slowly rotating, life-sized image of a white shark.

All the glass was bullet proof, of course.

The Managing Director liked glass. It made her feel secure. She could see other people and (if the glass was properly designed) they couldn't see her.

That was good.

She fingered the black diamond pendant at her collar and raised her eyes from the list of technical specifications she was reading. She examined her client. The woman was foreign; there would have been no doubt of that, even without the accent. The shape of her face, the cut of her green satin jacket, a certain elegance, a style that wasn't native.

But then a lot of the Managing Director's clients were foreign. It wasn't a problem, as long as they could pay.

And this client was a little bit obsessed. The Managing Director was sure of that. The way the client's eyes fixed on her own, the supreme confidence in her manner. It was more confidence than any sane person would have.

But a lot of the Managing Director's other clients were obsessive, too. And that wasn't a problem either.

'You understand it is only the linking equipment we require,' the client was saying. 'A microwave antenna, a relay dish. We already have the rest.'

The Managing Director nodded. Of course she understood. The specifications in front of her were quite clear. She also understood that in order for her client to require this kind of equipment, the stuff she 'already had' must be something very big. And very dangerous. She knew the woman must have stolen it, or at the very least imported it illegally.

All of which made it very saleable, thought the Managing Director. But first, of course, we have to obtain it. To persuade her to part with it.

The Managing Director glanced at the shark slowly rotating on the wall screen. She could be very good at persuading people to do things.

'We are willing to pay any reasonable price,' the woman was saying. 'All we ask is that you –' a small shrug '– don't ask too many questions.'

The Managing Director looked down at her hands on the glass desk. 'You needn't worry, Ms Johnson. Cyberscope never asks questions. In our business that often leads to many difficulties.' She met the woman's eyes. 'Difficulties that can be avoided. Now, the price –'

She named a figure. Five times the market price for the equipment that the client required.

But then nobody came to Cyberscope expecting the bargain basement.

Ms Johnson said quietly, 'Half that.'

The Managing Director smiled. Small operators often made this mistake, thought they could haggle with her.

She glanced up at the glass screens. No haggling.

'Ms Johnson,' she said. 'You must be aware that, if we go ahead with this deal, there are certain costs involved. There are legal requirements.' She smiled. 'If you understand what I mean. The paperwork has to be satisfactory.'

A stubborn, childish expression formed on the client's face. 'That's no reason to charge me so much! I will go elsewhere!'

The Managing Director had met this situation before. Many times.

'Where, Ms Johnson? How many companies will be willing to avoid asking – for example – why you need enough microwave power to call up every satellite above the Earth, all at the same time?' She paused, to let that sink in. To let the woman realise that she'd said enough already to leave her open to, at the very least, surveillance, and quite probably arrest, if the Managing Director chose to pass the information on to the relevant authorities.

The silence stretched. The Managing Director fingered the black diamond pendant – I'm a busy woman, she was telling her client, a woman with no time for small fry.

'Very well,' said Johnson at last. 'We will pay your price.' Her voice was sulky, dangerous. But the Managing Director was used to that, too.

Most of her clients were dangerous. In one way or another.

Johnson stood. 'You will deliver tomorrow. Before eleven a.m.'

'And the payment?' said the Managing Director delicately.

'Cash,' said Johnson simply. 'On delivery. Not before.'

The Managing Director nodded. At least they understood each other there.

As soon as the woman was gone, the Managing Director touched a key on her desk phone.

A man's face appeared.

Cold, green, businesslike eyes stared at her. Somehow they reminded her of the shark on the wall screen.

Her shark. Her man.

She smiled. 'Mr Marasco. I have a job for you.'

« Five »

Cottrell's office seemed darker than ever, though the windows were still letting in small slots of grey daylight. Beckett stood in front of the desk, aware of Moore pacing behind him.

Like a caged animal, thought Beckett.

Except that I'm the one in a cage, if I don't look out.

He looked down at the almost bald dome of Cottrell's head. Avoided the calm eyes, let his gaze slide to a point on the wall.

'Mr Dent called me on an internal line.'

No change in Cottrell's expression.

Cold fish.

And Moore, from behind him: 'Mr Dent is out for the rest of the day. I just checked with his PA.'

'That's impossible,' said Beckett. 'He just asked me to bring him a file.'

Cottrell stared at him, still without any apparent expression. Beckett wondered if the man had any normal emotional processes. He only seemed to get excited when he was playing with his electronic toys – SACROS, for instance. One of his operatives being pulled in on suspicion of burgling the controller's

48

office didn't seem to merit any concern at all.

'I'm sure there's some easy explanation,' Cottrell was saying. He glanced at Moore. 'Log it in the incident book and we'll say no more.'

Beckett felt a moment's relief. Cottrell might be a cold fish, but at least he wasn't stupid, and paranoid, as Moore appeared to be.

The security chief still hadn't given up. 'Sir, regulations state –'

'I know the rule book, Alan,' interrupted Cottrell, with a touch of exasperation. Then his eyes met Moore's, and he seemed to reconsider. 'OK, just search Mr Beckett, then. Satisfy yourself that there's nothing amiss.'

Beckett looked at Moore, got a hard stare in return. Reluctantly, he turned and faced the man. Moore's hands began rifling the pockets of his overcoat and the jacket underneath.

Beckett began to feel annoyed. This shouldn't be happening to him. He was a trusted operative. He looked at Cottrell, who was bent over his computer, typing something in. 'There's really no need for this, you know.'

But Cottrell ignored him.

And then Beckett remembered the DAT.

The DAT he'd been going to see Ros Henderson about. The DAT he'd taken out without authorisation – in effect, stolen. The DAT which he'd simply put in his pocket, without thinking there would be any problem.

And now he was being searched.

He moved his hand quickly towards the pocket that held the tape.

Too late. Moore got there first. There was a click of plastic as the security chief's hand closed over the tape.

Moore stared at him, the expression in his eyes harder than ever.

Cottrell looked up. 'Is there a problem, Nick?'

Moore pulled the tape out of Beckett's pocket, held it up just inches from his face.

The security chief spoke in a voice that dripped irony. 'I assume this was logged out according to the correct procedure, sir?'

Ros Henderson pulled the optical disc out of her computer and slipped it into her pocket. You never knew when a little inside info would come in handy. And there was lots of inside info on Nick Beckett's file. Lots and lots and lots.

Definitely an interesting end to the day, she decided.

She switched off the lamp, left the computer screen on, bits and pieces of Nick's file still showing in a couple of the windows, though the link to BHQ was broken.

Whistling softly to herself, she pulled on her outdoor coat and picked her car keys out of a mess of coffee cups and small pieces of electronic equipment. She checked the time: ten to five.

Ten minutes. And about six miles to go, through the city, in the rush hour.

She licked her lips, grinned.

No problem.

Might even be fun.

Beckett looked at his flat. Looked at the two Hive security men – Tim Edwards and another he didn't know by name – pulling up the carpet in his lounge.

CDs were stacked neatly on the floor. A brass statue of a cat lay on its side. His coffee table was upside down, as if they thought he might have glued a tape underneath it.

Beckett still couldn't quite believe that this was happening. He'd said as much to Cottrell already, twice at least, but the man had made no response. Now Cottrell was looking at the view from the lounge window: the pier, the river, the lights on the other side, which were beginning to stand out against the growing dusk.

'Smart place for a man on your salary,' Cottrell commented.

Beckett couldn't let that one past. He might be under suspicion, but surely Cottrell knew the charges were ridiculous. 'All paid for by stolen information, of course,' he said.

'It's no joke, Beckett.' Cottrell's voice was even colder than usual.

'Am I laughing?'

Cottrell ignored the remark. He turned and paced past Beckett into the entrance hall. Moore was there, staring at Beckett as if he were already under arrest.

Which I suppose I am, thought Beckett.

'Has anyone checked in there?' Cottrell gestured at the closed door of Beckett's study.

Moore nodded at Tim Edwards, who had just finished examining the floorboards under the carpet in the lounge. Edwards got up, walked past Beckett with an apologetic look, then opened the study door and went in.

Beckett cursed under his breath. There were things in there he'd definitely rather not let Moore or Cottrell see. He could only hope that Tim would exercise a bit of discretion.

Cottrell was talking again, his shoes making hollow clicks on the now-bare boards of the lounge, his voice weary. 'You should have signed the tape out. You know the procedure.'

And you know this is bloody stupid, thought Beckett. I haven't stolen anything. Not anything that matters. Yes, I bend the rules occasionally, but –

'I think you ought to look at this, sir.'

51

Beckett whirled round, saw Edwards standing in the doorway of the study. The apologetic expression on his face had intensified.

Beckett was suddenly worried. He tried to push past Moore, was stopped by an arm as rigid as iron. The security chief strode into the study, stopped over the desk, then turned round and gave Beckett his hardest stare yet.

'Mr Cottrell!' he said quietly.

Beckett went in, Cottrell behind him. They both stood and stared at the desk, at the five DAT tapes scattered across it, all officially labelled with the BHQ stamp.

'Didn't even lock them away, sir,' said Moore quietly. 'Very careless if you ask me.' He began picking up the tapes with his gloved hands, putting them one by one into a clear plastic bag.

Beckett looked at Cottrell but his boss only stared at him, his blue eyes stony.

I've got to get out, Beckett realised. This is a frame-up.

Someone in the Hive set it up. Ballantyne's last words to Beckett.

And they killed Ballantyne.

They're not going to wait for a trial – they won't want me in court, talking. They'll want me dead.

I've got to get out *now*.

He punched Moore in the face. Caught by surprise, the security chief fell backwards across the desk. Beckett turned and shoved the lightweight Cottrell out of his way. He saw Tim Edwards staring at him, heard Cottrell shout, 'Beckett!'

The other security man was in the lounge. Beckett kicked him in the crotch, saw him fall back into the shelving. Ornaments fell with a clash of metal and breaking china.

Beckett was already running for the window, jumping up on the sofa, pulling at the latch.

He heard Cottrell shout again, and Tim Edwards's voice. The latch gave, the window opened. Beckett jumped down onto the balcony and over the rail in one movement, holding onto the painted metal and twisting himself round so that he landed on the balcony below, which projected a little further than his own.

He looked down, saw the roof of the black official car which had driven him here.

He jumped again, landed hard on the car roof, then slipped down between the body of the car and the wall of the building. He tugged at the driver's door.

The car was locked. Of course.

Beckett looked up and down the road, saw nothing but bare cobbles.

And a car coming: small, red, fast. Headlights on.

Ros Henderson at the wheel. There was something different about her hair, but it had to be her.

He dived out in front of the car, forcing it to stop with a screech of brakes. He ran to the passenger door, pulled it open, jumped in.

'Drive!' he shouted.

'Mr Beckett?' Ros's voice sounded bewildered, which was, Beckett had to concede, understandable. But there wasn't time for a discussion.

'Drive!' he repeated.

'We did say five? Am I early? I –'

'You're just in time. Now for God's sake drive!'

Beckett could see Edwards emerging from the front door, all trace of apology gone, chasing the villain now. Ros had begun to move the car, but hesitantly, as if pulling out at a busy junction.

Edwards was running straight towards them.

'DRIVE!' yelled Beckett, yanking at the wheel to steer them away from the Hive man.

53

Too late. Even as Ros began to accelerate, Edwards leaped onto the bonnet, shouting, struggling to get a grip.

'Oi!' shouted Ros. 'Get off my car!' She floored the accelerator, swerved violently, then stopped suddenly, sending the unfortunate Edwards sprawling down a flight of steps that led to the river. He almost fell into the water, stopped himself just in time.

Ros was already driving again, across the bridge that crossed the mouth of the dock. Without looking away from the road, she said, 'You wouldn't want to tell me what the hell is going on, I suppose?'

Beckett looked over his shoulder. The Hive car was following them, Cottrell at the wheel. It had already reached the far side of the bridge.

'As soon as I find out,' he said, 'you'll be the first to know.'

He looked back at Ros, who was checking her mirror. She floored the accelerator again, almost throwing Beckett out of his seat.

'They from the Hive too?' she asked. They'd cleared the bridge. On either side, white stone arches raced past, framed in red brick.

'Yes, they're –' Beckett broke off, as he registered something. 'How did you know I'm from the Hive?'

Ros glanced at him, gave a small shrug. 'Checked you out.'

Beckett glanced ahead, saw bollards, a sloping pedestrian precinct beyond.

The end of the road.

He swore inwardly. They would have to stop, get out, run. Or at least, he would have to run. Ros would be OK. She was just a bystander.

He hoped.

But Ros showed no sign of slowing down. 'So what's the score here then?' she said casually, her voice betraying no concern at the fact that they were approaching three tall, solid metal pillars at more than sixty miles per hour. 'Not been paying your tea money?'

'Do I look dishonest?'

Ros glanced at him: a brief, appraising, glance. Then she said, 'Right.'

The car slowed, swerved. Beckett heard tyres screaming on tarmac, saw brick walls and metal bollards whirling round. He gripped the side of his seat as hard as he could, but even so almost lost his balance and fell onto Ros.

Where the hell's she going? he thought. There's no other way.

Then they were heading back up the road, the Hive car straight ahead of them on a collision course.

She's mad, thought Beckett. She's got to be.

'What are you doing?' he asked aloud.

No response. The Hive car was twenty metres away, ten, five.

'Watch out!'

The Hive car swerved, almost crashed into the buildings at the side of the road.

'Chicken!' said Ros, grinning.

Beckett looked back, saw the Hive car backing into an entrance, turning. He looked at Ros, saw her grin getting wider. She was looking forward to a rematch.

He began to put his seat belt on.

'Persistent, aren't they?' commented Ros.

'I blame performance-related pay, myself,' said Beckett, snapping his belt into place.

Ros flashed him a smile. 'So they think you're a wrong 'un, do they?'

'Someone's working very hard to make it look that way.'

They were driving over the bridge again. Beckett's

stomach was temporarily left behind as the car bounced over the hump in the middle. They passed his flat. The windows were still flapping open where he'd made his rapid exit.

'Wouldn't exactly be out of character, though, would it?' said Ros suddenly. 'Stealing the tea money, I mean. Or whatever.'

Beckett stared at her. Whose side was she on?

'Trespass at a US base?' Ros went on. 'Unauthorised leave? And –' her voice became heavy, judicial '– court martialled for failing to obey orders, no less.'

'That's classified!'

But Ros only winked at him. 'A mis-spent youth, Mr Beckett.' The car made a violent turn to the right.

'Me?' he asked. 'A mis-spent youth? What about you? Illegal phone tapping, bugging hotel rooms.'

'Never touch the stuff,' said Ros, glancing in the mirror.

'Phone phreaking. You hooked the Foreign Secretary's private line up to a knocking shop in Tokyo! That was a nice little job.'

'He deserved it,' said Ros crossly. Then she frowned. 'How did you find out?'

'Same way you did, probably – Hive files. Only I'm authorised . . .' He broke off as the car went over another of the dock bridges. He glanced over his shoulder, saw that the Hive car had caught up, was driving practically on their back bumper. He looked ahead, saw shops, pedestrians.

And metal bollards, blocking the road.

'Look out!' he yelled.

Ros swerved, barrelled the car down a narrow alley and into a courtyard between tall redbrick blocks of flats. A small fountain played in the middle of the courtyard, a statue of a boy on a dolphin.

'Not very original,' observed Ros, possibly of the

fountain, as she steered around it, tyres screeching. Beckett wondered if she was going to try and repeat her head-on-collision trick, but then saw that it was too late. The Hive car was already in the courtyard, skidding around the fountain behind them.

Beckett saw a grassy bank ahead of them, then realised that they were going to go straight up it.

'In the cross-country driver's club, are we?' he asked, as the nose of the car rose like an aircraft taking off.

Ros only grinned.

The bank levelled out. Ahead were lawns, flowerbeds dug over for the autumn, and a few small trees. Ros crossed the lawns, swerving around the trees. Beckett glanced over his shoulder again, saw the Hive car right behind them. Fans of mud from the rear wheels of Ros's car were spraying across the bonnet and the windscreen.

'They're still there,' he told Ros.

'Yes, but they're bigger than us,' said Ros, swerving through a narrow gap between two small birches. 'Which could work to our advantage.'

With a jolt, they reached the hard paved walkway around the block of flats. Ros turned the car round, the fastest three-point turn Beckett had ever experienced, then set off back across the lawns. Behind them, the Hive car floundered, skidded.

But made the turn.

'What do we do now?' shouted Beckett.

'Wait and see.' Ros was still grinning, as if all this were a ride in an adventure playground.

They were jolting and squelching along the muddy track they'd made on the way out. As they reached the bank, Ros swerved to one side and drove along the top of the bank, towards a flight of steps. The Hive car tried to follow suit, but it was too heavy. It went into a huge four-wheel slide, down the bank and over the courtyard, where it rolled onto its roof and landed in the fountains.

Ros stopped the car at the top of the steps and surveyed the scene. Beckett looked too. Cottrell was struggling to open the car door, which was no longer in any condition to be opened.

Ros turned to Beckett and grinned. 'Definitely an improvement, don't you think? Post-deconstructionalist sculpture at its best.'

Beckett grinned back.

Ros began driving again, slowly, carefully, nosing the car down the bank, then out of the courtyard and along the alleyway to the road.

'By the way, Mr Beckett,' said Ros quietly as they pulled out into the traffic.

'Yes?'

'Whatever you were going to pay me for this job, the price just went up.'

« Six »

The bike was fast. Fast enough to be thoroughly dangerous in the wrong pair of hands. But the present rider didn't consider himself to be the wrong pair of hands. He knew exactly what he was doing.

Lights sped past: front rooms, bedrooms, people watching TV, reading magazines.

Boring, thought the rider. A life I wouldn't lead in a million years.

Ahead, he saw the familiar semi-circular building. Red bricks, splashes of soft lighting, the illuminated sign in blue. The rider dropped down a gear, braked sharply, then swung off the road into the cobbled courtyard.

Business and pleasure, he thought. Not many people get to mix them in their lives, but I *always* do.

He switched off the engine, let the bike drift to a stop. Chocked it.

Lights off, helmet off.

Spiked overshoes on.

The rider stood on the pavement and looked up at the face of the building, surveying the task ahead of him. A few of the windows were still lit, thin lines of light edging around closed shutters. A figure moved in one of the windows. Someone working late. The rider ducked for cover under the wall of the building, waited a few minutes, then cautiously peered out again.

The figure was gone. But he was pretty sure who it had been.

'Target sighted,' he muttered. 'And confirmed.'

Time for a bit of climbing. Time for a surprise visit.

He was looking forward to this.

Ros Henderson turned from the window and looked at Beckett, who was sprawled on her sofa looking as if he'd very much like to go to sleep there. His unspeakable yellow tie – the same one with the green spots that he'd been wearing in the Hive photo ID – was loose around his neck. His collar was unbuttoned. A mug of coffee stood empty on the glass table in front of him. Behind the sofa, the partition window to the inner office was dark except for the faint sparks of LEDs on the clusters of gizmos within.

'So,' she said, 'what's on this tape that's so important?'

'That's what I was hoping you'd find out.'

Ros leaned over the table and picked up the empty cup. 'More coffee?'

'Yeah, thanks.' He looked up at her. 'That was very impressive, you know. The way you lost Cottrell.'

She looked at him for a moment, decided that he wasn't just being polite, nor was he trying to chat her up. She'd just received a professional compliment. From a professional.

She decided she liked that.

She nodded, moved away to the kitchen area, switched the kettle on.

Behind her, Beckett was talking, apparently half to

himself. 'Cottrell's a perfectionist, though. He won't just give up. If he thinks I'm a villain, he's going to get me.'

The air was cooler on the fifth floor level. The wind had found a way around the curve of the building, and it tugged at the climber. Not enough to be really dangerous, just enough to make things a little more interesting. The climber looked down at his bike, six floors below.

He grinned tightly as he pulled himself up, brick by brick, his hands grasping now a drainpipe, now the support stanchion of one of the balconies.

He took care not to touch the rails of any of the balconies. He might set off an alarm.

And besides, it would be too easy.

He looked up, caught a glimpse of light edging around shutters two floors above.

Target zone.

Sixty seconds, he decided. I can do it in sixty, easy.

He gave himself forty, and began counting.

Beckett closed his eyes for a moment. Just for a moment, he decided. Even a minute's sleep will help. Ros will wake me up with the coffee.

He heard the kettle begin to boil, then something else.

Something from outside.

He jolted awake, eyes on the window, on the narrow crack of darkness at the edge of the shutters.

He saw a pale flicker of movement.

Heard a faint hiss: cloth moving over metal.

Beckett was on his feet, running for the window. He was slamming the shutters up, even as the window swung open. He saw black leathers, a young man's face, blue-grey eyes.

He punched. Into the gut. Hard.

The man grunted, fell back onto the balcony.

Beckett was on him in a moment, punching, kicking, a knee in the groin.

'Oi!' shouted the man, his face twisting with pain.

Beckett dragged him upright, got an armlock around him, checked him for weapons.

Nothing. Or at least, nothing obvious.

He pushed the man through the open windows into the office.

Ros was standing in the kitchen door, staring.

'Ed!' she shouted.

The man in Beckett's arms shouted something. It was muffled by the hand Beckett had around his throat, but it could have been Ros's name.

Beckett began to wonder if this situation was quite what it seemed to be.

'You know this guy?' he asked Ros.

'Only for five years.'

Beckett didn't feel that irony was justified, in the circumstances. He let the man go, pushing him to the floor, then stood back so that he could get another good swipe at him if anything went wrong.

The man got up, quicker than Beckett had expected, whirled round and tried to hit him. Beckett grabbed him again, this time putting a slightly tighter hold on his throat.

'Beckett, Ed's a friend of mine.' Ros sounded genuinely angry now. 'Put him down.'

'Behave yourself,' Beckett told Ed, then pushed him to the floor again.

This time Ed got up more slowly, turned carefully, his hands by his sides. He stared at Beckett.

Beckett spread his arms in a gesture of apology. 'I'm sorry, all right? I thought you were someone else.'

'Obviously.' Ed drawled the word. Australian accent, Beckett decided.

Ed was young: in his late twenties, Beckett guessed. With his short cropped hair and biker's leathers, he probably fancied himself as a bit of a hard nut. Being beaten in a fight would have hurt his pride.

Beckett decided he'd made enough enemies for one day. He extended a hand. 'Nick Beckett.'

Ed hesitated, still staring. Finally he too extended his hand.

'Ed.' He didn't offer a surname.

They shook. Ros walked over and clapped Ed on the shoulder.

'You make a habit of this?' asked Beckett. 'Climbing in through people's windows in the middle of the night?'

Ed didn't smile. 'It's more interesting than coming through the front door.'

Ros put an arm round Ed's shoulders, slipped a blue bottle of mineral water into his hand. She looked at Beckett, smiling a little. 'He's always doing this. When I first met up with him he said he was a helicopter salesman. He didn't tell me he was Spiderman in his spare time.'

'A helicopter salesman?' Beckett stared at the younger man.

'It's one of the things I do,' said Ed casually, winking at Ros.

Ros shook her head. 'Ed, you would not believe the day we've had. Beckett works for – actually, I should say, he used to work for – OK, is on the run from – this place called the Hive. Now we were supposed to be –'

'The Hive?' Ed interrupted. He stared at Beckett again. 'I did a job for them yesterday.'

Beckett stared back at Ed. He realised that the younger man was probably thinking what he had been thinking earlier: has he been sent to kill me?

'You're joking,' Ros was saying.

Ed was still staring at Beckett. 'Got shot at for my troubles.' The suspicion in his eyes was growing fast.

Beckett didn't want another fight. And he'd already decided that he could trust Ed, hard nut or no. Behind the street coolness in those blue-grey eyes was an essential innocence, the sort of innocence that didn't survive if you took certain career options.

'Wait a minute,' he said quickly. 'You were Ballantyne's pilot, right?'

'Ballantyne.' Ed appeared to weigh up the name, the situation. Then he nodded. 'Yeah, that was the guy's name. Is he a friend of yours?'

Beckett swallowed, remembering the soft cough of the silenced gunshot over the phone.

'He was. He's dead.' Beckett paused, swallowed again, looking down at the carpet. 'At least I think he's dead. I heard this shot – at least, I thought I heard this shot – on this tape. The trouble is, the tape's back at the Hive –'

'Right,' Ros broke in. 'So that's the sound on the tape that you want me to enhance.'

'That's right,' said Beckett. 'Except that I haven't got the tape any more.'

Ed looked from one to the other of them. 'Maybe I'm concussed, but why don't you just go back and get it? I mean – you work there, don't you?'

'Because,' said Beckett, 'I'm a wanted man, and the Hive has got a security system that makes Fort Knox look like a playpen.'

Ed was silent for a moment, then he said, 'Sounds interesting.'

Beckett glanced at Ros, saw her raise her eyes to the ceiling.

'Meaning?' he asked Ed.

'Meaning,' said Ed, pulling the top off the bottle of mineral water and sprawling on the couch. 'I like a challenge. This Ballantyne – he seemed like an OK kind of guy. If something's happened to him, well – I'd like to help if I can.' He took a swig of the mineral water.

Beckett wasn't convinced. 'And how exactly could you help?'

Ros grinned. 'Don't ask.'

Ed took another swig of the mineral water. 'This Hive,' he said. 'It's got a helicopter landing pad on the roof, right?'

Beckett nodded, but then said quickly, 'Look, I don't want you getting yourself involved in this. It's my problem. If you try to break in there, you could be killed. Even landing an unauthorised chopper –'

'Could've been killed climbing up here,' interrupted Ed. He rubbed at his neck. 'Damn nearly was, but that was down to you.' He got up. 'I don't think you've got much choice, Beckett. You need some help in this. Do you want to give it a shot or don't you?'

Beckett tried to stare Ed down. But the man was right. He didn't have any choice. None of the Hive operatives was going to help him. Not in this situation.

'OK, we'll try it your way,' he said. Then frowned and added, 'What is your way?'

For the first time, Ed smiled. 'I told you. I don't just sell helicopters for a living.'

'Hello Alan, I'm glad you're in.'

Elena's voice on the phone was warmer than usual, as if something had pleased her. Perhaps, thought Moore, her other contact in the Hive had made a good report about him.

'I thought we could meet for dinner tonight. Do you like seafood?'

Dinner? thought Moore. Then – why not? It's better than meeting up a back street somewhere, and as soon as I get the money I'm away. Flight booked in the morning. Who cares if I'm seen with them? He looked around his almost empty living room, at the bare furniture, at the suitcases neatly piled in the middle of the floor, as if to reassure himself that he really was ready to go.

'Yes,' he said out loud. 'When do we meet?'

A light laugh. 'Ten o'clock. At the Waterfront. They do the most marvellous cajun fish. You like cajun cooking?'

Truthfully, Moore wasn't quite sure what it was. He bypassed the question. 'The Waterfront's all right with me. Will –' he broke off, decided to be careful. Mentioning names on the phone might not be a good idea. 'Will your friend be there?'

'No, he has some urgent business to take care of. You will bring the cards we talked about, though?'

The security cards, with tomorrow's codes for access to the secure store in the Hive. They were in a neat plastic wallet inside Moore's briefcase, their UV tags taped over so that they could be smuggled freely in and out of the building.

'Of course,' he said. 'And you will have my –'

'You do like cajun cooking?' Elena interrupted. 'There's no need to be polite – just say, and we will go somewhere else if you like.'

For the first time Moore actually thought about the meal. Wasn't cajun food supposed to be rather spicy? 'Well,' he said cautiously, 'I'm a cod and chips man myself.'

Another laugh. 'Don't worry, Alan. It will be all right. I will take care of you.'

'Fingers crossed, Ed.'

Ros's voice came through the headset loud and clear. Clear enough to show that she was worried. Ed didn't

66

reply, and didn't cross his fingers. He couldn't. He was too busy adjusting the wing trim of the microlite, making it drop towards the lights of the helipad on the roof of the Hive. He glanced down at the road below, saw the tiny green box of Beckett's 4×4, parked up on one of the quiet roads leading to the docks. He couldn't see Beckett or Ros from this height, but it was reassuring to know that they were in there.

'You're mad. You know that?' Beckett's voice. There was a note of admiration in it. Ed liked that. Beckett was a professional, an ex-Army man. It was a plus to be admired by a pro.

But best to stay cool about it.

'Nah, I just get bored if I don't risk my life at least once a day.' Ed made another adjustment to the trim of the microlite. 'Twice on Sundays.'

The Hive was close now, blotting out his view of the docks. He could see the half-lit shapes of the masts and dishes on the roof.

None of them were in his glide path, which was good.

'Picture coming through OK?' he asked.

'Camera's working all right,' said Ros. 'But something's getting in the way. We can only see half the field of vision.'

Ed thought for a moment. The minicam was attached to a headband. 'Probably the helmet,' he said. 'I'll take it off when I land.'

The wall of the Hive glided below, then the roof. There was about two metres clearance between his feet and the smooth concrete platform.

OK. Close enough.

He swung his legs forward, ready to take the impact, then pulled the cable that furled in the wing.

One, two, three – and his legs jolted as his feet hit the concrete.

'All right, I'm down.'

Even as the wing crumpled behind him, he kneeled down and unstrapped the motor unit. Then removed the offending helmet.

'Camera OK now?' he asked as he got up.

'Fine,' said Ros.

Ed looked around him, saw a landscape of steel dishes, spiked aerials, surrounded by a high parapet. The parapet was broken in several places by railed fire escapes. Beyond it, the city rose against the sky: white superstructures of light, green and blue signs flickering, the steady pulse of the red air-warning lights on the tops of the towers.

Beckett's voice came over the headset. 'You're on the right side there. There's a window in the tower below you.'

Ed looked around again, saw he was standing in the middle of one of the round towers. 'Right or left?' he asked.

'Straight ahead. The way you were looking a few seconds ago.'

Ed turned his head, slowly.

'That's it.'

Ed ran straight forward, looked down over the parapet. It was a sheer drop: fifty metres, maybe.

'Here?'

'Yes.'

'Right. I'm going over.' Ed uncoiled the end of the steel cable from his waist, hooked the grapple over the parapet and secured it. Then he jumped, releasing enough cable to let his body drop about a metre. He stopped himself with his feet against the wall, let the cable brace him, then released some more and jumped again.

He repeated the procedure until he was level with the window. It was tiny: about the size and shape

68

you'd expect on a tourist aeroplane.

'How am I going to get through that?'

'You'll manage,' said Ros, sounding amused.

And Beckett: 'Those are the only windows that open. There's a short corridor inside. No cameras.'

Ed clamped the abseiling cable, so that he could swing on it if he needed to, then peered through the window.

Shadows, half-shadows, a single beam of light.

'Ed.' Ros again. 'Don't break the contact on the window. Use the bypass I gave you. And make sure the contacts are clean.'

'OK, OK,' muttered Ed irritably. Sometimes Ros seemed to think she was the only person in the universe who understood how an electric circuit worked.

He took the bypass from the pouch on his belt and, working one handed with the cabling between his teeth, pushed it against the steel window frame. Then he clipped the other end to the metal surface of the wall itself and closed the switch. A red light flickered on the unit.

Should be OK. He pulled at the window.

It opened. No alarms. Good.

The cable on the bypass uncoiled as he pulled the window open wider. Ed looped it over the top of the frame to give himself a clear passage, then pushed himself away from the wall with his feet.

As he swung back, he brought his feet together. He slid into the window as far as his waist, then stuck.

'Damn,' he muttered aloud. He wriggled forward, curled his legs to grip the wall beneath the frame.

Something gave with a clink of metal. He slithered through, half-falling, then dropped to the ground.

He was inside the Hive.

A short corridor, just like Beckett had said, with no

cameras. A single round spot of light ahead: as his eyes adjusted, he realised that it was a window into a lit room. He took a few paces forward, keeping to the wall away from the light.

It occurred to him that if the room was lit, there might be somebody in there.

'The door on your left leads to a stairwell,' Beckett was telling him. 'The one in front leads to another corridor. That's how you get to the records room.'

The light was on his left. It was the stairwell that was lit.

OK. Well, probably OK.

He walked to the door, peered cautiously into the light.

Yep. Stairwell. Well lit – and empty.

He went to the other door, checked ahead. Saw a corridor spotted with dim lights.

'That it?' he whispered.

'There are cameras in that corridor, Ed.' Ros's voice. She seemed to know as much about the inside of the Hive as Beckett. 'Move as quickly as you can.'

He moved, running down the corridor, ducking in the hope of reducing his visibility.

'Records room on your left now.' Beckett this time. Ed pulled Beckett's passcard from his waist pouch, slid it through the lock, punched in the code Beckett had given him.

The lock clicked and he was in. Blue lighting, filing cabinets with electronic locks. This was it.

'If the night shift are as hot as the day lot,' said Beckett, 'you've got about twenty seconds until they come looking for you.'

Ed unclipped the mirror from his belt and attached it to the camera above the door. Then he looked around the room, stopping his gaze – and the minicam's – at each cabinet in turn until Beckett said, 'That one! Go!'

Ed went. He took the second card from the pouch and slid it through the lock. The light turned green, the lock chimed.

He pulled open the drawer.

He saw the gap in the rack of tapes straight away, heard an intake of breath from Beckett.

'It's not there, is it?' asked Ed.

'You're out of time, Ed,' said Beckett. 'Get out.'

Ed looked around the room in exasperation. 'It's got to be here somewhere.'

A door slammed in the distance.

'Ed.' Ros's voice. 'Get out.'

Ed went to the open door, looked up and down the corridor. He heard the sound of running feet, coming from the direction he'd have to go to get back to that window.

Coming closer.

They'll be looking in the records room, he thought. So I'd better –

There was a door opposite. He dived in, found himself in a darkened office.

I could hide, he thought. And then: damn, I didn't close the records room door. They're going to know I'm here, for sure. Any second.

There was a shout from outside, and an alarm sounded, shockingly loud. Suddenly the office was full of blue light, strobing across the walls. In the light Ed could see clearly: a desk, a computer, a couple of plastic trays with J COTTRELL stencilled on them in neat white letters.

Cottrell. That was the guy's name: Beckett's boss, the one who was after him.

Ed looked in the trays, saw a DAT tape with the word 'Beckett' scrawled on it.

'Hey!' he shouted. 'You won't believe this! I've found it – in Cottrell's in-tray!'

71

'I should have guessed,' said Beckett.

Anything else Beckett might have said was drowned by an explosion of machine-gun fire. Ed saw holes appearing in the door and the desk jolting under the impact of bullets.

He looked around for another door, saw one that looked suspiciously as if it led to some inner office with no other exit.

Chance it, he thought. No choice.

The door did lead to an inner office. Ed saw another computer. An anglepoise lamp. Red optical discs neatly filed in racks.

A barred door marked FIRE EXIT.

Ed grinned and blessed the safety regulations. He dived for the bar, pushed open the door. The glass signal point shattered and the clamour of a fire bell added itself to the whooping of the intruder alarm. Ed found himself on a platform with metal steps leading down to the paved courtyard at the front of the building.

He was about to start down the steps when he saw a pair of guards step out onto the courtyard, guns in their hands.

They looked around, then looked up and saw him.

Ed heard their shouts as he turned and ran up the open steps, two at a time, three at a time.

A patter of gunfire. Bullets clattered off the metal around him.

No 'shoot to wound' policy here, then.

'And sometimes I risk my life three times in less than an hour,' he muttered. He jumped the last metre and a half to the parapet, scrambled over.

Two more guards were standing on the far side of the roof, silhouetted against the illuminated towers of the city. As Ed watched, they started jogging towards the microlite.

72

Ed swore and ran flat out across the darkened roof, ducking down in case the men saw him and opened fire. He made it to the machine, heard the shouted 'Halt!' as he struggled into the harness.

Helmet. Where was the damn helmet?

Never mind. Too late. Ed ran for the edge of the roof, pulling at the starter cord of the motor in the same motion.

The motor didn't start.

Ed stopped on the very edge of the parapet, balancing precariously, and pulled desperately at the cord. Gunfire clattered behind him, amazingly loud. The metal rail of the parapet rang as a bullet hit it.

'I can't get the motor to work!' he yelled, though he knew there was nothing Beckett or Ros could do to help him.

He looked at the drop, at the wing crumpled behind him. Felt the light, cold wind blowing against his left cheek.

Just strong enough.

Ed unclipped the useless motor from its harness, hurled it back at the approaching guards. As he'd hoped, they stopped and ducked down, perhaps thinking it was some kind of bomb.

Then Ed was running along the parapet, into the wind. He felt the wing fill behind him, felt the fabric shudder as the air caught it.

The roof began to curve, the wind dropped away. Ed cursed, ran faster, grunting with the effort.

At last the straps tightened on his chest and his arms, as the dragging fabric became a true wing.

Ed jumped.

For a sickening moment, he fell: then, with a jolt that knocked the breath out of him, the straps tightened again. He adjusted the trim of the wing as best he could, watched the ground swing below him. The docks glittered, reflecting the street lamps around them.

And under one of the street lamps, the tiny green box of Beckett's car.

Ed whooped his victory. 'All right, guys. I'm coming home!'

« Seven »

The lab was quiet, and dark. The man hadn't turned the lights on, and didn't intend to. The small torch he was carrying was enough. He knew his way around.

He walked past benches, the torch flashing on white tiles, a microscope, a tank full of carnivorous fish, a gutted rat in a storage jar. His target was at the far end. The 'red cupboard' – actually a refrigeration unit, its door marked with red poison icons and warnings in several languages.

The door was locked. Which it should be. The man unlocked it, pulled out a rack of small, sealed, glass tubes.

He selected one marked 'V5'.

Yes. That would do it.

He took the briefcase he was carrying, opened it, took out the device within. It looked like a gun – a large, heavy, gun – but it wasn't.

It was something potentially more deadly than that.

And this was an opportunity to test its potential.

He took the sealed tube, pushed it into a socket above the barrel of the weapon, then closed the protective cover.

A faint vibration, a muffled hiss, told him that the loading had been successful.

He closed the red cupboard again, locked it. Then he put the weapon back into the briefcase, locked that, and made his way out of the lab.

In the glass corridor outside, he took a phone from his pocket, touched the button that added his own private encryption to the call, then dialled a number.

A woman's voice answered. 'Yes?'

'Marasco here. The field test you asked for is under way.'

'Good,' said the voice of the Managing Director. 'Let me know the results as soon as you can.'

« Eight »

'Someone in the Hive set it up.'

Ballantyne's voice. The words, the inflection, every spike and trough of noise in the background, were recorded as firmly in Ros's brain as in the RAM of the audio analyser in front of her. In fact she barely heard the words any more. Instead she watched the play of frequencies on the analyser, the movements of blue and gold and white lights that represented the sounds. She could feel Beckett's gaze on her, waiting for her verdict.

Though she was pretty sure he already knew what it would be.

The voice on the tape went on: 'I'm sorry, I'll just be a couple of seconds –'

And then the sound: a metallic cough, a muffled thud, and something else behind it.

Ros touched a fader, replayed the last half second.

Replayed it again.

Again.

Then she looked up at Beckett and said, 'No doubt in my mind, that's a shot into a body.'

77

Beckett looked away, staring at the display as if the flickering lights, the multiple sliders, the cabling, the huge speaker stacks, could somehow have told a different story.

Ros looked down at the console. 'Sorry, Beckett.'

'What's the sound just before, umm – Beckett broke off, made a vague gesture at the analyser. 'Just before that, in the background. There's a noise.'

Ros nodded. There were several noises, in fact: separating them would be the problem.

'I'll see what I can do,' she said. She reconfigured the manual faders, then typed some instructions into the analyser through her computer.

'What're you trying to do?'

Ed's voice, from behind her. She'd almost forgotten he was there.

'I'm telling the system to isolate anything that looks like a human voice. It's possible the killer said something to Ballantyne, before or after the shot.' She watched as the computer digested the data. The speakers made a few clicks and thuds.

Then a woman's voice: 'Excuse me, will you be long?'

Beckett stared at the speakers, swallowed.

'Do you recognise the voice?' asked Ros. 'The range is no more than a couple of metres, or we wouldn't be able to hear it at this level. She's probably the killer.'

Beckett shook his head. 'There's another sound. In the background.'

'It sounds mechanical, Nick,' said Ed. 'Could be a train, a truck going past – anything. Why do you want to know?'

'Because it might help us work out where Ballantyne was shot, which could lead us to the killer.'

'How?' Ros asked.

'Ballantyne – he'd followed his suspect, right? And

he'd bugged her car. If we can pick up the signals from the bug, then we can find her.'

'But the range of that sort of bug is strictly limited,' said Ros.

'Exactly. He can't have been far from her location when he made the call. He probably had her address – where she was staying. Something. Or he wouldn't have broken cover.' Beckett was speaking rapidly, words tumbling out in a heap.

A man grasping at straws, Ros realised. She tried to think of something to say, something that would make Beckett's plan seem anything other than wildly unlikely to work. She couldn't.

Judging by his silence, Ed couldn't either.

Beckett's gaze flicked around from Ros, to Ed, to the speakers, back to Ros again. 'Come on,' he said. 'This is all I've got.'

Ros looked at him. His face was pale, the skin under his eyes dark.

If we don't find out what's going on here, thought Ros, if we can't *prove* what's happened is real, then, sooner or later, the Hive will find Beckett. He'll be discredited – at least.

More likely he'll end up like Ballantyne.

And he knows that.

She heard the sound of the shot, almost as if the system was playing it again. The metallic cough of the silenced gun. The dull thud of the bullet hitting Ballantyne's body.

She reached for the faders, said, 'I'll see if I can get the background any clearer.'

The first attempt brought up a rumble of trains: light transit, Ros guessed, rather than mainline. She told the system to eliminate both the voices and the trains.

What was left was a scratchy noise, echoing, oddly familiar.

'Sounds like a station announcement,' said Ed. 'You know, one of those you can't hear because it echoes too much.'

Ros glanced at him, nodded. She cut in an echo filter on the amplifier, then used the deck to boost the frequencies in the mid-range area you'd expect to come out of a station tannoy.

On the next replay the voice was clear: 'Central Junction. This is Central Junction. Change here for Riverside Gardens.'

Beckett's face broke into a broad grin. He reached out and clapped Ros on the shoulder.

'Thanks.'

Ros smiled. 'Don't mention it. All we need now is to do the impossible a few times before breakfast, and we'll be home and dry.'

Ed jumped up off his chair. 'Sounds OK to me,' he said. 'Let's get going.'

The station was quiet, which Beckett supposed was normal at 9.30 on a Tuesday night. Central Junction was a commuter station, a daytime place. Not many people going out for the night would be using this line. He looked around the floodlit platform for a phone box, but couldn't see one.

'Perhaps it's on the bridge,' suggested Ed.

Beckett nodded and started up the ramp. The bridge was new and clean, a tube of glass supported by steel hoops and lined with white sun blinds. He saw the phone box about halfway along. He ran up to it, crouched down and examined the ground.

There was nothing. No trace of blood, no mark at all on the pale floor tiles. Whoever had killed Ballantyne had cleared up thoroughly afterwards.

Which was only to be expected.

'This where she shot him?'

Ed's voice made Beckett jump. He stood up, said quietly, 'Looks like it.'

'But no proof, right?'

Beckett looked out at the railway lines and the night. 'No proof,' he said.

An electronic beeping from the direction of the ramp made them both look round.

'Guys?' Ros's voice. She was approaching, carrying a RaSearch screen unit in her hands. 'I think I've got something.'

'Ballantyne's bug?' asked Ed.

'Yes.' Ros gestured at the RaSearch display.

Beckett looked at it over her shoulder. Orange and blue LCDs, backlit. The bridge showed up, a faint double trace, a little blurred by Ros's motion. Somewhere beyond it, amongst the random dots of echoes from nearby houses, a bright cross shape flickered in time with the beeping. A string of numbers was printed next to it.

'Is that the frequency he was using?' Ed asked Ros.

'Probably. It's one of the ones the Hive uses, anyway.'

Beckett decided not to ask Ros how she knew that. There wasn't time. Instead, he said, 'Log the direction, in case we lose it.'

Ros punched a couple of keys on the RaSearch. Beckett stared out across the platform in the direction the machine had indicated. It certainly wasn't far. It looked like it was the Central Park Estate.

Very rich, very exclusive.

But then anyone who could buy their way into Hive security, as this person evidently had, would have to be rich.

And if they were rich already . . .

For the first time, Beckett started wondering about motives. They were after SACROS and it wasn't just money that they needed.

Which left the other thing. The other thing that SACROS offered.

Power.

Unlimited power.

Beckett glanced at Ed and Ros, who were talking quietly by the phone box.

'Come on,' he said, 'Let's get in the car.'

'You're sure it's this one?'

Ed was sitting in the back seat. He couldn't see the RaSearch screen on Ros's lap. But from behind the steering wheel Beckett could see enough. Blurry echoes of the garages they'd just passed. The shape of the house slowly forming out of blue specks.

And the clear cross of the bug signal, just outside the walls.

Beckett looked up, saw grey stone walls, a wooden gate, a white 4WD car parked on the hardstanding.

'That's the car,' he said. 'It matches the description on Ballantyne's initial report.'

'Ballantyne had reported all this officially?' Ed again. 'So – maybe I'm just stupid, but won't someone follow it up?'

'She was only a witness at that stage, a witness to yesterday's incident. Someone he was going to interview. He had a registration, a description. That was all.' Beckett paused, shrugged. 'He may not even have made that official report. He told me about it in the tea room – it was just casual chat. By the time he was killed he knew a lot more than that of course, but only I know about it. And I'm on the run.'

Whilst Beckett was talking, Ros had produced a palmtop computer from her bag and clipped it to the RaSearch. She typed quickly on the tiny keyboard.

'What are you doing?' asked Beckett.

'I'm into the phone company's records, trying to

find out who lives here.'

Beckett nodded. It was the obvious thing to do. Illegal, of course, if you weren't a Hive operative. But it was too late to worry about legality now. He watched the data fade in on the palmtop's screen.

'Well, the house is alarmed and the phone's in the name of Elena Johnson,' said Ros. 'Mean anything to anybody?'

Beckett shook his head, then looked over his shoulder at Ed, who shrugged.

Beckett picked up his torch from the dash, grabbed his lock picking kit with the same hand. 'Let's take a look around.'

'Hang on a sec.' Ed, again. Beckett looked round, wondering what the matter was *now*. 'We know she did it, why play spy games on her?'

Beckett closed his eyes for a moment, remembered what he'd thought a few hours ago when he'd first met Ed. That he was essentially an innocent.

It was obviously true. Ed really didn't understand.

Well, now was the time to make it crystal clear.

'Look, Ed,' he said firmly. 'Someone at the Hive has framed me. If I go to Cottrell with an illegally obtained name and a few pretty pictures, they'll just lock me up and throw away the key. I need to find out who did it, who's working with this woman. Right?'

Ed stared for a moment, then nodded slowly. 'OK.'

Beckett put his hand on the door to open it, then saw movement from the corner of his eye. He froze, turned his eyes – just his eyes.

He saw the woman in the royal blue coat walking out of the house.

'Down!' he whispered, ducking under the steering wheel.

Ros slipped down in her seat, almost onto the floor. Ed, he hoped, had vanished in the back.

Beckett waited. He heard a car door slam. A faint rattle of keys. The chatter of a starter motor, the rumble of an engine.

Bright light filled the car. The door banged again.

'What's she doing?' whispered Ed.

'Opening the gate,' said Beckett tersely.

A moment later, there was a faint rattle, and the creak of wood on wood.

'I can tell you've done this kind of thing before,' whispered Ros.

Beckett shushed them. This was no time for chat. The woman could well be a killer, and doubtless wouldn't hesitate to kill again if she discovered them spying on her. He listened carefully as she got into her car again, drove through the gate, got out, closed it behind her. It seemed to take for ever.

At last, the car swung past them, only metres away. For a moment, it seemed to pause right by them, then the sound of its engine receded.

'She didn't see us,' muttered Ros.

'Hope not,' said Beckett, sitting up. 'Right. Ed, you follow her. Me and Ros'll go take a look inside.' He got out of the car and ran around the front towards the gate. As he did so he looked down the road, saw Elena Johnson's car turning left.

Beckett turned back to relay this to Ed, who was already getting into the driving seat. But Ros was speaking to him, handing him a small object that looked like a steel comb.

Ed frowned at it, and Beckett heard Ros's voice. 'It's a tracer. So I can find you if you get lost.'

Not a bad idea, thought Beckett. This Ros is at least as smart as Ballantyne said she was.

But Ed was arguing, again. 'I am out of short trousers now, you know.'

Ros shrugged, took the device back, got out of the

car. Beckett was about to intervene, but decided that there was no more time to argue. If Elena Johnson's car got out of the one kilometre scanning radius of the RaSearch, then they'd lose her until she came back.

Ed started up the engine, gunned it, roared away with a screech of tyres.

'What was all that about?' asked Beckett.

She shrugged. 'Just sometimes,' she said, 'I wish Ed would grow up.'

'Oh, he will,' said Beckett, looking at the tail-lights of the retreating car. Then he looked back at Ros and grinned. 'I reckon it'll happen when he gets to retirement age.'

« Nine »

Marasco watched.

He propped the night vision binoculars against the windscreen of his car and watched as the two people left outside Elena Johnson's house proceeded to break in.

It was a very professional job. The woman disabled the alarm, then the man picked the lock on the front door. The whole process took no more than a minute.

Marasco was a little surprised that they seemed to find it so easy, but he wasn't surprised that they were there. Not given what he knew about the likely contents of the house.

He was only annoyed that they'd got there first.

Still, he thought. It was possible to do something about that.

One by one, he undid the three catches on the briefcase in the passenger seat, holding them with his thumb so that there was no sound when they opened.

He looked inside. Next to the device that looked like a gun was a tiny sealed plastic bubble and a pair of power controlled tweezers. He picked up the tweezers, used their pointed legs to puncture the bubble, then picked up the object within.

He loaded it into the muzzle of the launching device. Waited, as the intricate machinery prepared the tiny missile for launch.

After a while, the red light on the launching device changed to green.

Marasco wound down the window of the car, and aimed the device at the house, slipping his finger over the trigger. A small screen showed the cross-hairs neatly positioned over the front door, which had been left ajar by the burglars, presumably for a quick getaway.

Now, there wouldn't be any getaway.

Marasco smiled at the thought.

Then he pulled the trigger.

« Ten »

Ros swung the flashlight around, saw a wood-panelled room with walls of bare grey brick. Wooden beams across the ceiling. A piano; a huge swiss cheese plant; a vast, strange shape that on closer inspection turned out to be a stuffed camel.

Beckett was ahead of her, examining, with apparent interest, a Zulu shield hanging on one wall. Then his flashlight beam moved to a pair of toy horses, child-sized, on a dresser.

'I suppose you people from the Hive do this all the time,' commented Ros.

'Only in the national interest,' replied Beckett. But his tone of voice made it clear what he thought of *that*.

Ros grinned. 'Of course.'

'I'll take upstairs,' said Beckett. He started up the open wooden steps without waiting for a reply.

Ros prowled around the room. She rooted in her pockets for the digital minicam, took a couple of test shots of the dresser.

Then she saw the photograph. A young man and a young woman, smiling at the camera.

She zoomed in, took a snap.

Behind her, she heard a buzzing sound.

She jumped, turned round, saw nothing. But the buzzing continued, weaving in and out like the sound of a circling insect.

Except that it wasn't an insect sound. It was metallic, mechanical.

Some kind of alarm system? thought Ros. But it seemed to be mobile.

'Beckett?' she called.

No response.

Suddenly the buzzing stopped and there was a faint, metallic click.

Ros approached the source of the sound, saw something glinting on the bookshelves at the back of the room. She raised the camera, zoomed in, caught a glimpse of something rather like a mechanical mosquito with a very long sting.

It seemed more absurd than dangerous.

She zoomed in closer, but before she could take a picture there was another click and a faint hissing sound.

Ros felt a burning sensation in her nostrils, then in her throat. Her vision blurred.

What −?

Then she realised.

She tried to call out to Beckett, tried to shout the word, 'Gas', but her throat was burning too much for her to speak.

It was nice to have technology on your side, thought Ed as he watched Elena Johnson and the heavy-set man walk across the gangplank to the floating restaurant. All he had to do was get a table on the same floor as theirs − and Ros's little bug would do the rest.

He got out of the car and strolled as casually as he could towards the restaurant. The smell of food wafted across the water, rich and spicy. Ed looked up at the red and gold lettering above the gangplank, saw the words, 'Cajun' and 'Seafood'.

My favourite, he thought. Hope I get a chance to eat some of it.

Inside, a waiter dressed in white shirt and bow tie greeted him.

'Table for one,' said Ed. From the corner of his eye he saw Elena and her companion start up the stairs. He quickly said, 'Upstairs, for preference.'

'Inside or outside?' asked the waiter.

'I don't know. Let me take a look.'

Upstairs, the restaurant was fairly busy: but the tables on the inside, which had a view of the road and the dark buildings rather than the river, were mostly empty. Ed saw red satin tablecloths, golden napkins folded on them, plum coloured candles.

Elena and the unknown man were seating themselves there, in a corner well away from everyone else.

They don't want to be overheard, thought Ed. Which means either they want a romantic evening, or they're up to no good. And considering what we know about Elena so far –

'Inside,' he said to the waiter. 'But –' he gestured at the couple, now seating themselves, Elena handing her coat to a waiter '– down the other end from those two if you can. I expect they'd like a bit of privacy.'

The waiter nodded and smiled. Ed slipped his hand into his pocket, checked the connection between the pen mike and the recorder.

All ready.

'I'm starving,' he said to the waiter. 'Do you know that I haven't eaten since twelve o'clock?'

Beckett had started moving as soon as he heard the sound. It had been a *wrong* sound. Metal popping. A hissing noise.

By the time he reached the bottom of the stairs, Ros was halfway to the front door, doubled over with a hand across her mouth. When she saw him she straightened up, gestured at her throat.

Beckett opened his own mouth to speak, was stopped by a frantic gesture from Ros, her other hand clamping over the first, her eyes widening.

He remembered the hissing sound, and understood.

She was miming: face mask.

Something in the air.

Beckett stopped breathing and clamped a hand over his mouth, though he was well aware that if the atmosphere contained any sort of neurotoxin this would do him no good at all.

He would just have to hope it didn't.

He ran after Ros out of the building. He slammed the door behind them, then kept running across the hardstanding, though his lungs were straining for air. Ros had already given up and was breathing in great gulps, leaning on the gate.

Beckett held his breath a little longer, waited.

'It's OK,' Ros said after a few seconds. Her voice was thick, clotted with phlegm. 'It was a tiny thing. Some kind of surveillance bug, I think. I saw a lens. Then it exploded in my face.'

Beckett nodded, took a gulp of the clean air, then said simply, 'Run. It might spread.' He ran through the gate and down the road.

At the junction with the main road he stopped again.

'All right?' asked Ros, breathing hard, her lungs wheezing like a forty-a-day smoker's.

'I should think so. If it didn't kill you when it first went off, it isn't going to be able to do it from this range.' *I hope.*

Ros leaned against the wall at the side of the road,

closed her eyes. 'I tasted this – stuff in my mouth, and my throat seemed to catch fire. It was horrible.'

Beckett glanced at her. 'You feel OK now?'

Ros nodded. 'My throat's a bit sore.'

'You were lucky. That must have been a low dose, and only of old-fashioned gas – probably intended to work only at a very short range. Maybe just a deterrent. If they'd been using neurotoxins you'd be dead.' *And so would I.*

Ros pushed herself upright again and looked over her shoulder, up the slope to Elena Johnson's house. 'Well, at least we've found something out about her,' she said. 'She doesn't mind killing people – and she's got something to hide.'

'We knew that already,' said Beckett, suddenly gloomy. In the excitement of the escape, he'd completely forgotten that they hadn't found anything in the house. Not one single useful thing. 'The question is, what's she hiding?'

Ros touched his shoulder. 'Cheer up,' she said. 'I got some pictures. There might be something on one of them. Let's get a cab back to base and have a look.'

She took her phone out of her bag and started dialling.

In different circumstances, Alan Moore might have thought that Elena liked him. She was friendly, almost flirtatious, in her smart green jacket and trousers. She was touching his hands as she talked, smiling every time he spoke.

But in these circumstances all this only made him suspicious.

Professionally suspicious.

He interrupted Elena's prattle about the relative merits of salmon and sea bass to say, 'What about our business?'

Elena looked up at him, her eyes sharp. 'You *have* got the access cards?'

Moore reached into his pocket. 'Of course.' He pulled the card out, handed it to Elena under the table without looking at her. There was only one person in their half of the restaurant, a young man in a leather jacket sitting on his own, and he had his nose in the menu – but it was best to take no chances.

'And this is tomorrow's?' asked Elena.

'Look. I program them. No one else knows the codes. Now, have you got something for me?'

Elena smiled. It was a charming smile, but Moore didn't like it. He didn't want charm, he wanted cash.

'Your payment,' she said, reaching inside her handbag.

'Yes,' said Moore, not attempting to hide his exasperation. If she hadn't got it this time . . .

Elena pulled out a package, wrapped in fawn coloured paper and tied with a gold ribbon. 'The money's being arranged, don't worry.' She pulled at the lapel of Moore's jacket, pushed the package into his inner pocket. 'In the meantime, a little something extra. To thank you for being so patient.'

Moore stared at her. Did she really think he was going to be fobbed off with a present? A bit of fancy aftershave, or a pair of 22 carat cuff links? He opened his mouth to say it – 'I want my money' – but Elena got there first.

'Open it later. Now, let's enjoy our meal.' She began examining the menu, then frowned suddenly. 'I'm sorry, but you must excuse me. I've left something in the car. I won't be a moment. Order for me, will you?'

Before Moore could say anything, she was gone, hurrying across the restaurant and down the steps.

Moore looked at the menu for a moment, then looked back at the stairway. He didn't like this. He didn't like it at all. The woman had got what she wanted, and now she was leaving.

He was suddenly sure that she wouldn't be back.

He got up to follow Elena, then saw another movement from the corner of his eye. The young man in the leather jacket had got up from his table and was also hurrying down the steps.

After Elena.

Moore froze. Elena was being watched. *They* were being watched. He didn't recognise the operative, but the man had to be something to do with the Hive.

Feeling suddenly sick, Moore sat down again and pretended to study the menu. His only hope was to pretend not to be involved, to pretend this was a social occasion, that he'd been trying to chat her up. Something like that. He would think of something. As long as he didn't admit –

But Alan Moore never did get the chance to work out what he shouldn't admit, because at that moment the package in his inside pocket received a signal from a device held, somewhere outside the building, in Elena Johnson's hand. A contact closed, a small electric current flowed for a fraction of a second.

Then half a kilo of high explosive detonated, pulping Moore's body, ramming his spine and fragments of his skull into his brain so quickly that he didn't even have time to realise he was dying.

He was just gone, transformed into several pieces of inert meat surrounded by a cloud of flame and smoke.

No longer a person.

No longer a problem.

Taken care of.

« Eleven »

The photo filled most of the computer screen. It showed the dresser in Elena Johnson's lounge, the two toy horses, a ceramic pot of some kind, and a photograph in a frame.

Beckett watched as Ros dragged the enhancement box over to it, clicked on the mouse.

There was a second's pause, and then the photo and a small part of its frame filled the screen: a young couple, some kind of lake in the background. The girl was clearly Elena, much younger but still fundamentally the same. The boy . . .

Before Beckett could examine the boy, Ros had clicked on the mouse again, and Elena's face filled the screen.

Beckett suddenly remembered the coffee he was carrying and plonked one of the mugs down on the desk beside Ros.

'Thanks, Beckett,' she said absently, tapping away at the keyboard.

A set of vaguely familiar icons appeared on the top line of the screen.

'What are you doing?' asked Beckett.

95

'I'm updating a photo I found at Elena's house. With computer ageing.'

'Oh, yeah,' said Beckett. 'The Americans invented it to find missing kids. We've got one on the mainframe at the Hive.'

Ros just glanced at him, then took a gulp of coffee.

'Hang on a minute,' said Beckett, suddenly realising why those icons on the top line looked so familiar. 'This is the one on the mainframe at the Hive.'

Ros smiled. 'You're catching on.'

Beckett decided not to ask how she'd got it. Instead, he looked back at the screen. The picture of Elena already looked a little older, a little more like the woman he'd seen leaving the house.

He frowned. 'Can you age the bloke up instead? He looked kind of familiar.'

'That's what I was about to do.' Ros tapped at the keyboard and the original photo returned. She enlarged the boy's face, engaged the ageing program.

'How long's it take on your system?' asked Beckett.

'Couple of minutes.'

Beckett didn't believe it. 'That's faster than the mainframe!'

Ros looked at him. ''Course it is. Ever heard of government spending limits? You know how old the motherboard is on that thing?'

Beckett just shook his head.

'Excuse me a minute.' Ros got up and walked in the direction of her workshop. Beckett glanced after her. Through the half-windowed wall he saw the light switch on, revealing a cluttered space full of electronic devices in various stages of dismemberment. He heard a few clattering noises; evidently Ros was searching for something.

He returned his attention to the screen. The boy already looked different; he was a young man now.

Beckett checked the 'Estimated Age' readout, saw that it had reached twenty-eight.

The guy definitely looked familiar.

At thirty-two he looked more familiar still. But there was something missing. Perhaps it was something to do with the hairline.

Thirty-six. The hairline receded.

Yes. He was sure of it.

The phone rang.

Beckett glanced at it irritably, looked up to see if Ros was around. He couldn't see her, only the white glare of the workshop. She must be out of earshot. Anyway, she wasn't answering the phone.

Beckett picked it up. 'Hello.'

A very familiar voice said, 'Beckett?'

Beckett's heart almost stopped. 'Mr Dent?'

'You've been rather a naughty boy, haven't you, Beckett?'

Beckett opened his mouth to say something, then thought better of it. If Dent was in on this . . .

'And I must warn you,' Dent's voice went on, 'beware –'

Beckett saw a movement from the direction of the workshop, saw Ros walking out into the section he could see through the window, with a phone against her ear.

'– of women who drive too fast.'

Except that Ros was speaking at the same time.

The same words.

Beckett held the phone away from his ear, stared at Ros.

'Across muddy lawns.'

As Beckett stared, Ros switched her phone off. 'Sorry, Beckett. Couldn't resist.' She walked back into the computer room. 'I've been trying to think how they set you up. I figured it had to be something like this.'

She showed him the unit she was carrying. Clipped over the mouthpiece of the phone she'd been using was a small black box with a smartcard slot and a couple of toggle switches. 'Someone's just sampled him, then used a voice synthesizer.'

Beckett squeezed his eyes shut, tried to take it all in. 'How did you get a sample of Dent's voice, then?' he asked.

'Do you really want to know?'

Beckett just looked at her.

She gestured at the screen. 'Voiceprint ID. On the mainframe.' She shrugged. 'Not very well protected, I'm afraid.'

Beckett shook his head slowly. 'So that's how Mr Dent made an internal call when he wasn't in the building, right?'

Ros nodded, took a sip of her coffee.

'But if he didn't make the call,' Beckett went on, 'who did?' He tried to think who would have access to the voiceprint system at the Hive.

Ros gestured at the computer screen with her coffee cup. 'Him?'

Beckett looked at the screen, saw that the ageing program had stopped at forty-five.

Beckett stared at the face. The hair was almost gone now.

'Hang on a minute.' Beckett picked up a marker pen from the desk, began drawing on the screen.

'Beckett!' Ros didn't sound pleased at the vandalism, but Beckett took no notice, just kept on drawing. A neatly trimmed beard. A moustache.

'Do you recognise him?' Ros had evidently realised what he was doing.

Beckett just grinned. Grinned even though his world should have been turned upside down by the revelation.

Grinned because he knew that he should have guessed it all along.

'Recognise him?' he said. 'I work for him. That's Cottrell!'

John Cottrell walked.

Something in his head whispered, *official car, you should use an official car. Undercover operation.*

But he knew that was ridiculous, so he walked.

In other circumstances, the night would have been pleasant. Cottrell didn't mind the cold. That, and the clear street lamps, the washed-looking fronts of the houses, reminded him of walking home from Elena's when they were kids.

All those years ago.

And now ...

Elena hadn't sounded frightened on the phone, but what she'd said had been frightening. The unlocked door, the bypassed alarm system.

'It isn't the Hive,' he'd told her. 'It can't be the Hive. Unless Moore –'

'Moore is taken care of.'

'So then who is it?'

Elena had laughed then. 'The One That Got Away?'

'Beckett?'

'Of course, Beckett. And his friend that you mentioned, with the fast car. Did you check the registration?'

Cottrell hadn't then, but he had since, and had found that it belonged to Ros Henderson, proprietor of Gizmos, a person well known to the Hive.

Too well known. And too clever.

He'd wanted to kill them at once, but Elena had said, 'We need to know how much they know. Keep one alive – the Hive man. And be careful how you dispose of the other one. We already have too many corpses.'

99

Elena had always been the thoughtful one. The one who considered everything first, weighed the risks. As usual, she was right.

Cottrell looked up, saw the complex ahead of him: shadowy curved brickwork, a few lit windows, the blue illuminated sign.

Yes. This was the place.

He reached under his jacket and touched the hard metal of the gun in its shoulder holster there.

All ready.

As with any well-planned operation, with luck he wouldn't have to use the weapon.

But if he did – well, that would just be too bad, wouldn't it?

'Voiceprint ID download complete.'

Ros stared at the words on the computer screen for a full second before they actually made sense to her.

I'm tired, she realised. It's past midnight and I haven't stopped once since five.

She clicked on the mouse, listened to the cold, precise voice through the speakers.

'That's him all right,' said Beckett. 'So what do you suggest we do with it?'

Ros smiled. 'I don't know. Make a phone call to Elena. Tell her the game's up, using his voice.'

'That won't work. He might even be there when we phone.'

Ros shrugged. 'OK, can you think of anything better?'

Beckett took a gulp of his coffee, shrugged. 'Uhh – no.' He paused. 'Perhaps Ed will have something.'

Ros glanced at her watch. 'Wherever he is. I told him to take that tracer.'

Beckett nodded, then said, 'You get some sleep. I'll –' he shrugged. 'I'll hang around.'

Ros opened her mouth to argue, then decided that she was too tired.

The phone rang.

Ros stared at it for a moment, then said, 'Ed.' She picked up the receiver.

'Is Nick Beckett there?' It wasn't Ed. The voice was the one she'd just heard from the computer system: John Cottrell.

Ros's surprise must have shown on her face, because Beckett said, 'What?'

Ros switched off the phone mike. 'Cottrell.'

Beckett took the phone without a word. Switched the mike back on.

'Sir?'

Ros touched a key that put Cottrell's voice through the computer system. She wanted to hear what was going on.

'. . . a mistake earlier today. I think we should talk. Now. Away from the Hive.' A pause. 'I think that Ballantyne was right.'

Ros felt goose bumps rise on her arms. She didn't like that voice. She shook her head at Beckett, but he only frowned and turned away. 'Where should we meet, sir?'

A pause. 'How about the Overlander?'

Beckett nodded. 'I'll be there in half an hour.' Then he put the phone down.

'Where's the Overlander?' asked Ros.

'It's a pub on the waterfront,' said Beckett, getting up and gulping down the last of his coffee. 'Not the sort of place Cottrell would normally be seen dead in, but I suppose he's desperate.'

Ros got up too. 'Beckett, I don't like this. I think it's a trap.'

Beckett was already halfway to the door. He turned and said quickly, 'So do I. That's why you're not

101

coming with me.' He took his coat from the peg on the door, and began putting it on.

She started after him, caught the door as he tried to close it. He turned again to face her, mouth open for an objection.

But Ros got there first. 'You might need a getaway driver.'

Beckett hesitated, met her eyes, then sighed and said, 'We'd better take your car then.'

'Done.'

In the lift, Ros said, 'I don't get it. If Cottrell is the mole, what the hell is he playing at? Couldn't he just take SACROS, if he wanted to?'

Beckett shook his head. 'No. He hasn't got the authority. He'd need passcards, codes, that kind of stuff.'

The lift doors opened, revealing the bare lighting of the lobby. Ros walked to the back and through the doors that led to the car park.

'So what's going on?' she asked.

'I don't know. I know that SACROS can be used to blackmail companies – even governments I should think. I know that Cottrell's obsessed with the potential power it has. What I still don't have is proof.'

They reached the car. Ros unlocked the doors, got in.

And heard a movement that shouldn't have been there.

She drew in a breath to speak, but it was too late. Beckett was jolting upright. Someone was in the back seat.

A gun was against Beckett's neck.

The man holding the gun had the face of the man on the computer screen. He had the beard and moustache that Beckett had drawn.

And he had the voice, too.

'Start the car,' he said.

Ros felt every muscle stiffen. No, she thought. I won't do this. I won't be caught this easily.

But she knew she had no choice in the matter.

'Start the car,' the cold, precise voice repeated. 'Start it now.'

The hotel bar was comfortable, and almost empty. Real leather seats, velvet curtains across the windows, air conditioning. The sweet scent of gin and tonic, the occasional clink of glasses, the gleam of soft lights on the bottles behind the bar. The night outside didn't exist any more, was only a backdrop to murmured conversations.

All that was good. The Managing Director liked comfort, liked warmth, liked silence. The protective cocoon of wealth. Yes.

She touched the black diamond that hung around her neck and smiled.

The man sitting opposite her smiled too, but the Managing Director doubted that it was because he was comfortable. Something in the shape of the lines on his face, in the set of his eyes, told her that he was rarely comfortable.

He spoke slowly, his asiatic accent heavy. 'We are interested in all the systems you offered to us yesterday.'

The Managing Director nodded. She'd hoped as much. She sipped her wine, waited.

'We need to know if they have been tested adequately.'

The Managing Director lowered her glass, smiled again. 'Of course. One of my colleagues has made field trials of the surveillance apparatus – the "flybugs". They perform according to specification. They're almost undetectable, even in flight.'

'And your colleague has tested the neurotoxin release mechanism?'

The Managing Director inclined her head.

'It was – fairly effective. But of course we couldn't test it with a full strength agent. Not here.'

'I was coming to that. We require the –' he too paused '– the loan of one of the full strength pheromone-specific agents. And the delivery system. To perform our own test of its effectiveness.'

The man's gaze was level, icy. Just for a moment, the Managing Director felt cold, as if the night outside had somehow sneaked through the velvet curtains.

The Managing Director let a slight frown form on her face. 'That would be difficult,' she said. 'If the device remains our property, any *test* could create severe difficulties for us.'

The man gave his tight, uncomfortable smile and leaned forward over the low glass table. 'We would take full responsibility if any difficulties should arise.'

The Managing Director took another sip of her wine. 'There would have to be an additional payment.'

The man nodded, named a sum.

The Managing Director smiled, touched the black diamond at her throat.

'I'm sure we could do business on those terms,' she said.

« Thirteen »

Ed had decided to use the front door this time. For starters, he had the key. Secondly, he didn't feel much like any climbing tricks now. What he'd seen at the restaurant had sickened him. OK, Moore had been up to no good. Betraying his own side, and for money by the sound of it. But Elena. Elena was a killer. First Ballantyne, now her own allies.

For the first time, Ed was hit by the full seriousness of what he'd got himself mixed up in.

It wasn't nice. It wasn't nice at all.

He'd followed Elena after the bombing, keeping a safe distance, but she'd gone straight home. He'd waited for a while, then made his way back. Somehow he hadn't felt like telling Ros and Beckett about this over the phone.

He opened the door to Gizmos with Ros's passkey and walked into the reception room.

Darkness. Silence. A few faint smudges marked the positions of the couch, the chairs, the door to the kitchen.

'Ros!' he called. 'Beckett!'

No answer.

They'll be in the office, he thought. They probably found some evidence at the house, and they're working on it now.

He started up the stairs, his feet ringing on the bare metal treads.

The office was dark, too. Only the computer screen glowed. In its faint light he could see that the room was empty. Ros's coat was gone from the stand, so was Beckett's. Ed checked the screen for messages, found nothing, only a photograph of two toy horses and a dark, irregular blob.

Ed frowned, looked closer at the mark. It wasn't part of the display. Someone had physically scribbled on the screen with a marker pen.

Had someone kidnapped them? Was this doodle Ros's or Beckett's way of telling him they were in trouble? It didn't seem impossible after what he'd seen tonight.

'Ros!' he shouted again, but without much hope. He tried to remember the number of Ros's mobile phone, but couldn't. He looked around the desk, in the drawers, for anything that might be an address book. There were pieces of cabling, electrical and optical, silver boxes full of EPROMs and PCMIA cards, bits of LCD displays trailing wiring, but nothing on paper.

Ed sighed. Knowing his luck, Ros kept the number on the computer.

Then he remembered the tracer. Ros offering it to him. Him giving it back to Ros. Ros pushing it into her coat pocket.

'In case I get lost,' he muttered.

He set off for the car at a run.

'Where are we going?'

Ros was trying to keep the shakiness out of her voice, but it was hard work. The road they were driving down was narrow and dark. High walls of corrugated iron rose on each side, topped by distorted shadows that looked like the wrecks of cars.

Cottrell didn't answer her question. Ros hadn't really expected him to. She could guess the answer anyway: somewhere dark and empty, near the river. A place where bodies could be disposed of easily.

She wondered what they had done with Ballantyne's body.

'Turn left here,' said Cottrell suddenly.

'Where?' said Ros. Then Beckett made a gesture from the passenger seat and she saw it: a gap in the corrugated iron, a holographic notice that glittered into life under her headlights.

BILL KNEBB'S *ECOLOGICALLY FRIENDLY* CAR RECYCLING PLANT. BEST PRICES FOR METALS, PLASTICS, CABLING. WIDE RANGE OF SPARE PARTS AVAILABLE.

Ros swallowed, glanced at Beckett. He raised his eyebrows, shook his head slightly.

Ros slowed down, pulled in to the narrow entrance. She half hoped there would be a gate, a night watchman, something. But there was only bare concrete, a darkened control building with a railing, and towers of wrecked cars. Some were already crushed, neat half-metre cubes of metal. Others were just stripped down, waiting.

Ros pulled up, bit her lip. There had to be some way out of this.

'Get out,' said Cottrell.

Ros opened the door, got out. The air was cold and smelled of oil and rust.

The back door of the car unlatched, flew open at a kick from Cottrell.

'Get in here with me.'

Ros heard Beckett's voice: 'Now hold on a minute, what are you doing?'

'Oh, don't worry, Beckett.' Cottrell's voice was level, calm, utterly cold. 'I'm not contemplating anything improper.'

No, thought Ros. Nothing improper. You're just going to kill me.

She wondered what would happen if she made a run for it. Would he kill Beckett and come after her?

Maybe.

Was that better than just letting him kill them both?

Yes.

But she couldn't do it. She couldn't move. She couldn't *leave* Beckett, hear the gunshot, know that she had allowed him to die like that.

A hand grasped her arm. Cottrell.

'Get in. Now.'

Ros sat down. Something hard and cold touched her neck.

The gun.

'Beckett!' she said. 'Run for it!'

But Beckett didn't move.

Ros's arms were dragged behind her back. She felt rope rub against her wrists, bite into her flesh as it was secured.

'Beckett, for God's sake get out of here!' she yelled. 'You've got a –'

A piece of cloth descended over her mouth, cutting off her speech, almost choking her. It tasted bitter, dry. Perhaps drugged?

But no, she could still breathe. She struggled to twist around, to see Cottrell.

And then he was in front of her, standing outside the car, with more rope in his hands. He bent down to tie her feet, working one-handed, the gun in his free hand and aimed at her body. The car's internal light made long, soft shadows on his face.

Ros knew it was almost impossible to aim a gun

109

properly firing one-handed. She took the chance and kicked out as hard as she could.

She felt her foot connect with Cottrell's flesh.

The gun went off, there was the sound of a ricochet, some smoke, then near silence. Beckett was moving, then he wasn't.

He had his hands up, and Cottrell had the gun trained on him. Blood trickled from Cottrell's lip.

'You'll have a nasty bruise in the morning,' commented Beckett. His voice sounded faint, tinny, over the ringing in Ros's ears.

'Tie her feet,' said Cottrell to Beckett.

'No.'

Ros felt the snout of the gun, still warm from the shot, touch her knee.

'Now or I shoot her in the knee.'

Ros closed her eyes. I will not scream, she thought. Though she knew she would, if Cottrell pulled the trigger.

She heard Beckett get out of the car. She tried to speak, almost choked on the gag. Shook her head violently instead. She was dead anyway. She would take the pain, whatever, if he would just *get himself out of here*.

But Beckett was leaning over the car doorway and the rope was tightening around her ankles again. She saw Cottrell moving somewhere in the shadows outside.

'Tight.' Cottrell's voice. Ros felt the ropes bite.

'*Tight.*'

The ropes bit harder.

Then Ros heard something she'd never thought she would hear again.

The sound of an engine.

Of wheels on concrete.

If it hadn't been for the gag, she would have cheered.

110

She saw Cottrell step back, Beckett whirl round.
Heard a car door open, and slam.

Heard a voice. A very familiar voice. A woman's
voice.

Elena's voice.

'Hello darling. I thought you might like a lift home.
When you've finished your work.'

Ed stopped the bike at the top of the hill. From here
he had a good view of the whole area. The lights of
the docks gleamed, white and green. A boat moved
slowly along the river. Ed heard the distant thud of
music.

Someone was having a party.

This was as good a vantage point as any, he decided.
If he couldn't pick up the tracker from here, then he
probably wasn't going to. He stared at the screen of the
RaSearch, trying to make sense of it. Who in the world
would choose orange and blue for the colours of a
display?

The blue, he supposed, represented solid objects. But
the resolution was erratic. Nearby buildings were
clear. Everything else was just dots. With the range
turned up to maximum, he could see a few faint
shadows forming at the edge of the screen, represent-
ing the high-rise towers of the city across the river.

But there were no bright points. The bug in Elena's
car was out of range – or out of juice – and so,
apparently, was Ros's tracker.

Unless the machine didn't scan on all frequencies at
once.

Ed looked at the controls on the machine, hoping for
a knob marked TUNING.

No such luck. There was a whole panel of buttons,
some with integral LEDs, some marked + and –. But
everything was labelled with icons, not words, so it was

111

impossible to tell what any of the buttons actually did.

'Frequency, I want frequency,' he muttered, aware that he was wasting time. Ros and Nick could be anywhere. Could be in danger. Could be dead. He'd moved the RaSearch to the bike because he'd figured the bike would be faster.

But that was no good if he didn't know where he was going.

He jabbed one of the buttons at random, and the whole screen faded out. He must have hit the screen contrast control. He jabbed the corresponding + button and the screen came back.

'Come *on*,' he muttered to himself. He saw a pair of buttons marked with an arrow-like icon, remembered something from a circuit diagram Ros had once explained to him.

He pressed the + button, held it.

Nothing.

He tried '−'.

Nothing, except that after a while the words 'minimum frequency' appeared on the screen. So, he had the right control, but he was still out of range. Or something.

Then Ed saw a button marked 'PROG', hiding out on the edge of the panel. He smiled. Knowing Ros, if it was programmable, she'd programmed it.

He pressed the button, and instantly a bright, flashing, blip appeared, apparently almost next to the bike. He adjusted the range downwards, then looked around to orientate himself.

South west. The industrial estate.

He gunned the engine and started the bike down the hill.

'Five minutes, Ros,' he muttered. 'Give me five minutes.'

* * *

112

Beckett watched the conveyor belt start with something akin to horror. On the bottom of the belt was Ros's car, just driven there by Elena. At the top was a long drop to the car crusher.

In the back of the car, tied up, was Ros.

Beckett turned to Cottrell. 'You can't do this.'

Cottrell didn't reply, just turned away and got into the back seat of Elena's car.

'Why not?' said Elena, who was still standing by the bonnet of the car, gazing at Ros's car ascending the conveyor belt. 'This way, it will be some time before they find her body. And some time after that before it's identified. Which gives us long enough to ask you a few questions, to get SACROS, and to leave the country.'

She explained the whole argument in a slightly amused, patronising tone, as if Beckett were stupid because he hadn't anticipated her reasoning.

Beckett looked into her calm, dark eyes. He realised that she was utterly unscrupulous. Utterly inhuman. He had no hope of reaching her, with logic or anything else. Desperately, he turned again to Cottrell.

'Look, sir,' he said, deliberately phrasing his request as far as possible as if he was still an operative and this was still a normal Hive operation. 'Can't you just leave her here, tied up? She hasn't done anything – she's a civilian! No one will find her till morning. You could be in Rio de Janeiro by then.'

'But not with SACROS,' said Cottrell. 'I'm sorry, Beckett, but it's going to take too long. She has to die. It's unfortunate, I know. But you shouldn't have involved her.'

'You can't blame me!'

'We're wasting time,' interrupted Elena. 'We need to ask you some questions, Mr Beckett, and this is not the best place.'

Her hand closed around Beckett's arm. He tried to pull it away, felt the gun against the back of his neck.

'Just get in, Beckett,' said Cottrell. 'Don't make any more unnecessary trouble.'

At that moment Beckett realised that Cottrell was as ruthless as Elena.

And always had been.

Ros was going to die, and there was nothing he could do about it.

Ros didn't hear the car go, but she saw the pattern of light from the headlights move across the misted up windows of her car, saw it fade and die, and knew that her last chance that Elena and Cottrell would somehow change their minds, or that Beckett would somehow escape and rescue her, was gone.

The motion of the conveyor belt was a steady, deep vibration. Ros struggled, though she was fairly sure it wasn't going to do any good. Her only hope was that Beckett had somehow made the bonds on her feet easy to loosen.

But so far there was no evidence of that.

Ros moved her head, tried to catch the knot at the back of the gag on the door handle. If she could just get the door open, perhaps she could wriggle out.

On the third try, the cloth caught. She pulled. The door handle moved, the door didn't click.

Locked.

She pulled harder, felt the knot give way. Suddenly she was free of the gag.

'Help!' she shouted. 'Somebody help me!'

But there was no one to hear. Ros knew that, knew she needed to save her breath. She sat up, saw the top of the conveyor belt sinking below the bonnet.

No time. There was no time.

Struggling against panic, Ros closed her teeth over

114

the rope that held her hands. She pulled, felt something give.

Not far enough.

Try again.

The car was shifting under her.

No time.

« Fourteen »

Ed saw the gate to Bill Knebb's scrapyard, looked at the screen. The tracker could only be in there.

Dark, deserted, close to the river.

A good place to dump a body.

He went in anyway, saw the conveyor belt moving, saw Ros's car on it, looked at the screen again.

The bright point indicating the tracker was moving, slowly, in just the same way as the bug.

She was in the car. She had to be.

And she'd be dead if he didn't get to the car in time.

He jumped off the bike, clambered up the tower of wrecked cars next to the belt. Rusty metal caught at his gloves, gave way under his boots.

He reached the conveyor belt, just behind the car. Saw the car shifting, nose-diving.

Gone.

'Ros!' he shouted.

The sound of crushing metal, breaking glass.

'Ros!' he shouted again, though he knew it was too late. Ros was dead. Beckett too, probably.

Ros . . .

Ed put his head in his hands. Ros had been his

116

friend. Now she was dead. What the hell was he going to do?

The conveyor belt stopped.

Ed turned, suddenly aware that he too might be in danger. There was a control shed of some kind next to the belt, a small brick building with a balcony. A light had just come on there.

A voice shouted his name.

Ros's voice.

As he stared, she appeared, leaning against the railing of the control shed.

'Five minutes earlier would have been better,' she said in a hoarse, shaky voice.

Ed still didn't quite believe it. 'Ros! You're all right!'

'Which is more than can be said for my car!' She managed a grin. It was a bit lopsided, and Ed noticed now that there were tears on her face, but she was grinning nonetheless. Somehow that was what really convinced him that she was still alive, that he wasn't suffering from some kind of strange delusion.

'Thank God!' he said. Then, almost as an afterthought: 'Where's Beckett?'

Ros shook her head. 'I don't know. Cottrell and Elena took him somewhere.'

Ed nodded, struggled to think. 'OK. We know where to find Cottrell – the Hive. We know he'll be there, because he's got to get SACROS. So we go there too, nail him, and find Beckett that way.'

'If he's alive.'

The thought sobered Ed. 'You think he might not be?'

'They wanted to ask him some questions. But considering what they tried to do to me . . .' She gestured at the now-silent car crusher, 'I think he might not last long.'

* * *

117

The sky was beginning to get light as they arrived at Elena Johnson's house. Elena had talked all the way, in that beautiful, calm, mad voice, about SACROS and how much money it would make them and how they would be the most powerful and – more importantly to Elena, as far as Beckett could judge – the cleverest people on Earth.

Cottrell had said little, but the light in his eyes had spoken for him. Beckett could hardly believe that he had worked for this man for more than three years and not *noticed*.

In the grey dawn the house looked starker than it had at night. The furniture was scattered. A chair here, a coffee table there. Beckett wondered if Cottrell and Elena actually lived here, or simply used it as a base.

They took him upstairs to a loft which had been converted into a living room. An overstuffed white couch was pushed against one wall. A thick white pile carpet filled most of the floor, surrounded by bare, polished boards and scattered with coloured cushions. A Latin American print was mounted on one of the roof pillars, jagged splashes of primary colour against a blue background.

Beckett noted the positions of the windows, noted whether they were locked or not.

Just in case he got a chance.

Elena lifted his arms and tied them to one of the bare wooden beams that crossed the ceiling. The ropes were tight enough to cut off the circulation to his hands. He protested, once, and Elena simply said, 'Don't worry, you won't be needing your hands again.'

'Is that supposed to make me talk?' said Beckett. 'Doesn't it occur to you that if I think you're going to kill me anyway I might not tell you anything?'

Elena, who was sitting on the couch sipping a cup of coffee, looked up at him and said, 'It is not a matter of whether we kill you, Mr Beckett. It's a matter of how painfully we kill you.'

Beckett thought about that for a while, then said, 'I'm not going to talk.'

Elena only smiled. 'Who else at the Hive knows about us?'

Beckett said nothing.

Elena stood up, put down her coffee, picked up the gun from a side table. 'Come on, Mr Beckett. We need the answer to this one before John goes to work.'

Beckett glanced out of the window at the growing daylight. 'Oh, yes, mustn't be late for work,' he said. 'It's OK to kill people, but you've got to log in on time.'

Elena walked up to him with the gun, smiling sweetly. She pushed it against his kneecap.

'*Who knows*?'

Beckett decided on a bluff. 'Moore, Dent.' He tried to shrug. 'Half the people in there, I should think, by now.'

Elena shook her head. 'Moore's dead, Dent doesn't know. You're lying.' She pushed the gun harder against his knee.

Moore's dead. 'I thought Moore was on your side.'

Elena shrugged. 'That's a matter of opinion. He expected to be *paid*, you know.' She giggled, as if at the childishness of such an illusion.

'How much are you paying Cottrell, then?'

The giggle turned into a laugh, which at least meant she took the gun away from Beckett's knee.

'Pay him? John and I are in love, and have been for a very long time. With the help of SACROS we are going to become very rich.'

'So you've said. Several times. But —'

There was an explosion of pain in Beckett's knee. For a moment he thought she had really shot him, then he realised that she'd just hit him with the gun.

'Who broke into my home last night?' Elena was shouting now, almost hysterical. The emotion itself was less frightening than the suddenness of her change of mood.

Beckett hesitated, unsure what to say to calm her down.

'It was you, wasn't it? You! Little bee from the Hive! How could you possibly have the presumption to try and be cleverer than me?' Elena laughed again, for far too long, far too hysterically, as if she were at a party and someone had made a very good joke.

Then, quite suddenly, she sobered.

'You don't know anything,' she said calmly. 'I think I will kill you now.'

She put the gun against Beckett's head.

« Fifteen »

The Managing Director watched the images on the wall screen. The man tied to the beam. The woman shouting at him, putting the gun against his knee, then against his head.

Then walking away, laughing, the man clearly amazed to be still alive.

On the notepad computer in front of her she made occasional notes: 'Hive', 'SACROS', and, more obscurely, 'Love?!!'. She glanced at Peter Marasco, who was standing in front of her glass desk, his arms folded, with a triumphant look on his face.

When the playback was finished, she asked him, 'Where is this Hive place? Is it real?'

Marasco nodded. 'It's a government listening agency. It's supposed to be top secret, but –' He let the sentence remain unfinished.

The Managing Director allowed herself to smile. 'You have ways of finding out. Yes. And SACROS is the code name of the device Ms Johnson wanted our microwave links for?'

Marasco nodded again. 'I suppose so. I thought it might be possible to – acquire this technology.'

The Managing Director raised her eyebrows.

Marasco said: 'Since our clients have acquired it illegally, there's no reason why we should have to limit ourselves to legal means.'

The Managing Director looked down at her desk, focused on a tiny irregularity in the glass surface.

'Just do whatever you think is necessary, Peter. And let me know the results, won't you?'

Marasco nodded, then turned and left the office.

« Sixteen »

Cottrell often had to hurry to work. He liked to give the impression to his colleagues that he was disciplined, organised, always on time. In fact, he was usually a few minutes late and had to hurry to catch up. This morning was no exception.

And this morning, of all mornings, he couldn't afford to be late.

He walked along the waterfront as quickly as he could, only just resisting the temptation to run. He barely saw the concrete arches of the shopping centre, the lights on the main road. He only saw the steel towers of the Hive, and how far he was away from them. He nearly walked out through a red light, straight in front of the traffic.

Elena was right, he thought. I have to get in there *fast* – and out again. He made a mental note to sign out an official car as soon as he got his hands on SACROS. He couldn't hang around waiting for Elena to pick him up.

The lights changed, and he crossed the road. On the other side there was another infuriating delay. A man was selling remembrance poppies, the plastic kind, right at the entrance to the Hive compound. Two old women had stopped to buy one and were fiddling around in their purses for change. Cottrell had to stop or walk through them. He stopped, but made no effort to conceal the impatience on his face.

The poppy seller turned to him. 'Morning, sir! Buy a poppy? It's only once a year.' He was young, wearing a leather jacket and a red polo-neck shirt. He had an Australian accent.

Cottrell fished in his pocket, found a coin and put it in the collecting box.

'Thank you. I'll just put him in there for you –' The man began fiddling about, attaching the poppy to the lapel of Cottrell's jacket.

'Come on!' said Cottrell. 'I'm in a hurry. I've got a meeting in five minutes.'

'Sorry, sir,' said the man, giving the poppy a final tweak. 'Decent of you to buy one!'

Cottrell shook his head, then pushed his way past the old ladies with a muttered 'Excuse me.' He'd been held up long enough. It might be too late already.

When he showed his pass to the guard at the Hive gate, he noticed that the poppy seller was gone. Ordinarily, Cottrell might have thought that strange. He might have wondered why the man had left when there were still plenty of people around.

But this morning, he was in too much of a hurry for that.

Ros looked at the tiny screen clipped to the dash of Beckett's car. The picture showed the main doors of the Hive opening, then the reception area inside. A young woman smiled and said, 'Hello Mr Cottrell. Mr Dent wants to see you urgently.'

'Ten minutes, Linda.'

Excellent. Cottrell's voice was coming in loud and

clear. She looked at the DAT, saw the counter ticking over.

Soon they would have all the proof they needed.

The passenger door opened and Ed got in. He dumped the poppy appeal box and tray on the back seat.

'OK?' he asked.

'Fine.' Ros gestured at the picture, which now showed a corridor in the Hive.

'Fine as long as he doesn't take his jacket off, you mean,' Ed pointed out.

Ros shrugged. 'We'll just have to hope he doesn't.' She thought of something, looked at him with a grin. 'Why should he? Is it hot in there?'

Ed shook his head, apparently taking her remark seriously. 'Didn't hang around long enough to find out.' He gestured at the screen. 'Hey look!'

Ros looked, saw a pass card sliding through a lock.

A door opening.

A storeroom: steel crates stacked up on shelving, with various labels, too small to read. The shelving got closer, until only the top of one of the boxes could be seen.

Cottrell's hand came into the picture, stroked the smooth metal.

Then someone spoke. 'Mr Cottrell? What do you want?'

The picture shifted violently. Ros saw a man in his forties, balding hair, a white storeman's coat, a smile on his face.

'I want SACROS.' Cottrell's voice. 'We're doing some more tests.'

'Mr Dent said there was restricted access to it.'

'Of course. But –'

'I can't let you take it without authorisation from Mr Dent.'

125

'Oh.' A pause. The picture shifted to show SACROS again, then blacked out for a moment. 'Will this do?'

The storeman again.

Then a gun appeared in the picture, Cottrell's hand around it, his finger squeezing the trigger. Ros opened her mouth to speak, to shout some useless protest, but before she could do even that the distorted sound of a shot came over the speaker and the storeman dropped to the ground.

The picture shifted again as Cottrell walked forward to inspect his victim. Ros saw the white coat with blood leaking across it, a still, waxy face.

'He's killed him!' she said.

'Like Elena killed Moore,' said Ed. 'Or like both of them tried to kill you. Anyone that gets in their way, by the look of it.'

Ros swallowed. 'What chance has Beckett got?'

Ed shrugged. 'Not much, I shouldn't think.'

Not exactly ten out of ten for tact, thought Ros. But that was Ed: take him or leave him.

She returned her attention to the screen, which was filled by the surface of the box that held SACROS. As she watched, an air ticket wallet was dropped onto the metal and opened to remove the luggage stickers.

Cottrell's hands placed a sticker over the BHQ security label, gummed it down.

'Looks like they're planning to leave the country,' said Ros.

'It figures,' said Ed.

Ros thought quickly, made a decision. Two crooks: two people to follow them. And one of them had to have Beckett.

She was glad now that she'd insisted on Ed bringing his bike to the Hive.

'You'd better get over to Elena Johnson's,' she said. 'Keep an eye on her. I'll try to stay with Cottrell. And

126

this time, keep in touch, all right?'

She looked at Ed, who nodded. 'Don't worry, Ros, I will. We don't want to see two cars crushed in one day, do we?'

Ed could hear the phone ringing as soon as he stopped the engine. He jumped off the bike and ran across the paved courtyard, trying to make as little noise as possible.

The phone kept ringing.

She's not here any more, thought Ed. This is a waste of time.

Then the phone stopped.

Ed opened the bag he was carrying, took out the guided microphone.

'Most powerful piece of listening apparatus there is,' Ros had told him when they were kitting out at Gizmos. 'Illegal, of course.' It was half a metre long, and looked like a light rifle with laser sights. The laser was real, a targeting aid for the listener. Correctly targeted, Ros had assured him, the thing could hear a bee four kilometres away.

Ed flicked on the laser, saw a red spot appear on the brick wall. Almost immediately, he heard a voice.

'You have it? Wonderful! Then I'll meet you as planned. Then we can –' A pause. 'What's happened?'

A longer pause. Ed turned up the gain, heard a faint, distorted voice that might have been Cottrell's: 'There's something strange.'

'Damn.' Ros's voice, over the headset that connected him to the radio link. 'They're onto us, Ed. He's seen the bug.'

'I know,' muttered Ed. 'I'm listening outside Elena's now.'

In Ed's other ear, Cottrell's scratchy voice said, 'They could have heard every word.'

127

'He's flattened it.' Ros. 'I've lost the signal at my end. What's happening?'

'Listen.' Elena. 'I'll kill Beckett. Now. Then we go. All right?'

Ed swallowed.

'Ros, listen,' he said quickly. 'Beckett's here and he's in trouble. I'm going in.'

He switched off the link before she could tell him to be careful.

« Seventeen »

Beckett flinched.

He knew it was useless. Flinching wouldn't save him from a bullet. But the instinct was there: if I shrink back, if I make myself as small as possible, then I might survive.

But Elena was in front of him now, taking careful aim at his head.

This time he knew she wasn't kidding.

'Time's up, Beckett.'

Beckett heard the crash of the explosion, knew at once that it wasn't just a gunshot. He saw glass flying behind Elena, then past her, scattering over the floor.

Saw Ed, leather jacket wrapped around his face but definitely Ed, half running, half sprawling and Elena turning.

'Ed! Look out!'

The gun cracked again. More glass shattered.

Beckett saw that Ed had a gun. A huge thing, some kind of rifle, laser sights glinting – no wait –

But Elena wasn't waiting. She was running past Beckett, down the stairs, firing wildly. Beckett felt the wooden beam he was tied to shudder under the impact of a bullet.

Ed was gone, hurrying after Elena.

'Shoot to wound!' yelled Beckett, though he doubted Ed would take any notice, and wouldn't really blame him if he didn't.

More shots. A door slamming. An engine starting. Silence.

'Ed?'

A groan. A thud.

'Ed, are you hurt?'

'No, but I lost her.' His feet began clumping up the stairs. 'I *lost* her. She just drove off.'

'You should have shot out the tyres.'

'With what?' Ed moved in front of Beckett, waved the gun-like object in his face. 'This is a long range microphone.'

Beckett stared at the thing. From close range, it obviously wasn't a gun: the 'muzzle' was covered with a thin layer of steel mesh. 'Good job Elena didn't notice that,' he said, then made the mistake of trying to laugh. A wrenching pain crossed his chest.

Ed began working on the ropes that held Beckett to the beam. 'Yeah,' he said. 'I got it from Ros this morning.'

Beckett twisted his head around and stared at him. 'Ed, Ros was . . .' He shook his head. 'They killed Ros last night. I'm sorry, Ed.'

He stopped when he saw the broad grin on Ed's face.

'No they didn't.' He released the first rope and began on the second. 'She didn't tell you she trained with Harry Houdini, did she?'

Ros watched Cottrell's car leave the Hive, but resisted the temptation to follow it. There was nothing she could do on her own. These people were likely to be armed, and were certainly willing to kill.

No, to have any chance of winning she was just going to have to be cleverer than they were.

As soon as Cottrell was out of sight, she got out of the car and began rummaging around in the electronic equipment stashed in the back.

There had to be a way.

The courtyard was cold, a November wind blowing under a grey sky, but Beckett couldn't move his arms enough to get them into his jacket. He rubbed at them, winced as the blood returned and the nerves began to burn.

He looked back up at the house, the broken window.

'You said you left Ros at the Hive?' he asked.

Ed nodded.

'Well, get on to her and find out what's happening.'

Ed flicked on his headset. 'Ros?'

The faint squawk of Ros's voice over the headphones. Beckett heard it and thought: she's alive. *Alive.*

And so am I. It's a wonderful feeling.

'Ros says Cottrell's left the Hive,' said Ed. 'She thinks he's headed for the airport. He's got SACROS.'

'Is she tailing him?'

Ed asked her.

'No. She says she's going to come and pick us up. She says she's got a better idea.'

The two men looked at each other.

'Tell her –' Beckett scratched his head, winced at a renewed stab of pain from his arm. 'Tell her it had better be a good one.'

Complications, thought Cottrell. There were always complications.

He looked at the red brake lights of the car in front and watched as its progress slowed from a crawl to a stop. He had to follow suit.

This ought to be the happiest day of his life. He had SACROS. He was on his way to the airport. He and Elena would be on their way to Rio de Janeiro in under an hour now.

But there were always these sordid details. Flights to be booked, traffic to negotiate, people who got in the way and had to be killed. The storeman. That woman last night. Ballantyne. Beckett.

Deaths. Complications.

He wound down the car window, leaned out and tried to see where the queue ended.

He couldn't see an end. A solid mass of cars rose up over the flying bridge, either stationary or crawling very slowly.

Obstructing him.

Him! John Cottrell! With SACROS on the back seat of the car! He felt like blaring his horn, felt like screaming at them, telling them he was the most powerful person on the planet and could they get out of his way.

But he couldn't. He wasn't the most powerful person on the planet.

Yet.

Never mind. The Traffic Master system that controlled the orbital motorway was satellite based, wasn't it? He would get his own back on these people, sooner or later.

He smiled.

Slowly, the traffic began to move. Cottrell eased the car forward, into second, into third gear. Up onto the flyover. Grey buildings slipped by, grey sky, grey earth. A gantry crane, huge, a startling yellow.

The phone rang.

He picked it up straight away, nerves jumping. Had they found the body of the storeman at the Hive? Had Beckett escaped and reported in?

But it was Elena.

'Hello, darling,' he said. 'You've disposed of Beckett?'

'He's dead.'

'Wonderful.'

'I don't think we should risk the airport. They'll be looking for us there. Now listen, I have a plan.'

Cottrell smiled. Elena always had a plan. And it always worked.

He listened. He liked the plan, if only because it meant he could get out of this traffic.

He turned off the motorway at the next exit.

Elena was angry. She waited in the queue at the traffic lights, barely able to contain her anger. She had been cheated again! How could she have known that someone had contacted the Hive and told them where Nick Beckett was being held?

If she ever found out who had done it, who had thwarted her, then she would kill them.

Painfully.

If only she knew.

She always knew best. She always knew everything. Why was no one telling her the things she needed to know?

The lights changed, and Elena pulled away, irritably attempting to dodge around a large truck. Its horn blared.

'Shut up!' she shouted. 'Shut up shut up shut up!'

John had better have SACROS, she thought. He'd better have got out of the Hive. She reached out to the phone, was about to dial Cottrell's number when it rang.

She picked it up, heard Cottrell's voice and sighed with relief. 'Darling! Is everything all right?'

'Yes. I'm on my way. But we need a change of plan. We'll never get through customs.'

Elena could hardly believe it. 'You mean you won't,' she said. 'They haven't got my name on their computers. Look, we –'

'It's all right,' interrupted Cottrell. 'I've got it all worked out. I know a man with a helicopter. He can take us across the border. We'll pick up a flight from there.'

'I've not had good experiences with helicopters, darling. And we've had enough changes of plan.'

Again, Cottrell interrupted her. 'It will be OK this time. I trust this man. Believe me, darling, it's better this way.'

Elena sighed again. John didn't often get into these moods, but when he did, he was stubborn.

She knew when it was best to give in.

'All right,' she said. 'Where do we meet him?'

'At a place called Walden Hangar,' said Beckett, speaking carefully and slowly into the mouthpiece of the voice synthesiser. Outside the car, brown fields sped by, and grey sky. Ros was driving. She'd taken over after she'd made her call to Cottrell as 'Elena'.

'Walden Hangar?' asked Elena over the phone. 'Where is that?'

'It's an old airfield,' said Beckett. 'Take Junction 14 off the motorway, and you'll see it signposted.'

'Very well, darling,' said Elena. 'I will see you there in ten minutes.'

'Goodbye, darling,' said Beckett, then hastily cut the line before he cracked up.

'Spoken like a true romantic,' said Ros, grinning. She glanced at the clock on the dashboard. 'Just about the same ETA as Cottrell – and us. Let's just hope Ed can get there in time.'

As she finished speaking, Beckett's radio headset crackled and Ed's voice came over the link. 'OK, we're in a go condition. Just lifting off. Do you copy?'

Beckett stared at Ros, who shook her head sadly.

'What are you on about, Ed?' he asked.

'Isn't that the sort of thing you say in these situations?'

'I never do, no.'

And I'd probably be disciplined if I did, thought Beckett. Oh, to be a freelance!

Then he remembered his current position with his employers – or rather, on the run from his employers – and realised that he was, in practice, a freelance anyway, for today at least.

Well, it was certainly more exciting this way. He hadn't photocopied anything all day.

'How long before you get to Walden Hangar, Ed?' asked Ros.

A pause. 'Fifteen minutes, perhaps a bit longer.'

'Well, step on it!' said Beckett. 'We're going to be there in ten – and so are Cottrell and Elena.'

'Nine minutes, now,' muttered Ros.

'Sure, I'll just climb outside and fit the rockets now,' said Ed.

Ros spluttered.

'OK, OK,' said Beckett. 'Just get there as fast as you can.'

Ros seemed to take this as an instruction to her: her foot went down on the accelerator, and Beckett's car was suddenly travelling faster than Beckett felt entirely comfortable with. Certainly faster than everything else on the road.

'Hold on, hold on –' began Beckett.

But Ros just glanced at him and winked. 'T minus eight minutes, and counting,' she said. 'Do you copy?'

Cottrell pulled up the car under the concrete wall of the hangar building and cautiously got out.

There was no sight or sound of a helicopter. Just an empty sky and a cold wind. He opened the back door, took out SACROS, and stood there, waiting, feeling like a tourist at the wrong bus stop.

Was this the right place? What if he'd misunderstood Elena's directions?

He was just about to go back to the car to phone her and make sure when he saw her car swing out from behind the building and on to the tarmac. He hurried across to join her, running awkwardly with the unbalancing weight of SACROS.

By the time he got there Elena was out of the car and looking around at the sky.

'A good idea of yours to order the helicopter,' she said.

Cottrell frowned. What was she talking about? 'I didn't order the helicopter.'

They stared at each other.

'You phoned me and told me to meet you here,' she said. 'You said –'

She broke off, obviously reading the incomprehension in his face.

Suddenly she shouted. 'You idiot!' They've duped us!'

Cottrell retreated a step. He still didn't understand. It had been her voice on the phone. Hadn't it?

Then he remembered the voice synthesizer. The device he had used to trick Beckett in the Hive.

'I –' he began.

'Never mind the explanation!' Elena was still shouting, her face distorted by anger. She opened the back door of her car. 'Put the machine in there, then we get out – now!'

Cottrell knew about Elena's anger. He hadn't faced it many times in his life, but each occasion had been memorable.

He did as he was told.

« Eighteen »

« Eighteen »

Ros heard the screech of tyres from ahead as they approached the hangar. She saw Elena's car accelerating down the runway.

'OK, Ros,' said Beckett from the passenger seat. 'Be careful. It looks like they know we're on to them.'

I can see that, thought Ros irritably. Aloud she said, 'Don't worry. They won't get far.'

'Yes, but keep your distance. Remember, they're armed, we're not. And don't ram them, you'll damage SACROS.'

'Anything else you don't want me to do?' She flung the steering wheel over, taking the 4×4 off the road, through a break in the hedge and into a field. 'Shall I keep to the speed limit? No U-turns?' She wrenched the wheel over again, sending the car skidding down an embankment and onto the end of the runway. 'Perhaps you'd like me to stay in second gear? Beckett, we've got to catch them!'

'Yes, but not at the cost of getting killed – or damaging SACROS. All right?'

She felt his eyes on her. Hard, serious. 'OK,' she said, reluctantly.

Elena had seen them by now, was pulling up hard, skidding to one side. She turned wide, sending up a spray of mud from the grass by the runway. For one lovely moment Ros thought she had got her car stuck, but no, she was away, back towards the hangar.

Ros flung the car into reverse, looked over her shoulder to check their progress through the field.

'Oh, my poor clutch!' wailed Beckett. 'I knew it was a mistake to let you drive my car.'

But he did sound as though he was joking this time.

Ros kept her eyes on the rear window. Wrestled the wheel over.

They went through the hedge backwards.

'I mean, don't worry about the paintwork,' protested Beckett.

She glanced at him, was rewarded with a grin.

The car lurched, throwing them together for an instant.

'We really must stop meeting like this,' he said.

'At least you don't get car sick.'

The car lurched again. Ros saw Elena's car on the road in front of them. It swerved, mounted the bank on the other side, almost turned over.

'Let's hope SACROS doesn't either,' observed Beckett.

The car gave a final lurch and settled on the road.

'Yes. It'd be a shame to go through all this and only pick up pieces fit for the recycling skip.'

By the time she'd finished speaking they were doing forty miles per hour. But it wasn't enough. Ros realised she'd misjudged it. Elena's car was well ahead, already pulling out onto the main road.

'They're getting away,' Beckett pointed out.

'No they're not,' Ros snapped. 'It only looks like it.'

By the time they reached the main road, the gap between the two cars had widened to almost half a mile. Ros put her foot to the ground, but Beckett's car could only go so fast.

And Elena's was faster.

Damn.

Beckett was peering out of the window, examining the sky. 'Ed, where are you? We're losing them!'

Ros wasn't about to let that one past. It was a straight road. They could still see the opposition. Anything might happen yet.

'We're not,' she said, glancing fiercely at Beckett.

'Easy, easy,' he said. 'We're not losing them, Ed. We're just – umm – very much in second place.'

Over the radio link, Ros heard Ed's voice, 'Roger. Wilco. Estimated time of arrival's about – er – well, pretty soon.'

'Just get here, Ed!' shouted Beckett.

'Now's the time you wish you'd bought one with a turbocharger,' murmured Ros.

Beckett gave her a poisonous look. 'Just drive,' he said.

Elena smiled, because she was the cleverest after all. Despite all the trickery they had thrown at her, despite her lover's stupidity, she had won. She had got away.

'We are still in time for that flight,' she said.

'Look out!' yelled Cottrell.

Elena looked up, saw a helicopter flying straight down the road towards them, low enough for a collision. Instinctively, she swerved. The car mounted the bank, almost turned over. Elena stamped on the brakes, skidded back onto the road as the helicopter soared overhead.

She glanced at Cottrell. He was pale, sweating.

'Don't worry,' she said. 'We will be all right. I know the way out of everything.'

There was a roundabout ahead. Elena slowed down,

aware of the helicopter still somewhere above her, near, out of sight. Its engine, and the clattering of the turning blades, were clearly audible.

Then, as she drove onto the roundabout, it was suddenly in front of her, fluorescent colours gleaming against the grey road.

She swerved again, found herself travelling off the roundabout towards a sign that said ROAD CLOSED. She wrenched at the wheel, skidded for a moment, smashing aside several plastic bollards.

She looked over her shoulder, saw that the other car was already on the roundabout. There was no way she could turn back.

'Where are we going?' asked Cottrell.

She ignored him, put her foot down further on the accelerator. The road sloped gently upwards, curving as it did so.

There were more barriers, lightweight ones with red and white stripes.

Elena drove straight through them.

'Where are we going?' repeated Cottrell.

Elena ignored him.

The helicopter was ahead of them again, hovering impossibly low over the road.

You want a crash, thought Elena. I give you a crash. I am cleverer than you.

She pushed the accelerator all the way to the floor.

Cottrell spoke again, his voice almost a scream. 'Elena! It's not worth dying for!'

Dying? thought Elena. Better than being caught. Better than being put into prison where she wouldn't be the cleverest. Where she would be stupid, just like the others. Where she would be no good.

But she knew she couldn't say that to John. He would panic. So she said, 'Don't worry, we'll be safe soon.'

The helicopter came closer. It still hovered there, didn't move, didn't lift.

'Stop! For God's sake – Elena – the road's not finished!'

And she could see that he was right. The helicopter was hovering over an open space: the road finished in mid air.

There was time to stop. Just. Elena knew there was. If she put on the brakes now.

But she didn't.

Cottrell made an inarticulate sound of terror and tried to grab the wheel from her.

Elena hung on, fighting him off.

She knew best. She knew more than everyone.

The road was gone from beneath them. They were falling.

Cottrell screamed.

But Elena smiled.

Smiled as the ground approached, faster than was believable.

I know more than everyone. I got away. I really did.

Then the world crumpled inwards, became dark.

« Nineteen »

Peter Marasco surveyed the wreckage as best he could from the far side of the security tape. He noticed that the guards were military, not civilian.

So he had the right place.

He supposed he looked pretty much like the other vultures: the local TV news team fussing around their camera, the passers-by hoping for a glimpse of blood.

It was probably just as well if he did.

He slipped the pen mike from his pocket, aimed it at the three people – two men and a woman – talking underneath the silent rotors of a bizarrely coloured helicopter.

'– back to the Hive –' A man's voice.

'Whatever's left of it.' The woman.

'Ten years' work went into SACROS. Now look at it.'

'Well, I guess that's your chances of getting your job back gone up in smoke.' Another man, with an Australian accent.

'Yes. I'd better get the old interview suit out again.' The first man.

'Not necessarily. I've got a proposition to put to you. You too, Ed.'

143

Marasco permitted himself a smile. This was almost too good to be true.

If that young woman could offer the Hive man a business proposition, then so could he.

But his would be a better one.

« Nineteen »

« Twenty »

Mr Dent's office looked pretty much the same as it had the last time Beckett had been there: the plush carpet and leather chairs, the LED traffic monitors, the big desk with a few paper files laid out between the computer and the gold-plated lamp, the filing cabinet with the green 'unlock' light glowing.

Beckett swallowed and tried not to think about that.

Mr Dent was sitting at his desk, his hands steepled on the polished surface, his face shadowy. A rare stripe of sunlight from the windows behind him lit his thinning hair, creating a kind of halo effect.

'You know,' he said slowly, 'you're lucky to have kept your job after this incident. You should have reported the matter directly to me.'

'You weren't there!' Beckett was astonished at the injustice of it. OK, so SACROS had been destroyed. OK, so the Ministry was making rumbling noises about the cost of a replacement – effectively suggesting it might be cheaper to leave the thing on the drawing board.

So what? He'd done everything he could.

'I can always be contacted on my mobile phone,

Beckett,' Dent was explaining in his pedantic way. 'My secretary knows the number.'

'I couldn't ask your secretary anything, sir. I was on the run. It was the middle of the night. Ros and Ed agreed to help me.'

'By breaking into the Hive?'

Beckett stared at Dent's half-shadowed face. Obviously, the man simply couldn't understand what it was like to be on the run, on your own.

'Sir, I didn't know who I could trust. Ballantyne had said it was an inside job. He was dead. For all I knew it might have been you, not Cottrell.' He stopped suddenly, realising that what he'd said was hardly tactful.

'Beckett!' Dent looked up at him, a severe, headmasterly expression on his lined face. 'You must try and control these melodramatic tendencies of yours.' A pause. 'I've decided that I want you to take charge of the Recording Facilities department for a while.'

'The filing department?' Beckett's head began to spin. This was impossible. They couldn't be doing this to him. 'But that's a clerical job, sir.'

'That's right.' A slightly amused expression crossed Dent's face, as if he'd made a terribly clever joke and was wondering why Beckett didn't get it. 'You're being temporarily demoted to clerical grading, Mr Beckett, whilst an investigation is carried out.'

Beckett looked away, stared at the filing cabinet, then looked down at Dent's steepled hands. He knew what the use of the 'Mr' in Dent's last words meant: the demotion was official, had already happened, was not up for discussion.

'In that case I'll resign, sir. With immediate effect.'

The words were out almost before Beckett knew he was saying them. He opened his mouth to say something else, some justification, but Dent got there first.

'Are you sure, Mr Beckett?'

146

That 'Mr' again. Beckett realised that this was it. He had to make the decision, here and now.

He also realised that Dent wanted him to resign, that the demotion had been no more than a means of provoking him into leaving. He had become an embarrassment to the Hive.

Beckett remembered the feeling he'd had the previous morning, on the run with Ed and Ros.

Glad to be alive. Oh, to be a freelance.

Well, now was the time to find out what it was really like. Ros's offer was still open, as far as he knew.

And if not? Well, he could always be a helicopter pilot.

Dent was watching him, waiting, his expression carefully neutral.

Beckett took a deep breath.

'I'm sure,' he said.

The Managing Director was uncomfortable. She was sitting in the reclining leather chair behind her custom-made glass desk in her air-conditioned office, but she was uncomfortable even so. Her office was full of strangers, milling about, randomly searching files. Her contracts were in jeopardy. They'd even searched her car.

The Managing Director didn't like being uncomfortable. She didn't like this invasion of her cocoon of wealth. She wanted somebody to do something about it.

Now.

She stared up at the architect of her discomfort, still not quite able to believe how suddenly it had happened. The man had just marched in, with his brown suit and his slightly untidy blond hair and his vague expression and his 'government authority', and told her that he was going to close down her company.

Now he was standing there, in front of her desk, hands in his pockets as if all that remained was for her to leave and let him get on with it.

'You haven't got a case,' she told him. 'Not a shred of evidence, and you know it, Mr Batty.'

'Blatty,' said the man quietly. 'And I do have evidence. One of my men was in the bar of the Hotel Superior on Tuesday night.'

The Managing Director only smiled. But inwardly she was furious. How could she have been so careless? How could she have failed to notice there was someone watching her?

Blatty said, 'You were there. And you did a deal with a certain person.'

The Managing Director's smile broadened, as if this revelation hadn't bothered her at all.

'I had a conversation, perhaps,' she said. 'I didn't know that was against the law.'

'No, but the deal you made may have been. We have enough evidence to impound your files. And that's exactly what we're going to do.'

The Managing Director raised her eyebrows. 'You'll at least let me speak to my legal adviser, I assume.'

Blatty's expression didn't change. 'You can speak to who you like. But I must ask you to leave your office now.'

'Leave!' Her outrage wasn't faked. She was so angry she could barely speak.

Blatty only looked mildly amused.

Which made it worse, of course.

'He's within his rights.' Marasco's voice. She hadn't noticed him come in. And from the slightly startled way Blatty turned his head towards the glass doors, she decided that he hadn't either. 'And we're within our rights to sue him for loss of business if his investigation doesn't come to anything,' Peter Marasco went

148

on. He walked up to Blatty. 'Which it won't, I can assure you.'

Blatty said nothing.

The Managing Director made a decision. She wasn't going to be stripped of her comfort, her position, so easily. She got up, gave a last glance at the wall screen, at the slowly rotating image of the white shark.

'Very well. But I trust you'll allow me to consult with my legal adviser – in private.'

Blatty gestured at the door. 'Be my guest.'

Outside in the corridor Marasco said, 'It's the computer records that are the problem. The off-site files I can take care of easily enough. But we need to do something about the on-site files.'

The Managing Director looked at him. She felt the tension, the discomfort, of her situation in every bone of her body.

She didn't like it.

'I pay you to take care of these things,' she said. 'I don't know how this was even allowed to happen. I want something done about it, and I want it done at once.'

Marasco raised a hand. 'I know.' He paused. 'I do have a plan. But I think it might be better if you made the initial contact with the people I have in mind.'

The Managing Director looked away. 'I'm not dealing with any "people". I can't afford to be –'

'These people are quite legal,' said Marasco. 'That's why I want you to be the one to contact them. It will look better.'

They were in the games room now. It was empty. The Managing Director looked around at the various machines, the glittering lights, the 3D displays.

Then she looked out of the window, from where you could see the high blue glass tower of the building.

It was her building.

And she wanted it to stay that way.

'Very well,' she said to Marasco. 'Tell me who these people are, and what we need to do.'

Ros clamped the screwdriver between her teeth and applied the soldering iron to the circuit board, carefully placing its fine tip on the thread of silver metal marked AV546. With her free hand, she brought the braided end of the copper wire up to the pin, watched as the solder already on it melted.

Just a little bit of cross-linking, she thought, and it'll be as good as new.

Actually, rather better.

'Looks as if I really will have to get the old interview suit out, then,' said Beckett from somewhere behind her.

Ros made a non-committal noise, which was all she could do with a screwdriver between her teeth.

AV546, pin 20, she thought, touching the soldering iron to the metal again. The wire was wriggling about, as wires usually did. She grabbed the screwdriver and pinned it down with that.

'I didn't think for one moment they'd really do it,' Beckett went on. 'I mean, I didn't cock it up that badly. But when Dent told me I was being demoted to a clerical grade, I thought . . .' His voice tailed off, obviously wishing to leave unspoken what he thought of Dent.

'My offer's still open,' said Ros.

'Were you serious?'

The wire seemed to be steady now. Satisfied, Ros removed the soldering iron and put it down on its rest. She twirled the trackerball on the computer that was attached to the rig, watched as the system sent microcurrents through the new circuit, testing it.

Everything read OK. She took the screwdriver away from the joint, racked up the power from the test unit.

Still OK. Good.

'Of course I was serious,' she said to Beckett. 'I've already put an ad on the Net.'

Beckett stared for a few seconds, cradling his coffee cup in his hands. 'But you didn't know whether I was going to leave.'

She smiled, then turned back to the circuit board and picked up the soldering iron again.

At that moment, the phone rang.

'Could be our first customer,' said Ros without looking up. 'Would you care to take the call, Mr Beckett? I'm rather tied up at the moment.'

The café was quiet. Beckett would have preferred it otherwise. He knew it was easier to discuss private business in a crowd, rather than with just a few people around who could hear every word. But the client had insisted. She would be here, she'd said, at six, dressed in black.

Beckett looked around, at the matt black tables and chairs, the delicate china cups and silvered cutlery, the chequerboard floor, the stylised chess pieces painted on the walls. He couldn't see any sign of a woman in black, so he settled himself at a table and ordered a cappuccino.

Our first customer, he thought. And I've got to deal with her. He had to admit he wasn't feeling too sure of himself. He'd never exactly handled customers in a commercial sense. Government work wasn't like that. But Ros was out at some kind of party with an old university friend and Ed had mysteriously said he had to see a man about a helicopter.

So it's down to me, thought Beckett, whether I like it or not.

The door of the café opened, and a tall, elegant woman came in.

Dressed in black.

She looked around, then her gaze settled on Beckett, sitting alone, and she approached him with a slightly uneasy smile.

Yes. This was it.

Beckett swallowed nervously. The whole thing reminded him rather too much of going on a blind date.

She looked quite fanciable, too. Long black waistcoat, black skirt to the ankles. The waistcoat was open at the throat in a distinctive star-shaped cut, displaying a black diamond pendant. A cape, rather than a coat; she slipped it off and draped it over her arm as she approached the table.

'Nick Beckett?' she asked.

Beckett nodded.

She sat down opposite him with evident relief. 'I'm Irene, Irene Campbell. We spoke on the phone.'

Beckett grinned. 'Actually I agreed to meet several women in black in this place today. But you were the only one booked for six, so I guess you have to be the computer games one. Yes?'

Ms Campbell gave a slight, abstracted smile. The joke had obviously gone straight past her.

Oh well, thought Beckett, we can't all have a sense of humour. And Ms Campbell obviously has other things on her mind.

He began to feel rather sorry for her. He decided to get straight to the point. 'How can we help you?'

'As I told you, I run a computer games company. In fact, I'm the managing director. I need some help in recovering lost property.'

Beckett nodded. 'We'll do anything we can, Ms Campbell.'

'Please, call me Irene.' The woman smiled, this time with her whole face. Nick stared, fascinated. She really was quite fanciable. Perhaps after the job was over he might ask her . . .

No. She was probably married, knowing his luck. And this was business.

Irene went on: 'We sold a program last week to a company called Cyberscope. A new game. Very original. But the cheque bounced. Apparently, they've gone bankrupt.' She looked down at her hands. 'They owe millions, Mr Beckett. I'll never get my game back, not until it's far too late for it to have any market value. Unless –'

She broke off, looked up at him.

'Unless we get it back for you,' supplied Beckett.

'Yes. Actually, it will be quite sufficient if you delete it from Cyberscope's files – thoroughly – so that no one would know it had ever been there. I don't know how you would go about it.'

'That's easy. All we need is an address, and the name and location of the file your game is stored in. The deletion won't be a problem with our –' Ros's '– computer skills.'

The woman smiled again. 'I think I can provide the details you need.' She drew a piece of paper from the pocket of her jacket. 'That's a map of the premises. I've marked the MD's office in red.'

Beckett scanned the paper, nodded. Compared to breaking into the Hive, this should be easy. 'And the filename?' he asked.

'It's called . . .' She hesitated, looked around, although no one was within earshot '. . . the Assassins file.'

Beckett grinned. These computer games always had such melodramatic names.

Anybody would think they were real.

« Twenty-one »

Roland Blatty hadn't changed, thought Ros. Standing on the dockside in the dark in his full evening dress, he looked faintly ridiculous. His straw-coloured hair was still a little less tidy than it should have been, his face still wore that expression of perpetual vagueness that made you wonder how he got any work done.

But at Uni he'd ended up with a First, and now . . .

'So what's this secret party you couldn't tell me about on the phone, then, Roland?'

Roland gestured at the warship docked a little further down the riverside. The deck and superstructure were floodlit, making the vessel stand out in the night, its lines almost too clean and perfect; more like a huge illuminated model of a ship than the real thing.

'The party's on there,' said Roland. 'It was hell getting you clearance, I can tell you.' Without offering any further explanation, he took her arm and led her towards the ship. As they got closer, Ros could see the people gathered on deck, the men in evening dress, the women in long coloured gowns.

154

'Good job I put my posh togs on,' she said.

Roland glanced at her. 'Very smart. Black and silver always did suit you.'

Ros decided not to be distracted by flattery. Instead, she tried an indirect approach to get the answer to the question she'd already asked. 'So who are you working for these days?'

'The Bureau of Weapons Technology,' said Roland impressively.

'I don't know it.'

'It's new.' A pause. 'I'm in charge of it.'

Ros stared at him, frankly amazed. 'You're kidding!'

'Why should I be?' Roland seemed offended, but not very. Ros had never seen Roland very offended.

Still, it was worth a try. 'Oh, come on Roland. You couldn't even run the student chess club. They rioted.'

'I've matured,' protested Roland, his good nature unshaken.

They had almost reached the ship by now. Ros could see several sailors in uniform. Some of them seemed to be lined up in an honour guard.

Roland certainly wasn't *that* important, thought Ros. 'So what do you do at this Bureau?' she asked him.

'Well, I could tell you.' Roland stopped walking, turned to face her, lowered his voice to deliver the old cliché. 'But then I'd have to kill you.'

When Ros didn't react, Roland went on in a more normal tone, 'We police all exports of high technology. Weapons, stuff that could be used in weapons. We can't just sell anything to anyone any more, you know.' He took her arm again, steered her towards the gangplank of the warship. 'And that really is all I can tell you.'

Thwarted, Ros let herself be escorted onto the ship. The honour guard ignored them, standing stiffly to attention. An elderly man in an Admiral's uniform nodded to Roland, and bowed slightly to Ros. She smiled back and wondered who the hell he was.

'This is certainly turning out to be one of your classic mystery tours, Roland,' she said.

Behind her, there was a rustle of uniforms and a clicking of heels as the honour guard came even more to attention. Ros turned, saw a short man with Asiatic features and an orange sash across his evening dress stepping off the gangplank onto the deck. He bowed to the Admiral as the sailors whistled him aboard.

'Who is it, then?' she whispered to Roland. 'You've got to tell me now!'

'He's the Regent in Exile of . . .'

Roland was interrupted by the arrival of the Regent himself, in the company of the Admiral. He bowed; Ros made what she hoped was a reasonable imitation of a curtsey. The Regent smiled and nodded at both of them, then pressed on into the ship. Roland and Ros followed, pushing their way along narrow, gloss-white corridors. Ros didn't think of herself as tall, but she had to duck several times to avoid clouting her head on a length of pipe or heavy duty ducting.

Finally, they arrived at a brightly lit mess room, crowded with well-dressed people. The Regent and the Admiral were standing at the front. A woman in a blue sari, who Ros guessed was the Regent's wife, stood with them.

'Less of a party, more of a diplomatic reception,' she said to Roland.

'Sort of,' he replied. 'We don't officially recognise the Regent, remember. He's in exile.' He grinned. 'Champagne's still free, though.' He lifted a glass from a tray held by a nearby waiter and handed it to Ros, then took one himself and downed about half of it in one gulp.

Ros rolled her eyes. Roland obviously hadn't

changed his views about how to make a party go with a swing.

The assassin was waiting on the quayside. He didn't think of himself as an assassin – few assassins do. He was a patriot, a liberator, even a hero, in his own eyes.

He raised the binoculars, scanned the deck of the warship once more. It was empty, save for a single rating on guard in the bridge who were scanning the surroundings slowly but was too far away to see anything.

By the time he did see anything – if he did – it would be too late.

The assassin smiled and reached for the box at his feet.

An ordinary, wooden box, that might contain fishing tackle.

It didn't.

He prised open the lid, took the launcher out of the foam-padded lining. It looked a bit more like a gun than he would have liked, but he was far enough from the ship that it shouldn't matter.

And if he was seen, what did it signify, so long as the weapon was launched first? He was a patriot. He was a hero.

And besides, he had diplomatic immunity.

He checked the launcher, then popped open the plastic capsule that held the device. He took the power tweezers as he had been instructed to do, let them grip the tip of the tiny machine – the toughest part, so he had been told.

Holding it by the tip, he loaded it into the launcher.

A shutter whirred open. A tiny needle attached to a cluster of thread-like capillary pipes moved down, touched the dart.

157

Red lights on the side of the launcher slowly changed to green.

The assassin smiled again, and, though he knew it wasn't really necessary, aimed the launcher crudely at the ship.

The last light went green. The shutter whirred again.

The assassin pulled the trigger.

'My Lords, Ladies and Gentlemen,' said the Admiral, in a voice loud enough to bring the crowd in the mess hall to immediate silence. 'Welcome to Marine Command HQ. We are honoured tonight by the presence of one who knows only too well that the burdens of state are no less heavy when carried in exile.'

Ros had taken one sip of her champagne, no more. She wanted to keep her head on, to concentrate. There was something odd about this gathering, she decided. There was a clear division between the ex-patriates, their formal wear decorated with sashes and medallions proclaiming their Royal or quasi-Royal status, and the locals, who were mostly business people by the look of them. The two groups were not mingling, but were watching each other, almost warily. She glanced at Roland, to see if he'd noticed, but he was gazing at the Admiral, with a vague expression on his face which seemed to signify that he'd forgotten something, but couldn't quite remember what.

But Ros was pretty sure it didn't signify that at all. She noticed the surreptitious eye movements, a slight tension in his hands. He was watching the audience. He had noticed, too. She wondered again why Roland had invited her to this party. One thing was sure: it wasn't for her skills in international diplomacy. She'd known that from the outset.

Ros discreetly prised open the small, apparently

158

decorative, handbag she was carrying, had a look at the pop-up screen inside.

A constellation of red and amber traces glowed on the screen, each trace flagged with its own frequency and ID.

Ros nodded to herself. This room wasn't just bugged: it had bugs on its bugs. There were at least ten separate sources, only one of which – a minicam she could see mounted near to the Admiral's head – was likely to be legitimate. A couple of others might be bodyguards, of course, and perhaps there was a reporter or two here on the quiet, but –

Not all of them. No way.

She turned to Roland, but he was looking to the front of the room. Ros realised there wasn't anything more she could do without attracting attention, so she touched a button which told the scanner to record the information it had displayed, then quietly closed her bag again.

The Regent himself was speaking now, in slow, measured phrases, with only the slightest of accents. 'It is a terrible thing when power is seized by the openly corrupt. But it is a source of hope for my people, I know, that they can see their ideals and their sense of nationhood survive, protected here on foreign soil. The links between our two countries have always been strong and will surely, one day, be so again.'

The Regent paused, looked around. Ros noticed polite nods from the ex-patriates, glassy smiles from the local business people.

'But there is something I have to say, though it pains me to say it. The embargo on lethal technology is being openly flouted by certain companies.' He was looking directly at the business people now. Ros abruptly realised what business these people were likely to be in, and why they were here. 'I am here tonight to beg you,' the Regent went on. 'Do not allow yourselves to be fooled by the claims of those in my country who say they need these weapons for defence. Do not be silent partners in the genocide that may lie ahead for my people.'

There was a murmur from the business half of the crowd. A not entirely friendly one. They felt they were being accused, and they obviously didn't like it.

She glanced at Roland, saw him furtively examining the same phenomenon, whilst ostensibly facing the Regent. The vague expression was still on his face, like a mask.

She grinned. He really hadn't changed.

'You know,' the Regent was saying, 'if my Irish great-grandfather were here tonight, I'm sure he'd say –' He broke off, looked up. There was a ripple of laughter from the audience: they were clearly expecting the Regent to attempt an Irish accent.

But then there was a startled expression on the man's face, and he was diving sideways – the bodyguards were on the move –

Ros looked at the crowd, tried to see a gunman. Nothing: just people staring in open-mouthed shock. But she couldn't see everyone.

'God help me!' The Regent's shout started a ripple of noise, words, shouts, rustles of clothing. Roland dived forward through the crowd. Ros started to follow him, was blocked by a heavily built Asiatic man with a white sash over his evening dress.

She took a step back, opened her bag, had a look at the electronic situation.

There was another source. A new one. She spotted it at once because it was moving – jigging about wildly, somewhere near the front of the room.

She heard a woman shouting: 'He's having convulsions. Somebody's poisoned him! Please help!'

160

And someone else: 'Give him air!'

She thought quickly: if it's sending, it must be some kind of tracking device. Either that or someone guided it to the target. Either way it's slow, which means it can't hope to kill him by force of impact alone.

Yes. They'd poisoned him all right.

She started to push her way through the crowd. 'Roland! Roland! Look for a bug. Some sort of dart.'

Then she looked at the screen again, and noticed something.

The bug had stopped moving. And it was no longer directly in front of her, but to one side.

In fact it was . . .

She jumped sideways, pushing an astonished businessman out of the way.

There! A tiny piece of metal, no bigger than an insect. It must have shaken loose, skidded across the floor. She crouched down to take a closer look, saw something very familiar.

The same thing she'd seen at Elena Johnson's house. The bug that had tried to gas her. Only, this one was slightly different.

She reached out, but her hand was pushed out of the way by a black, polished, shoe.

Before Ros could react, call out, shout, the shoe went on to crush the bug.

'Damn!'

Ros became aware of eyes on her. She looked up, saw the Asiatic bodyguard who'd blocked her earlier.

'I beg your pardon?' he said.

'You just trod on it. The bug they used to attack the Regent.'

The man frowned, then seemed to grasp what Ros had said. He lifted his shoe, revealing fragments of metal, now bent and unrecognisable.

He looked at Ros solemnly. 'We should recover the

pieces,' he said slowly, his English awkward and accented. 'We will need the evidence.'

Ros became aware of a growing silence in the room. 'The Regent –' she began.

The man bowed his head. 'The Regent is dead.'

« Twenty-two »

'Ros is probably dancing on the table by now,' whispered Ed. 'Presuming she isn't under it.'

Beckett shushed him, of course. Ed had expected that.

He looked around the dark, silent room that by day was the goods reception area of Cyberscope, and repressed the urge to sing 'Oh What a Beautiful Morning' in a very loud voice.

No. That might really get them into trouble.

Beckett was halfway across the room, sticking close to the wall. He beckoned, mouthed something that Ed didn't understand. Perhaps all Hive agents could lipread, or something.

He edged around the wall, watched as Beckett prised open a service panel.

'Video links,' muttered Beckett as Ed drew closer. 'Give me some light.'

Ed pulled the penlight torch from the pocket of his shirt, shone it into the space behind the service panel. Several rows of electrical cabling were revealed, and a couple of scart sockets.

'OK,' said Beckett. 'Now watch.'

'Do I get much choice?' asked Ed. 'Mind you, if we'd brought a portable TV I could be watching the football.'

Beckett ignored him, took a small grey box from the bag he was carrying over his shoulder. Coloured leads ending in croc clips trailed from the box. Beckett began fixing the clips to exposed junctions on the cabling exposed beneath the service panel. 'Don't try this at home, kids,' he muttered.

'Wouldn't dream of it,' said Ed.

As each connection was made, a red light on the box signalled that it was clean. When there were three lights on, Beckett said, 'Now, this is the clever bit. Three security cameras – one picture. One, two, three.' At 'three' he flicked a switch on the box. A green light came on next to it.

'So how do you know it's worked?' asked Ed.

Beckett pointed at the green light. 'Circuit's OK,' he said. 'So it's working.'

Ed shook his head slowly. 'What if they've got a back up or something?'

'It would have shown up on the circuit test,' said Beckett. He looked round at Ed. 'You have to trust these machines to do their job. There isn't any choice in this business.'

'I hope you're right, my friend,' said Ed.

But Beckett was already looking at the map.

'The door on the right at the end should be the one,' he said, taking his lock picking kit out of the bag. 'Let's just hope there aren't any bolts on the inside.'

'And if there are?'

'Then we try the one on the left. Come on.'

He hurried off along the wall, leaving Ed to follow.

Ros looked at the readout from the scanner in her bag, now connected to a computer screen in a radar control room inside the warship. The room was dark, apart from the light from the screen and a little seeping in under the door.

'That's the one,' said Ros, indicating a trace that moved in rapid steps across the screen from one sweep to the next.

Roland just nodded. The expression on his face was entirely different now: tense, angry. In fact, it was the first time Ros had ever seen Roland angry in some ten years of friendship.

'And you say you'd seen this type of machine before?' he asked.

Ros made a slight shrug. 'I can't be absolutely sure, but I'll swear it was practically identical to a bug that nearly gassed me the other night. Now that one belonged to a woman called Elena Johnson – or at least, we think it did. Unless someone was trying to bug her. She was after this thing called SACROS.'

Roland looked at her sharply. 'You'd better tell me the full story.'

Ros did. When she'd finished, Roland said, almost conversationally, 'Elena Johnson was on the client list of a company called Cyberscope. Heard of them?'

Ros shook her head.

'They're under investigation. For –'

'– the export of illegal technology,' guessed Ros.

Roland nodded. 'Voice-activated bombs, mostly. We knew that Cyberscope had done a deal with these people, but we weren't quite sure of the nature of the weapon.' He looked grimly at the screen. 'We'd hoped we could prevent this, but –' he shook his head slowly. Suddenly, the old vague expression was back. He looked at his shoes, then said, 'Actually, the reason I asked you out in the first place was to get you to give us some help there. I saw on the net that you were setting up some kind of confidential investigation service. The Bureau would like to employ you.'

Ros looked at him. 'To do what?'

'To get into Cyberscope's files.'

Ros stared at the flickering screen, the information frozen at the moment of the poison bug's arrival. 'Any particular files?'

'The one we're after is called "The Assassins".' He looked at her apologetically. 'Hardly original, but graphically descriptive.'

Ed stared at the room in some confusion. It was full of games. The familiar purple cuboid holoscreen of RamRaider; the interlocking blue diamond symbol of Shoot-M-Up; a closed box that looked like a sub-VR Flight Simulator; and a couple of You Are The Pinball machines, complete with loop-the-loop arches stretching up to the ceiling and a slam-hammer for That Real Sensation Of Impact!TM. And lots more.

'Wow! Grab this rec room!' he said. 'What do they do here?'

'They develop and market computer games. Software and hardware. The lot. This isn't a rec room – it'll be the main working area. Where they get the new product ideas.'

Ed looked around. He couldn't see any new products, just a lot of old ones. He experimentally touched the SETUP button on Shoot-M-Up, saw the same old familiar screen with the fifteen robot turkeys (or aliens, or whatever they were meant to be). He touched BESTSCORE?, saw that it was only in the tens of millions.

And these were games designers?

'This is a place for serious timewasting, my friend,' he told Beckett.

Then looked around.

'Beckett?'

Torchlight shone through the window, and Ed

suddenly realised that there was a guard outside, and a dog was barking, and that he shouldn't have been trying to play computer games whilst raiding a factory in the middle of the night.

He ducked down and ran, caught up with Beckett in a corridor outside the rec room.

'Thought you were on holiday,' commented Beckett.

'Nah, just a couple of minutes' unpaid leave.'

Beckett gestured ahead, at a wide glass door sealed shut with yellow tape marked BY GOVERNMENT ORDER in recurring capitals. Beyond, Ed could see a glass desk, a glass chair, and a stacked computer system with a display of flickering lights. Behind it, the huge image of a shark slowly rotated on a wallscreen.

'This it?' he asked Beckett.

Beckett nodded.

Ed stepped towards the door, put his palm against the tape. 'Well, this won't stop anyone.'

Beckett caught his arm. 'No, but they will.' He gestured at the ceiling of the office: Ed saw an insignificant looking black box with a winking red light. 'Motion detector,' explained Beckett. 'And it won't be the only one. Anything bigger than a mouse gets in there and we're blown.'

Ed looked around. There had to be another way in. Suddenly, he had an idea. He jumped up, banged his fist on the ceiling tiles.

'Careful!' said Beckett.

But Ed was triumphant. 'It's hollow! There's a false ceiling! Now all we have to do is find a way in.' He looked around, saw a ventilation grille a few metres back down the corridor.

Beckett followed his gaze, nodded. 'We ought to be able to shift that pretty easily.'

Closer inspection showed that the grille had only two of its four screws intact. Obviously it was removed regularly, and the service engineers weren't too careful about how they put it back. It only took a couple of minutes to remove the cover, then Beckett lifted Ed up on his shoulders, grunting with the effort, and Ed lifted himself inside.

There wasn't much space. Less than a metre of headroom, and a framework of light steel girders and foam panelling gave the area the appearance of a maze. Worse, a large ventilation fan a little further down the corridor created a dust-loaded draught. He began crawling forward in what seemed to be the direction of the office, hoping that he wouldn't get lost.

After a moment Beckett's voice came over the headset. 'Ed? Can you hear me?'

'Loud and clear, Houston.'

'Don't start that again. Listen, I'm setting up the vid now. You got that connector?'

'Nah, I think I left it at home.'

There was a pause, and for a moment Ed thought Beckett had taken him seriously. There was an audible outlet of breath, then, 'You won't get your bonus this way, you know.'

Ed laughed.

'Where are you now?'

'About sixty-three west by twelve north. Entering cannibal country.'

Another sigh. 'Ed? Do you actually know where you are?'

'Yeah.' Ed had found another ventilator grille. He peered through it. 'I'm above the glass desk.'

'Good. Can you see the ribbon cable on there?'

'The black thing? Got it.'

Ed reached into the bag of tools at his waist, pulled out the connector. It looked like a miniature rake with too many prongs. He found that it would fit nicely through the slats of the ventilation grille. He gradually extended it to its full length, hoping that the motion detectors wouldn't pick up the movement if he was slow and careful enough.

They didn't.

The pins made contact with the ribbon cable.

Beckett's voice came through the headset. 'Right, I've got an enlargement on the computer display on my system. All I need you to do is speed it up. Push the pins in.'

Ed pushed.

Nothing happened.

'No good,' said Beckett unnecessarily. 'Try again.'

Ed tried.

And tried.

And tried.

On the fourth attempt, he said, 'This is like trying to circumcise a gnat. Isn't there a simpler way? I mean, can't your friend Irene just tell them the computer game's hers and get it back?'

'Ed, if you'd ever had anything tied up in a company that went bust – it's a nightmare. Now try again.'

Ed lowered the connector one more time.

Beckett said, 'And she isn't "my friend Irene". She's a client.'

'Sure,' said Ed, still struggling with the connector. He could see it was going to miss again.

'I never met her before tonight!' Beckett was protesting.

Ed grinned to himself. 'It was love at first sight, then.' He pulled his body a little more upright, in an effort to get a new angle on the connector.

Something hit him on the back of the head.

The roof.

'You in pain?' asked Beckett.

'I certainly am!'

'Good.'

Ed rubbed his head, shoved down on the connector. To hell with finesse. It was just going to have to connect.

There was a rapid bleeping noise from below.

'That's good,' said Beckett. 'I can work with that.'

'What now?' asked Ed, trying to hide his amazement at the fact that the thing had actually worked this time.

'We have to remove all Irene's material. Overwrite every sector on every disc with garbage so that there's no record of it ever having been there.'

Beckett's voice was interrupted by another. Ed jumped, and almost hit his head on the ceiling again.

'Voice identification,' it demanded.

It was the computer.

'That's one hell of a realistic voice,' he muttered.

'Yeah, it's one of Dave Young's systems. Ros says he's good at voices. Does them himself.' Beckett raised his own voice, said, 'Designer override.'

'Designer password?' prompted Dave Young's voice.

'City of Tiny Lights,' said Beckett, with every appearance of total confidence.

'How'd you know that?' asked Ed, bewildered.

'Easy. Dave Young always uses Frank Zappa song titles for his passwords.'

Ed didn't quite believe it but, sure enough, the computer was saying, 'Designer access approved. Name of file?'

Beckett's voice was triumphant. 'The Assassins.'

Ros stood with Roland Blatty, looking at the glass towers of Cyberscope Ltd. Dim blue security lights shone from some of the windows.

'So what's in this Assassins file then?'

'Well, we don't know for sure, of course, or we wouldn't be asking for your help. But I'd guess it included the names and bank account numbers of quite a few of the Regent's enemies. Plus the real audit trail for Cyberscope's hi-tech weapons sales.'

Ros nodded. 'It figures. Want to go in and have a look now?'

Roland shook his head. 'It'll wait until morning. Get your new business partners on to it. Beckett was a good man at BHQ, one of the few there from what I've heard. He could be quite useful, I think.'

Ed had suddenly thought of something.

'How do we know this is all right?' he asked. 'If we're going to eradicate the files from Cyberscope's computer – I mean, we could just be sabotaging the competition.'

Beckett's voice came back over the headset. 'Watch this.'

A clicking of buttons, then electronic greeting noises from the computer. Ed flattened his head against the ventilation grille, caught sight of part of a huge face on the wallscreen.

A woman's voice spoke: 'This file is confidential. It is encrypted and protected. Do not proceed without full clearance.'

Beckett spoke again. 'Eradicate this file.'

The computer replied in Dave Young's voice: 'Specify procedure "eradicate" to be used.'

More clicking, as Beckett used his notebook computer keyboard to enter the necessary instructions to run Ros's erasure program. The woman's voice abruptly vanished from the screen.

'Process terminated,' said Dave Young's voice.

'Exit,' instructed Beckett, adding a muttered, 'Gotcha.'

At that point, the alarms went off.

'Guards must've spotted our triplicate pictures,' commented Beckett.

That much was obvious, thought Ed. Aloud he said, 'Look, Beckett, don't wait for me, just get the hell out of here. I'll meet you at the car.'

He pulled in the connector, slammed the cover back on the ventilation grille, then crawled as fast as he could for the place where he'd come in.

When he got there, three security guards were standing below it, holding a shouted conversation. A dog was with them. It looked up at Ed and barked. Ed ducked out of the way, heard shouts behind him.

'. . . hole in the ceiling . . . someone's up there!'

Ed crawled faster, banged his head on the roof again. This time it wasn't funny. The ventilation fan was ahead – no way out there. Hell, what was he going to do? He scrambled into the maze of roofing panels, looking for a hatchway, a hole, anything that went down. He could hear clattering and banging behind him. It was rapidly becoming totally dark, and he was losing all sense of direction.

Then he saw it. A line of blueish light.

A proper ceiling hatch, marked EMERGENCY EXIT.

Well, thought Ed, this is certainly an emergency. He hit open the hatch, scrambled through, landed in the middle of a room that looked like some sort of lab. Rows of microscopes, red cupboards on the walls. A gutted rat in a glass case. Ed made for the exit, struggled with the lock.

The dog was waiting for him in the corridor.

Ed kicked out at it, ran for the open.

He almost made it, would have made it if there hadn't been another door with one of those fiddly locks. In the couple of seconds it took to get the door open, the dog had caught him up and got its teeth into the seat of his trousers.

The door opened at last, and Ed managed to shake off the dog, though it took some of his trousers with it

– and, by the feel of it, some of his backside too.

It hurt.

He slammed the door on the brute and ran. He ran fast, across a courtyard dotted with antique-style lamps and neatly trimmed small trees. He saw Beckett and the car, already on the move, saw the passenger door open and dived for it.

'You OK?' Beckett was already shoving the accelerator to the floor. The car took off in a screech of tyres even before Ed had got the door closed.

'Mostly,' said Ed, wincing as his backside made contact with the car seat. 'Just don't ask me to ride a pushbike for a few days.'

Beckett stared at him.

'I think that dog took a piece right out of my bum,' explained Ed.

'Now that,' said Beckett, swerving the car out onto the main road, 'is something I don't want to see.'

'– and this is where the alarms went off, and we had to get out of there pretty fast. But not before we removed every trace of your Assassins material.'

Ed watched as Beckett packed away the microcam viewer he'd been using to show the evening's recordings to their client. Then he watched as Beckett looked up and smiled at her. 'Irene.' Yeah. There was no doubt about it, the guy was hooked. Client she might be, but Beckett was definitely hoping for more.

Ed took a look around the café, at the chess pieces painted on the walls, the chequerboard floor. Definitely a bit upmarket for me, he decided. And 'Irene', too.

He decided to add a little businesslike caution to the conversation.

'There still might be some back ups,' he said.

Irene glanced swiftly at him, then looked back at Beckett. 'Oh, no, they were stored off site. They were easy to take care of.' She smiled. 'I don't know what to say.'

Ed wondered if 'Will you kiss me, my prince?' would be appropriate, but decided to keep his mouth shut.

Beckett was still all doggy grin. You could almost see his tongue hanging out. 'Well, as soon as you make a million out of this little game of yours, then –' He shrugged. '– we'll send you a bill.'

Irene extended a hand, touched Beckett's. 'Thanks, Mr Beckett.' She glanced at Ed. 'Thank you, too.'

'Er – thanks,' said Ed.

Irene stood up. So did Beckett.

Christ, he wasn't going off with her, was he? He'd better leave the car keys if he was.

Beckett put Irene's cape around her shoulders, making quite a performance of it. At last Irene left, Beckett following her with his eyes, but thankfully not with the rest of him and certainly not with his car keys.

When she reached the door, she waved.

Beckett waved back.

Ed decided it was time to say something, man to man. He stared at Beckett, said slowly, 'You should see the look on your face, my friend.'

Beckett took a slurp of his coffee, coffee which Irene had paid for. 'Oh yeah?' he said. 'Well, look on the bright side. At least I've got an arse in my trousers.'

« Twenty-three »

Irene's smile floated above the clouds.

Not her face, just her smile. It was fixed, ironic, and the Hive was underneath it, just where her chin should be. As Beckett watched, a fluorescent helicopter – Ed's heli – lifted off from the Hive roof and flew behind the smile. Then it began banging on the roof of her skull, trying to get out.

Ed was such a smart-arse. Couldn't he see they were stuck inside Irene's head?

But the banging went on, until Beckett had to admit he wasn't asleep any more, that he wasn't inside Irene's head either, and that someone was knocking on the door and he was going to have to wake up.

He pulled a towelling robe around himself, went to the door, opened it and peered around.

It was Ros.

'Your country needs you, Beckett.'

'What, now? It's only –'

'– half past nine,' Ros finished for him. 'I know, you had a late night. But this one's urgent.'

She gave him five minutes to shower and dress. He took three. He was used to getting ready in a hurry, a

175

legacy from late mornings at the Hive. He took half his coffee with him to the car, another familiar time saver. The caffeine began to brighten the edges of his vision, though he couldn't quite shake off the notion that all this was happening inside Irene's head.

Ed was right, he decided. The woman must have made an impression on him.

Ed was waiting in the car. As Ros drove them across the river, she explained what had happened to her last night.

'And we thought we were having an exciting time!' commented Ed.

Ros glanced over her shoulder at Beckett in the back seat.

'The man was killed, Ed,' said Beckett quietly. 'That isn't excitement, it's murder.'

Ros went on: 'The Regent-in-exile was almost certainly killed on the orders of the Generals who drove him out. Now, this company called Cyberscope –'

Beckett felt his stomach lurch.

'– has been supplying weapons to repressive regimes in defiance of all international embargoes.'

Ed looked over his shoulder at Beckett, then back at the glass towers of the factory in front of them. Beckett was staring too. It was all beginning to look rather familiar.

He remembered his dream, about being inside Irene's head. And realised that his subconscious had been trying to tell him something.

Too late.

'Now, Roland's new bureau had enough confidence in its information to shut them down yesterday, but now they can't get into the records to establish proof of supply.' She looked over her shoulder and grinned. 'We're going to show them how it's done.'

No we're not, thought Beckett as he got out of the

car. We're going to make first-rate fools of ourselves.

He felt a nudge on his shoulder. Ed. 'This place look kind of familiar?'

Beckett's anger boiled over.

'Don't!' he snapped. He strode off after Ros, who was talking to a blond-haired man in a brown business suit.

Ros turned as he approached. 'Guys, meet Roland Blatty, ex-chess club senior, currently with the government.'

Roland shook Beckett's hand. 'I've heard a lot about you. Glad to have you aboard.'

You won't be, thought Beckett, when you find out where I was last night.

Somehow, he managed to smile.

Roland led them through the building, explaining as he went.

'I put our own guards on the place, so that Cyberscope wouldn't have a chance to interfere with the evidence. We've been looking in the labs.' He waved down a corridor. 'They specialise in miniature anti-personnel devices. Vicious, really vicious stuff. And they're niche marketing to the tyrants because they'll pay more.' He looked at Beckett. 'I'm not saying we don't have the skills to get to the information, but we're running out of time.'

Beckett couldn't think of anything to say. He felt physically sick.

'You can't just close them down for good?' That was Ed.

'It's not illegal to make what they make,' explained Roland. 'The crime's in who they sell it to. That's why we need the records. We know they're kept in a file called "Assassins", but –'

Beckett didn't hear the rest of the sentence. He was staring at the wallscreen in the office ahead of them.

At the rotating display of a huge white shark.

How appropriate, he thought.

But that didn't make it any better.

Roland led the way into the office, which was full of technicians. One had a connector linked up to the ribbon cable. Another had the back off one of the computer cabinets and was fiddling with the circuitry. A third held a scanning device against the wallscreen, as if she hoped that the shark might be able to tell them something.

He looked over his shoulder, noticed Ed peering at the loose ventilator grille where he'd climbed up the night before.

'What's the hardware?' Ros was asking.

The technician who was investigating the interior of the computer answered. 'It's a connection machine with R-A-I-D memory, that's –'

'– a Redundant Array of Inexpensive Devices.' Ros was grinning broadly, obviously absolutely confident of her ability to get into the system.

So was Beckett. It was what she was likely to find when she got in there that he was worried about.

Why hadn't he *realised*?

'– voice activated, and security protected,' Roland was saying. 'It'll only respond to the company chief. And we're getting no cooperation there.'

'Designer override,' said Ros.

The white shark froze.

Just as it had the previous night, thought Beckett. Except that this time Roland's equipment was doing the connection work.

Not that it would do any good. There was nothing left to connect with.

Ros was explaining to Roland Blatty and his staff: 'Nearly all these systems have back doors. Once we know what we're dealing with, we can get hold of the

178

designer's own cheats and passwords within an hour.'

Beckett decided that he couldn't stand another hour of feeling like this. If it was gone, it was gone. But he had to know.

'This looks like one of Dave Young's systems to me,' he said aloud. 'Why not try – "City of Tiny Lights".'

The shark vanished from the screen, just as it had last night. And a city of tiny lights appeared – a schematic representation of the computer's own circuitry.

'Access approved,' said the computer, in Dave Young's voice. 'Name of file for review?'

Ros looked round, frowning at Beckett, a little embarrassed. 'He – uhh – usually uses Frank Zappa songs.'

Roland Blatty was obviously impressed. 'We were trying to crack this all day yesterday!'

'Do you have a file name to look for?'

'The Assassins files.'

'I have no such files.'

Ros wasn't fazed. She just turned to the screen and said, 'Recover deleted files.'

'I have no trace or record of any such files.'

Beckett winced. He'd hoped that by some miracle Blatty's deeper, more organised probe into the system had reached areas that last night's operation had left unscathed.

No such luck.

The technician who had spoken before looked up again. 'They existed yesterday, we just couldn't get into them.'

Roland frowned. 'How've they done that?'

'How tight was your security?' asked Ros.

That does it, thought Beckett. I'm going to have to say something. I'm going to have to explain this – this – monumental cock-up. Somehow.

'A couple of thieves did get into the offices, but they didn't get in here.'

'Well, someone's been interfering. What about back-ups?'

'Kept off site in a warehouse by the river. Which was destroyed in a very convenient fire two nights ago.'

A new voice spoke. A woman's voice. 'I hope that's not an accusation, Mr Blatty.'

Beckett jumped, turned, saw the face to match the voice.

Irene Campbell.

He saw Ed looking at him, returned the glance. Ed gave the slightest of shrugs.

A man stood next to Irene, holding aloft a small, gold-plated DAT recorder. 'I should warn you, I'm recording this conversation,' he said.

Ros spoke. 'Introduce us, Roland.'

Blatty stepped forward. 'This is Irene Campbell. Founder, sole shareholder and Managing Director of Cyberscope. And this is her legal director Peter Marasco.'

Blatty was asking Irene Campbell what she'd done with the evidence. Beckett heard Marasco murmur, 'You don't have to answer.'

But the Managing Director answered anyway. 'There is no evidence. Get your people out, Mr Blatty. I want my company back and I want it now. I'm going to sue you for every penny of lost business. You've no case, you never had a case, you never will have a case.'

Beckett barely heard the words. He was concentrating on the smug look on Irene Campbell's face. He was thinking of the man who'd died last night, whilst he, Beckett, had been busy protecting the perpetrator from the consequences of her actions.

It was time to speak up.

He stepped forward, touched Ros on the arm. 'Excuse me – Roland – I'm sorry.' He looked from Ros to Ed and back again, briefly glanced at Irene's smug face. 'We need to talk. Now. In private.'

Ros frowned, then looked at him and started walking. Ed tagged along behind. Roland looked from one to the other of them.

Beckett took a deep breath. 'You'd better come too, Roland,' he said.

He pushed his way out of the room, passing Irene Campbell, passing her glassy smile without a word.

Ros couldn't believe it. It was impossible.

Nobody could be that stupid.

She tried to catch Beckett's eye, but he just kept marching up and down in front of her, head bowed, miserable, like a little boy called before the head teacher at school. Ed leaned against one of the games machines, arms folded, looking at nothing in particular. Roland stood some distance away from them, hands behind his back, looking out of the window. So far, to Ros's immense relief, he hadn't said anything.

'Look, Beckett,' trying to keep herself from actually shouting at him. 'I put my reputation on the line for this. Our reputation. The reputation of the new company that we set up yesterday, OK? I told Roland we could achieve the impossible. I did not expect to turn up and find you'd been here first and wiped the slate clean!'

Beckett looked at her once, but didn't stop pacing. 'I'm not going to make excuses, all right? I'm just going to get her.'

'Get her how? That was my erasure program! It leaves nothing – nothing at all! We haven't got any evidence, we haven't got anything!'

Beckett carried on pacing. 'I don't know what we're

going to do, OK? But we're going to do something. Somehow.'

'Something like last night, you mean? Something you haven't even thought about before you do it, so that we all end up looking like idiots. What were you thinking of?'

Beckett stopped pacing, turned to face her at last. 'She conned me. All right? She conned me and I fell for it. I'm sorry.'

Ed spoke up. 'Listen Beckett, don't torture yourself. Anyone – I mean anyone – of your reduced mental capacity would have done the same thing.'

Beckett's face screwed up tight. Before Ros could intervene, he'd turned on Ed.

'That's funny, Ed. That's really funny.' He stalked off out of the room.

Helpless, Ros followed.

She caught up with Beckett in the reception area, at about the same time as Roland Blatty caught up with her.

She took one look at Beckett's face and decided to talk to Roland.

'Other people are going to die now, aren't they?'

'Very probably,' said Roland shortly. Ros remembered what she'd thought last night, that she'd never seen Roland really angry.

Well – he was now.

She swallowed, looked at Beckett. 'Last night's show wasn't half of it. Cyberscope have been selling devices for assassination programmes. They've been helping to wipe out opposition groups across half the world. And, by erasing those files, we've just given them the means to carry on doing it.'

Roland shook his head slowly. 'I have to talk to the Minister,' he said, and walked off.

As Ros looked around helplessly, she saw Irene

Campbell and Marasco walk out of the lift and across the lobby. Outside, they nodded pleasantly to Roland, who ignored them, then got into a red Ferrari.

'I bet she doesn't have a stain on her conscience,' said Ros.

'That makes her one step better off than me,' said Beckett.

Ros touched his shoulder. 'Come on, let's get away from this place and do some thinking. There has to be something we can do.'

The Managing Director settled into the driver's seat of her car and smiled. She looked over her shoulder through the tinted glass of the rear window, saw Beckett and the others standing there.

For the first time in more than a day she felt comfortable.

'We may have another use for Beckett,' said Marasco suddenly.

The Managing Director looked at him.

'SACROS,' he said simply. 'He works – or, at least, worked – for the Hive. He may have contacts. Access to blueprints.' A pause. 'It's worth pursuing.'

The Managing Director looked over her shoulder again, saw Beckett walking away, hands in his pockets, defeated.

'Why not?' she asked. 'We should have put paid to his little "independent company". Let's see if we can make him a better offer.'

Marasco glanced at her. 'How much?'

The Managing Director put the car into gear, looked out at the car park through the protective glass of the windscreen.

'Cash.' She named a sum. 'And if that fails – do whatever you feel is necessary to get him.'

« Twenty-four »

The roof of the shrine was plain black wood, the walls plain white plaster. Under the roof, housed in a white alcove within the walls, the statue of the Regent's God was made of solid gold, engraved with Sanskrit characters painted black. The image held one hand up, palm outward, the other down by his knees, fist clenched.

Peace and welcoming above anger and distrust.

Yes, thought Beckett. A neat philosophy. Shame the opposition weren't listening.

He adjusted his elbows on the rickety windowsill of the shed they were using as cover, and lowered the track of the binoculars so that he could get a look at the action in front of the shrine. The shaven-headed Master in his russet robe stood in the same position as his God, while four lesser priests in saffron robes each held aloft a single white lily, as a symbol of death and rebirth. The mourners too carried white lilies, and wore saffron armbands over the formal black of western mourning. Each one bowed before the Master and the icon, then laid the flower down before the shrine, bowed again, and withdrew. It was a long, slow, progression: the Regent-in-exile had been a man with many friends.

184

A slow, quiet rain fell on everything.

'I don't know whether we're watching a state funeral or a dress rehearsal for the Mikado,' said Ed suddenly.

Beckett couldn't think of any way to adequately communicate to the younger man the devastating inappropriateness of this remark, so he simply said, 'Shut up, Ed.'

But Ed was in no mood to shut up. 'Who's the guy in the uniform?' he asked.

Beckett panned the binoculars until he saw the uniform, the familiar face under the peaked cap. 'That's Admiral Lansdale. He's the government's semi-official liaison man.'

'Why only semi-official?'

Beckett put the binoculars down, turned to the younger man. Rain, falling harder now, drummed on the wooden roof of the shed. 'We can't openly encourage the downfall of another nation's rulers, Ed,' he explained. 'Not even if they are a bunch of murdering square-bashers.'

Ed nodded, then looked back at the small screen in front of him which was relaying the picture from the binoculars.

'Beckett, there's someone coming. Take a look.'

Beckett put the binoculars back to his eyes, saw the priests, the icon, the Admiral bowing to the Master.

'Swing over to the right.'

Beckett panned right, and at once saw a new arrival whose face looked familiar.

Familiar in the wrong sort of way.

Two of the more heavy-set mourners, the ones who had remained watching on the fringes of the crowd, had moved to block his way.

As Beckett watched, an argument began. One of the 'mourners' reached under his jacket.

'Is that guy on Roland's list?' asked Beckett swiftly.

'I'll have a look.' Beckett heard keys click as Ed scanned the file on the laptop, searching for a face that matched the man. Then came the information he was half-expecting. 'He's a security attaché at the embassy.' A pause. 'Says here that if there's an assassination programme going on, chances are he's behind it. What the hell's he doing here?'

Whilst Ed had been speaking, Admiral Lansdale had intervened in the dispute between the security attaché and the others. The embassy man now withdrew, throwing the white lily he was carrying to the ground in evident disgust.

'Stirring things up, by the looks of it. Under the guise of honouring a former statesman.' He lowered the binoculars once more. 'OK, Ed. You follow him. Try to find out what he was after. I'll wait this out then see if I can catch up with the Admiral.'

Ed was already packing up the camera and screen. 'What're you going to say to the Admiral?'

'I don't know,' said Beckett. 'Warn him, I suppose.'

'Warn him?'

Beckett looked at Ed steadily. 'This is serious stuff, Ed. These people are killers, big time. If anyone gets in their way, the going could get rough.' He paused. 'Fatally rough.'

'Anyone who gets in the way,' said Ed steadily. 'Anyone including us, right?'

Rain drummed on the roof. 'You can back out if you want to,' said Beckett carefully.

But Ed only smiled. 'I risk my life twice on Sundays, remember.' He paused, frowned. 'Hey, it's Sunday today, isn't it?'

Beckett couldn't help but smile back.

Ros sat back and watched as the computer dialled the next number on the list.

This is boring, she thought. Boring as hell and I've been doing it for two hours now and I want a break.

On the screen, the words, 'Welcome to Comfortworld Exclusive Health and Fitness Club Membership System. Please enter password.'

Ros waited as her computer gently interrogated the other machine with various options.

After about ten seconds the screen cleared, and an alphabetical list of members appeared. Ros grinned at some of the names. It was funny who popped up in these sorts of places.

Then she saw it. 'Irene Campbell/2 yrs/PAID Cyberscope Co Acct'. The computer had already highlighted the entry, because it contained the name it had been told to look for.

'Jackpot!' shouted Ros, though there was no one around in the Gizmos office to hear her. She pushed her chair up to the desk, then noticed for the first time in half an hour the mug of cold tea standing by the computer.

Tea can wait, Ros decided.

She pulled up the keyboard and entered a couple of control characters. The screen went blank, then the prompt AMEND DATABASE (Y/N)? appeared. Ros typed 'y'.

Time to have some fun.

The hotel plaza was full of glass angels.

They stood between the thick boles of the date palms, perched on the rocks of the little waterfall, flew under the tinted sun dome suspended on barely visible threads. Their names were painted in white gothic letters across their wings: Gabriel, Baradiel, Uriel. Piano music echoed around the angels, played live on a white concert grand.

No cheapjack hotel this one, thought Ed.

His target was weaving his way through the coffee tables scattered around the plaza, his air of purpose looking out of place amid the hubbub of conversation and laughter.

Out of place enough to make him easy to follow.

Suddenly, the embassy man stopped, looked round. Ed almost ducked, then remembered that the man didn't know him, couldn't know him. He was safe enough.

Then Ed saw the person that the embassy man had come to meet and realised he wasn't safe after all.

Tall, elegant, with a dark cloak over a dark business suit.

Irene Campbell, Managing Director of Cyberscope.

Ed ducked down behind a decorative palm in a pot, quickly unshipped the pen mike from the inside pocket of his jacket and pointed it at the couple.

Just to make things more difficult, they didn't sit down, but began wandering around the waterfall display in the middle of the lobby. Before Ed heard a word of the conversation they were out of sight, and out of range of the pen mike. He was forced to follow them.

When he caught sight of them again, the embassy man was speaking, his English heavily accented and slow.

'– the Admiral's voice on tape at the funeral. Does it matter what he said?'

Irene shook her head. 'Do your people still want to go ahead?'

'Your price is very high.'

'But cheaper than a war. And cleaner. There's no risk to any of your own people.'

As she finished speaking, Irene looked up. Ed quickly turned away, pretending to scan the plaza as if looking for a friend.

When he turned back, Irene and her companion were gone.

Ed cursed, hurried between the tables, then caught sight of them again by the doors of the hotel. He took cover behind a pillar, aimed the pen mike again.

'There is one final requirement,' the embassy man was saying.

'What's that?'

There was a pause. Then: 'Human testing. For the final weapon.'

Another pause, so long that Ed thought that they'd moved again and he'd lost the signal. He peered around the pillar, saw Irene facing him. But she didn't seem to see him.

Suddenly she spoke. 'There's no need. It works in tissue cultures and in computer models. It will work in practice, believe me.'

'No. I need you to test it for me. This virus is a crucial element in our plan. It is not enough to know it kills. We need to know that it kills the people we want it to kill. Is proving this a problem for you?'

Again Irene hesitated, this time facing away from Ed, her head down. Finally, she straightened her cloak around her shoulders and said quietly, 'Not at these prices.'

Ed couldn't be sure from the distance, but he thought the embassy man smiled. 'Thank you.' The man opened the door, held it to let Irene pass. Ed heard one last snatch of conversation before the door closed. 'Our ambitions go way beyond controlling a few dissidents, Ms Campbell.'

He hurried to the door, just in time to see the embassy man getting into a black car with diplomatic plates. Irene wasn't in the car, was nowhere in sight.

Ed watched the diplomatic car recede, wondered about following it, then decided against the idea.

He had the Cyberscope connection. That would be enough.

The assassin closed the door of the embassy car quietly, and then walked to the dockside slowly, hands in his pockets, as if he were no more than a tourist.

One of his hands touched the smooth chameleon coating of the bomb.

As if he were no more than a tourist, he gazed at the warship that was Marine Command HQ casually, never letting his eyes give away his intention. After a while he strolled to the grey metal gate that guarded the entrance to the gangway and leaned on it, as if he were a little tired.

With his back to the ship, he slipped the bomb out of his pocket. As if he were stretching, he reached up with both arms, touching the bomb to one of the metal pillars of the gate.

'Test,' he murmured.

'You've no business here and I would ask you to leave at once.' Admiral Lansdale's voice, realistic enough to make the assassin glance around nervously, even though he knew it was coming from the device.

He looked at the gate pillar, saw –

Nothing. The chameleon coating of the bomb had blended perfectly with the grey metal.

The assassin nodded to himself and smiled, then strolled down the waterfront, away from the warship, to where the embassy car was waiting.

All things come to an end in time, he thought. It is merely a matter of waiting long enough.

The rain had stopped, and the sun was beginning to break through the clouds. The Admiral and the Regent's widow sat on a bench, talking quietly, their heads bowed. They had been talking for a long time.

Beckett watched, not sure whether he should intervene. Or what he would say if he did.

A faint vibration in his jacket pocket told him that his phone was ringing. He turned away from the Admiral, pulled out the phone and touched the ANSWER key.

'Yes?'

'Beckett, it's Ed.'

Beckett listened as Ed recounted what he had heard at the hotel.

'Did he say what he was going to do with the weapon?' he asked when Ed had finished.

'No, he just said it was a killer. What did the Admiral say to you?'

Beckett nodded. 'I haven't spoken to him yet. He's been with the Regent's widow. But if you say they've recorded his voice, that has to be for a reason. I think I'm going to have to –'

He heard the sound of a car door slamming behind him, turned quickly. Saw the Admiral raising his hand in farewell to a departing taxi.

Lansdale then strode off along the waterfront towards the warship that housed Marine Command HQ.

'Beckett?'

Ed's voice on the phone.

'Listen Ed, I've got to go. See you later.'

He put the phone away and started after the Admiral at a run, leaping over the waist high metal barrier that divided the military part of the waterfront from the rest.

'Admiral Lansdale!'

The Admiral glanced round, didn't stop.

Beckett hurried to his side. 'You're a difficult man to catch up with, sir.'

The Admiral strode on, pointedly staring out over the river.

Beckett thought he'd better introduce himself. 'Nick

191

Beckett, sir. We met once in Gibraltar.'

'Did we?' said the Admiral coolly, still not breaking his stride.

'I'm sorry if this is a bad moment, sir, but I need to talk to you. About your liaison work with the Regent-in-exile.'

'I don't think so.'

Beckett couldn't understand it. What was the matter with the man?

'But sir, I –'

'As far as all that's concerned,' interrupted the Admiral, 'I'm just a private citizen with private interests.' He still hadn't stopped his quarterdeck stride.

Beckett decided he'd had enough of this. He grabbed the Admiral by the arm, forcing him to look round, to acknowledge him.

'With all due respect, sir,' he said. 'That's baloney.'

The Admiral gave Beckett a hard look. 'That doesn't sound much like respect to me,' he said. Then walked on.

They were almost at the entrance to the narrow gangway that led to the warship. Desperately, Beckett called after the Admiral, 'The sanctions on weapons export are being openly flouted. The device that killed the Regent was probably made in this country – and the company that made it is willing to sell them more – and worse. The entire ex-patriate community is in danger and I have reason to believe that you are too, sir.'

The Admiral stopped, turned. 'Beckett,' he said. 'Surveillance, yes?'

'Yes, sir.'

'Well, stick to your skulking in the bushes and stay out of what you don't understand. The real issues are the big ones. Racial conflicts. Threats of territorial expansion. Not the odd fanatic out to pot himself a prince.' The Admiral took another step towards the gangway, then stopped again. 'The trouble with you people is you get carried away with spy toys. Most of them don't work – and when they do, it's pure fluke if they get the right person.'

He started to stalk towards the gangway once more.

Beckett stared after him, called, 'These aren't just spy toys, sir. And they work every time!'

The Admiral stopped once more, by the metal gate that sealed off the gangway from the waterfront.

'Rubbish!' he shouted.

Beckett wasn't quite sure what happened next. At first it seemed as if the gangway had started to detach itself from the quayside. Then Beckett saw the white glare of flame coming from beyond the spot where the Admiral stood.

For a moment, Beckett saw the Admiral's spare form silhouetted against the fire. Then the shock of the explosion threw Beckett to the ground.

The blare of a klaxon slowly made itself heard over the ringing in his ears. He struggled upright, aware of a sharp pain in his arm. Saw sailors running across the deck of the ship, some carrying guns.

He saw part of the gangway, sloping down to the water now, twisted, bent. Steam rising from the water around the end of it. A chunk of concrete was missing from the quay.

The Admiral was gone.

« Twenty-five »

'How do we know this is all right?'

It was Ed's voice, on the tape from the night of the raid. Even Ed – carefree, lackadaisical Ed – had possessed enough savvy to guess that something might be up. But not Nick Beckett. Not me, Nick Beckett, ex-Hive employee, Government trained, guaranteed expert in all logistical matters.

Nick Beckett, the one who got us into this mess.

The picture on the screen shifted slightly and Ed's voice spoke again. 'If we're going to eradicate the files from Cyberscope's computer – I mean, we could just be sabotaging the competition.'

Beckett glanced at Ros, who was curled up on the couch, watching the TV over the back of it, then at Ed, who sat on the arm of a chair, his back to the screen.

'Watch this,' said Beckett's voice on the tape.

He'd sounded so confident. So clever. So sure of himself. Oh, to be a freelance. Oh, to be able to make your own decisions.

So far, mostly wrong ones.

And there on the screen was Irene's picture, her warning about the file.

Encrypted and protected.

Suddenly, Beckett couldn't stand it any more. He strode across to the window, looked out through the sun blinds. Between the slats of plastic he saw glimpses of the city: slate roofs, concrete towers, a road glinting with cars, all clear, sharply defined in the low afternoon sunlight. The sky was blue.

The Admiral won't be seeing this any more, thought Beckett. Nor will the Regent. Nor will dozens – perhaps hundreds – of other people, killed with Cyberscope's weapons.

And it's all my fault.

Behind him, his own voice said, 'Eradicate this file.'

He turned, found the TV remote, turned it off.

'We're wasting time,' he said. 'We have to get after Irene. We have to do something.'

Ros looked up at him, said quietly, 'You can't blame yourself for this, Nick.'

Beckett ignored her sympathy. Sympathy wasn't going to bring anyone back to life. 'The bomb had to be voice activated. It had to be one of Cyberscope's. One that Irene sold to our friend from the embassy. But they didn't find any trace of the bomb. Well, nothing you could identify, anyway. Certainly, nothing you could trace back to Cyberscope.'

Ed spoke up. 'I hear they didn't find much of the Admiral either.'

From the corner of his eye, Beckett saw Ros punch Ed's arm. Hard.

She said: 'We could try that health club where I traced Irene's membership. If we can't get to her in her offices, perhaps we can track her down when she's off duty.'

'What, catch her selling a deadly virus on the cycling machine? Or manufacturing poison darts over muesli and fruit salad?'

'It's a lead, Beckett. It's all we've got.' She didn't say it, but Beckett caught the implication: stop being so negative.

'Well – OK,' he said. 'But what can we do?'

'We could plant a bug on her. Something she'll take back to the offices.'

'Wait a minute.' Ed. 'This is a health club, right? I mean, what's she going to be wearing?' He laughed. 'Plant a bug on a naked woman – there's a challenge for you.'

Ros just looked at him.

Beckett had suddenly had enough. 'This isn't funny, Ed. None of it's funny, right?'

He walked out of the door, not sure where he was going and not sure whether he cared.

Marasco waited.

The entrance to the station was quite crowded. Mid-afternoon shoppers walked past him, laden with their bags and bundles.

He watched them idly, glanced at his watch a few times.

At last Beckett appeared. Marasco recognised him at once, despite the shabby jacket and old jeans.

Beckett recognised Marasco, too.

'OK, so what do you want?' he asked, as soon as he was in earshot.

Marasco started walking quickly into the station, across the glass and steel bridge. Beckett tagged along behind. A train pulled away below them, almost silent on its cushion of air.

Beckett was getting impatient. 'You phoned me, asked me to come here and meet you. You said it was important. Now you'd better tell me what it is.'

Marasco turned to Beckett, said quietly, 'SACROS.'

'What?'

Marasco stopped walking suddenly, so that Beckett almost collided with him.

'You know what I'm talking about. You could help us to obtain it.'

Beckett stared at him. 'Do you really think I'd betray my country for you? You must be out of your skull.'

Marasco named a sum of money.

Beckett just turned away and walked.

Marasco followed. 'We could go higher – depending on the sales potential.'

Beckett stopped again, turned to face him.

The expression on his face told Marasco everything he needed to know. Money usually worked, but not always. This was going to be one of the times it didn't.

Never mind, there were other methods.

Beckett was saying: 'Look, Mr Marasco, we're going to get your outfit. We're going to find out what you get up to and we're going to get you. Don't forget that.'

Then he walked away. Marasco didn't bother to follow.

'That was a very useful piece of information, Mr Beckett,' he murmured to himself. 'Very useful indeed.'

Irene Campbell stretched out in the water and watched the reflections of ripples chasing each other across the ceiling. She liked her days off. They were few and far between, but they enabled her to enjoy the fruits of her hard work. Comfort. Warmth. Exclusiveness.

Like this health centre, for instance. The Comfortworld Club didn't allow just anyone in. You had to be a member. And you had to be rich to be a member. Very rich. That was why she was the only person in the pool this morning.

She liked it that way.

Irene turned over, swam a few lazy strokes to the edge of the pool and climbed out. The air was warm, humid, almost tropical. She found a towel and rubbed some of the water from her hair and her face, then headed for the changing rooms.

But at the door something made her pause. A sudden uneasy feeling, as if she were being watched.

She looked around, but saw only a heavily built man emerging from the men's changing rooms. He gave her a broad grin, as if he knew she'd recognised him. Irene felt a moment's panic, then realised with a start that he was a well known professional boxer. He was hardly likely to be working for the government on the side.

But the feeling of being watched persisted.

Irene went into the changing rooms, went to her private cubicle and spoke open the voice activated lock. She looked around carefully inside, but couldn't see any trace of disturbance. She took off her swimsuit, dried herself down, and put on a white towelling robe.

Then she hesitated, looking at her neatly folded clothes.

A little too neat.

She looked suspiciously at the voice activated lock. They'd only need a voiceprint to get in, after all.

No. This was stupid. She was being paranoid. This was her day off. If they were following her, all they would see her doing was meeting a friend for lunch, shopping in the city this afternoon, a night at the theatre. Let them get on with it.

Irene decided it was time for breakfast.

She left the cubicle, made her way to the main concourse. Here there were a few other people, mostly sitting at tables, chatting and eating. Everything was white: white tables, white floor with a few potted palms, white walls with carefully trained ivy growing here and there. Irene made her way to the self-service bar, filled a bowl with fruit salad and another with muesli, then found an empty table and sat down. There was no need to pay for the food, of course: her membership covered everything like that.

Suddenly, she felt the sensation of being watched again, this time stronger, more convincing. She looked up sharply.

And saw a familiar face. The woman – the one who'd been with Beckett. Ros Henderson. She was wearing a blue tracksuit and an orange headband. She waved at Irene, then ducked into the women's changing rooms. Irene got up and almost ran after her.

Inside, everything was quiet. A row of pristine white cubicles, a white tiled floor, white walls.

No movement.

Irene called, 'Ms Henderson?'

Her voice echoed from the tiles. There was no other response.

'If you're following me, I'll sue you for breach of privacy.'

Still no response.

Irene went to her cubicle, had another look inside. Nothing seemed to have been disturbed.

Henderson wouldn't have had time to get in here, thought Irene. Nonetheless . . .

She locked the cubicle, dressed quickly, then picked up her handbag and left. 'Nothing left in there now,' she said aloud to the empty changing room. 'I'd go home if I were you. You're wasting your time.'

A plump blonde woman emerged from one of the cubicles in a blue swimsuit and stared at Irene.

Irene ducked out of the changing room, angry and embarrassed. These people were making a fool of her. She had a strong inclination to leave now, but quickly realised that they would easily follow her outside.

She didn't want to be followed all day, even if her activities were innocent. She wanted privacy. She wanted comfort. Her cocoon of wealth.

Distractedly, she sat down at her table with her unfinished breakfast. She ate the muesli, glancing nervously around, wondering if she should call the manager.

She heard a commotion from the pool, looked up.

The club manager talking to a young man in a swimsuit. The young man had his back to her, but even so Irene was fairly sure who he was.

The one who'd called himself Ed.

Irene decided she'd had enough. Two of them?

She hurried out of the concourse, out through the glass and brushed steel door that fronted the club, and across the car park to the space reserved for her car. As soon as she was inside, she powered up the phone and dialled the number for Cyberscope.

It looked as if she was going to have to make an unexpected visit to the office.

The manager was young and heavily built under his suit – even more heavily built than Ed. Ros watched as the two of them argued.

'You must have your card with you at all times, sir. I'm afraid it isn't enough to have your name on the membership register.'

'OK, OK, I'll just go and get it.'

Ed sounded convincingly rich and bored, thought Ros. He could probably get rather good at it, in time.

As he passed on his way to the men's changing room, she peeked out from the pillar she was hiding behind and whispered, 'Time to go.'

Ed stopped, looked round. 'She's gone?'

Ros raised her eyebrows, beckoned. With a glance over his shoulder at the manager, Ed followed.

Ros went to one of the tables, held up a breakfast bowl with a few flakes of muesli adhering to it.

'Gone,' she said.

200

Ed grinned in triumph. 'Yes!'

'Excuse me.' The manager, from behind them. Close up, he seemed even bigger and broader than he had by the poolside. 'I think that you two ought to explain to me precisely what you are doing,' he said. 'Now.' A pause. 'Or I will have you escorted from the premises.'

Ros looked at Ed, who shrugged. 'Keep your hat on, my friend,' he said. 'We were just going anyway.'

Ros laughed.

'Mr Marasco?' Irene's voice over the headset was quite clear.

We're in business, thought Beckett. He looked out of the window of his car at the brushed steel frontage of the Comfortworld Club, and grinned in triumph.

'I want a meeting. Everyone – especially the R & D people. In my office at ten. Arrange it now.'

A faint, garbled, response. Beckett checked that the DAT was recording. With luck, Ros could enhance the replies later. And any other signals that needed enhancing.

This lot would be a gold mine.

'Be careful what you say,' Irene was saying. 'I think they've planted a bug on me.'

Yes, thought Beckett. Several. But you'll never find them all. And eventually you'll get tired of looking.

He saw a movement from the corner of his eye, looked up, saw Ed and Ros hurrying across the road. He opened the car door.

'How's it sound?' asked Ros.

'Loud and clear,' grinned Beckett. He started up the car and set off towards the offices of Cyberscope.

'Something's definitely transmitting.'

'Three devices on the car.'

'There's one in the wristwatch. And two in your clothing.'

Marasco listened to the babble of excited voices, but kept his back turned to them. Instead, he looked through the Managing Director's glass screens at the faint, refracted image of the city.

'This one's got a range of about five hundred metres.'

Yes, thought Marasco. And not many of them will be much further. Which means Beckett and his friends have to be in range.

Well in range for what I have in mind for them.

He nodded at the Managing Director, who ignored him. He left the office and walked to his own, locking the door behind him.

He picked up his desk phone and dialled a number.

He dialled it manually, because it wasn't the kind of number it was safe to keep on a computer database, however well encrypted.

A voice answered.

'Time for the operation,' said Marasco simply. 'The car's green. Four-wheel drive.'

The voice gave an appropriate response, asked about timing.

'Fifteen minutes,' said Marasco, and hung up.

202

« Twenty-six »

Irene had changed her clothes. She had emptied her handbag and thrown everything non-essential away. Her car, it seemed, was in pieces in the garage.

She was thoroughly uncomfortable, and she'd had enough.

'Surely there can't be another one, Elsa?' she asked the young woman standing in front of her. The woman was decked about with electronic apparatus: headset, several microphones and scanners, a flat LCD screen taped to her arm. Behind her, several other young men and women waved scanning devices around, or talked to each other in low voices.

'Seems to be something transmitting,' said Elsa. 'A regular pattern.'

Her voice trailed off.

'Cavity resonator device?' said one of the others.

'Yes!' Elsa's face lit up. 'That's it!'

Irene stared at her.

'You must have swallowed it,' said Elsa apologetically. 'Cavity resonator turns your entire body – well, your – er – belly region – into a microphone and transmitter.' She grinned brightly. 'That's really clever.'

203

Irene managed the ghost of a smile. She liked her bright young things, normally. They were where the ideas for the weapons came from, after all. And she knew they needed to be nurtured, encouraged.

But not today.

'Can they still hear us?' she snapped.

'They can hear you,' said Elsa. 'Probably not the rest of us. Not too clearly, anyway.'

Clearly enough, I expect, thought Irene.

'Find the frequency and jam it.'

'It's not that simple, it's a matter of wave resonance.'

'You mean you can't jam it?' Irene tried not to think about other possible means of getting rid of the bug. They were all likely to be uncomfortable, undignified. In short, impossible.

'Oh, we can do it,' said Elsa brightly. 'But it'll take a while.'

'Well, get on with it then!' snapped Irene. 'In the meantime, watch what you say, everyone.' She looked down at her stomach, then spoke loudly and clearly, for the benefit of those listening to the bug. 'Good attempt, but nowhere near good enough.'

Beckett started up the car as soon as he heard Irene's voice over the link to the bug.

'Steady on,' said Ed from the back seat. 'We might still hear something.'

As if in answer, a clattering noise came over the link, followed by a roar of static. Beckett looked at Ros, who shrugged.

'I'll keep monitoring, but –'

'Forget it.' Beckett put the car in gear and pulled away. Rows of parked cars slid past, then they were in a main street: bright plate-glass displays, racks of wine, bunches of flowers in tubs on the pavement, several colours of fish on slabs.

'Sorry, Beckett, I really thought this would work,' said Ros after a while.

'Not your fault,' said Beckett shortly. 'Look, why don't we all just go home and have –'

'Beckett,' interrupted Ed, 'I know that this isn't a good moment to bring it up, but there's someone following us. Pretty fast.'

Beckett looked in the mirror, saw the rounded nose of a black maxivan, almost on his back bumper. As he watched, the van slid to one side and pulled level with them.

The engine of the car cut out.

'What –?' began Ros.

The van pulled in front of them, forcing Beckett to jam on the brakes.

Another black van appeared behind.

Beckett swerved to one side so that he was driving up the wrong side of the road. He pressed the starter.

Nothing happened. Red lights lit up on the dash. A car appeared ahead of him, forcing him to swerve back, losing still more speed.

He looked across at Ros, who was struggling to plug her laptop computer into a socket underneath the dashboard.

'What's happening?' asked Ed.

The car had now stopped. It was still sandwiched between the black vans. A man in a camouflage jacket and black balaclava had jumped out of one of the vans and was running back to them, waving something that looked very much like a gun.

Suddenly, the car engine started.

'Drive!' yelled Ros.

Beckett didn't need any encouragement. He floored the accelerator, threw the car into gear, wrestling the steering wheel over.

There was a shout, then a gunshot. A dent – no, a

hole – appeared in the bonnet of Beckett's car, as if by magic.

Ros was shouting something: 'I've overridden their software, but I don't know how long the patch will hold. They're trying to –'

Another gunshot. Beckett saw people staring from the grey pavement in front of the shops, open mouthed. He wanted to shout at them to get down, take cover, but he knew that they wouldn't hear him.

'Whatever else they're trying to do,' said Beckett, swerving across into the wrong lane again, 'they're definitely trying to shoot out the tyres.' He swerved back into the left-hand lane, trying to put some traffic between him and the enemy.

Hopefully, they'd hold their fire then.

They're not trying to kill us outright, he thought. They could have done that just now, when we were stopped. Just fired from the two vans. So they obviously want us alive. Some sort of kidnap attempt? Blackmail?

He remembered his conversation with Marasco about SACROS. It looked like the man was trying other means to get what money hadn't bought him.

That seemed pretty much in character.

Beckett heard a blare of horns behind him, looked in the mirror, saw one of the vans dodging the traffic, catching up fast.

'There's a computerised engine control in this car,' Ros was explaining, perhaps to Ed. 'They've managed to get remote access somehow. I'm trying to override it but –'

The engine cut out again.

'I suggest we use our legs,' said Ed from the back.

'No, that's just what they want us to do,' said Beckett. He looked around. The main road sloped upwards, but there was an embankment on the left leading to a car park. The car park itself had a slight slope, and at the lower end a red tiled lane led to what looked like a pedestrian precinct.

Beckett judged the width of the lane, the width of his car, the width of the vans rapidly closing behind them.

He steered off the road, across the empty pavement, down the embankment. The car lurched and jolted. At the bottom of the slope there was a clang of metal as the exhaust grounded.

'You know, I really think I'm going to have to get around to telling my car insurance company I'm a business user,' commented Beckett as he wrestled the wheel around, steering through the narrow gap between an old man with a shopping trolley and the back end of a parked car. Glancing over his shoulder, he saw that one of the vans had stopped on the main road. The other was trying to follow them down.

He let the car roll down across the car park, hoping no one would take it into their heads to walk in front of him.

Suddenly, Ros shouted, 'Bingo!'

And the engine started.

Beckett floored the accelerator, aimed for the red tiled lane. As an afterthought, he jammed a hand on the horn.

They had just reached the end of the lane when Beckett saw the van which had been following them stop rather too suddenly at the narrow entrance. There was a satisfying crumpling of metal and shattering of glass.

Beckett put the brakes on and drove out into the pedestrian precinct as quickly as he dared. Fortunately, the place was almost empty.

'Have we lost them?' asked Ros.

'Not yet.' Beckett gestured up the slope, to where the main road crossed the red tiles of the precinct. The second black van was waiting there.

Beckett looked down the slope, saw nothing but

plate glass displays: computers and hi-fi, beds and three-piece suites, kettles and toasters.

No exit.

He swerved wildly around an island of ornamental maples, pushed the accelerator to the floor and started up the slope away towards the van.

'What are you doing?' yelled Ros.

'Just watch,' said Beckett, trying to sound more confident than he felt. What if they didn't –?

But it worked.

The van started down the slope towards them.

'They think they can still override the engine,' said Beckett triumphantly, swerving around the van. 'Thanks to you, they can't.'

He reached the main road, swerved wildly away from a bus, and rode up on the pavement. An elderly man waved a stick at them.

Then they were on the right side of the road, accelerating fast.

'Where to now?' asked Ros.

'Anywhere, as long as it's out of here,' said Ed. 'And quickly.'

Beckett floored the accelerator. 'I think I can agree with that,' he said.

'This is the last thing I need right now.'

Marasco stared at the Managing Director, then at the slowly rotating image of the white shark on the wall screen behind her.

'I thought we'd agreed –' he began.

'We agreed that we'd use them to get the Bureau off our backs. I didn't imagine that we'd end up taking them on instead.'

Marasco tried again. 'But I was expecting them to try something like this. I'd already organised the kid-napping –'

The Managing Director turned to him and snapped, 'I don't care what you'd organised. It didn't work. They got away. I don't want any more of these games.'

'But what about SACROS?' asked Marasco.

'It's not worth the risk. We're in enough trouble already. I don't want to lose this Asian deal because of a possible lead to some satellite toy. You've no idea whether this Beckett has access to any blueprints. And even if he does, kidnapping his friends might not be the best way of persuading him to hand them over. In any case, I'm not sure about the market for a thing like that. It's like trying to sell a nuclear warhead. It's just too risky.'

Marasco felt the anger rising, controlled it with difficulty. 'What do you suggest, then?' he asked her.

A pause. The Managing Director walked past her coloured-glass screens to the window, looked down at the real city outside, a strange expression on her face. Finally she said, 'You've still got the voiceprints, haven't you?'

Marasco nodded, tapped the DAT recorder in his inside pocket.

'And you can get their addresses, I suppose.'

Marasco nodded. 'You want me to –'

'Just get them off my back.' She turned and walked back to her desk. Marasco looked at her, met her eyes.

They were icy, furious.

He knew then that there was no point in arguing with her. He turned and left the office without a word.

Damn Nick Beckett, he thought. Damn Ros Henderson. Damn all three of them for humiliating him like this in front of the Managing Director.

He clenched one fist, hit it into his palm.

He was going to enjoy carrying out the Managing Director's instructions.

« Twenty-seven »

C major: C, E, G, C.

The piano sang. Simple, massive, dominant. The sound filled the room, rang against the square, leaded windows, wrapped around the walls, drawing the several colours of the medicine bottles stacked along the shelves into its harmony.

Good, thought Ralph. That was a start.

Now. Concentrate. Plagal cadence. This is how it works.

Your results were outstanding, Ralph.

Plagal cadence. Concentrate.

But Ralph's fingers were trembling on the keyboard, suddenly too long, too clumsy. He lifted them away before they could do any harm.

We'd like to offer you a place.

'No,' muttered Ralph aloud.

Thank you. I'd really like that.

'No!' shouted Ralph.

He put his head in his hands and began to cry, but it didn't do any good. The voice went on. The memory, the truth of it, wouldn't go away.

I've got this great job. Company called Cyberscope.

210

Somewhere, there was the sound of footsteps. Ralph sat up, frowned at the window, heard the steps come closer. He got up from the piano.

'Who's that?'

The voice that replied was familiar: the male nurse, Keith. 'You've got a visitor, Ralph. He'd like your help.'

A visitor. A visitor who wanted help. Ralph closed his eyes in pain. The visitors always wanted the same sort of help. Couldn't they see how much it hurt him to give them that? How much it hurt even to think about it?

But it was his duty. He knew that. More than a duty: it was a moral requirement. The only recompense he could make to the world for his years of evil.

Ralph put his glasses on, stood up straight in the light from the windows.

'Show him in, Keith.'

The door opened, and a familiar figure appeared.

But the request was not a familiar one. No. Not a familiar one at all.

Marasco pulled his car up outside the semi-circular building, surveyed the stepped balconies, the shuttered windows, the blue neon sign. Then he looked down at the building plan displayed on the screen of his laptop computer. He touched a key which brought up the ventilation and cabling ducts. Outlined in red, they looked just like a maze.

He smiled to himself. Time to introduce the rats.

He got out of his car and walked to the main doors. Brushed steel and glass, and an SCD in silver and black, showing the companies currently resident.

Fourth on the list was Gizmos. The block reference tied up with the information Marasco had obtained. He nodded to himself, then walked quietly around the curve of the building to the car park entrance at the

211

back. There was a security guard, but Marasco just nodded at her pleasantly and then walked in, computer in hand.

Inside was low, dim space, smelling of oil and concrete. Marasco walked to the nearest maintenance hatch, applied a device attached to his computer to the electronic lock.

It opened.

Marasco smiled, looked at the map outlined on the screen, and took the first of the two bombs from his pocket.

The unit's chameleon coating flushed with the pale colour of Marasco's hands. Marasco touched a key on the underside, muttered, 'Test.'

It wouldn't do to get the two bombs mixed up.

The bomb said quietly, 'Introduce us, Roland,' in Ros Henderson's voice.

Marasco smiled again. He sat the little device on the orange cables, then connected it to the computer. Using the trackerball, he moved the screen cursor to an area marked as living quarters for Ros Henderson. Clicked the trackerball.

A route appeared almost at once, flashing brightly. Marasco followed it with his finger, just to make sure, then okayed it by clicking again.

The bomb started to climb slowly and silently up the cables.

Marasco waited until it was out of sight before he moved to another maintenance hatch. Then he took the second bomb out of his pocket, and repeated the procedure for the second target.

When that was done he left, nodding to the security guard on the way out. Back at the car, he plugged the computer into the phone and accessed the net. He chased up and downloaded a couple of personal comms numbers.

It was time to make a few phone calls.

Rio de Janeiro? thought Ros. How on earth did he get there?

She stared at the postcard, which showed bronzed women in yellow and black swimsuits lazing on a seemingly infinite beach. Jules had always been one for unexpected globetrotting, but this?

She read the card, which simply said, 'Found music! Found <u>LOVE</u>!! Fantastic time, will tell you all!'

Ros grinned, shook her head slowly. Jules never changed. He was always finding 'love', double underlined, two exclamation marks. It never lasted.

She glanced at her other mail, which she'd picked up with the postcard, and decided from the envelopes that it was all junk. She filed it in the bin, threw the postcard down by the phone. There wasn't any kind of return address on it, but Jules's e-mail might get to him. She'd try to do something about it – later.

Right now, she needed a shower, and then about an hour's kip. Maybe two.

I spent too long searching databases last night, she thought ruefully. I just wish it had been a party, or something else worthwhile. And fending off an attempted kidnap is hardly the ideal way of spending your lunch hour.

Ros closed her eyes, stretched, then walked into the bathroom and turned on the shower. She left the door open as she undressed: there was nobody else in the flat to see her, after all.

She'd just got into the cubicle when the phone rang.

For a moment she considered ignoring it, letting the answering machine take the call. But no. It might be something important. It might be Beckett, or Ed, or Roland, with news.

She reached out of the cubicle and picked up the phone mounted on the wall outside.

'Hello,' she said.

In his car, a safe distance away, Marasco heard the sound of the explosion over the phone and smiled.

The experiment so far was a total success. Results as expected.

He hesitated for a moment, thinking about SACROS.

But he had his instructions. And anyway, he was enjoying this.

He dialled Nick Beckett's number.

The phone was ringing.

Beckett opened his eyes, stared at the ceiling for a moment, then reached for the phone by the bed.

Except that there wasn't a phone by the bed. He wasn't in bed. He was on the couch, asleep with his clothes on.

By the time he'd staggered upright and made his way to the phone, it had stopped ringing. The quiet whirr of the fax machine starting up told him why. He stared at the machine, watched as the paper started to come out.

'DON'T SPEAK.' Huge block capitals.

Beckett stared as more lines of the message emerged.
'GET OUT OF
THE FLAT
NOW
– ROS.'

Then he understood. Voice activated. The bomb that had killed Admiral Lansdale.

Someone had planted a voice-activated bomb in the flat.

He made for the door. As he opened it he saw Ros, hair wet, hurrying towards him.

'Beckett, don't.' She ran to the door. He saw something electronic in her hand, heard a rapid pipping noise. 'I can speak, you can't.'

Beckett opened his mouth to say it – *voice activated, I know* – then realised.

First time in my life I've wished I was gagged, he thought. He followed Ros into the flat. She moved around, watching the readout on the device in her hand.

'I was in the shower,' she said. 'They weren't expecting that. The bomb took out most of the living room floor. If I'd been in there when the phone rang I'd be dead.'

Ros moved to the wall that divided the living area from the kitchen section. The pipping noise from the device became a continuous tone.

'There it is,' she said.

The phone rang.

Beckett and Ros looked at each other. Beckett put a finger to his lips, went to the phone, picked it up.

'Beckett!' snapped Ros.

But Beckett knew what he was doing. He blew gently on the mouthpiece, then replaced the handset.

Ros frowned.

Beckett shook his head. It would have sounded like an explosion, he wanted to say. He tugged at his ear, then did his best to mime an explosion.

Ros spluttered with laughter.

Beckett shrugged.

Ros tapped the wall where the device had indicated that the bomb was hidden. 'Hollow,' she said. She inspected the ventilation grille at the bottom of the wall. 'Got a screwdriver?'

But Beckett had a better idea.

He went to the kitchen, found a heavy, green saucepan with twin handles, and a tea cosy.

When he got back Ros had removed the ventilation grille and was holding a beetle-shaped object in her hand. Its dark colour changed as Beckett watched, became the coffee brown of Ros's skin.

Silently, Beckett held up the pressure cooker and the tea cosy.

Ros stared at him for a moment, then laughed again.

Roland Blatty hadn't been entirely surprised when Ros Henderson had phoned him at the Bureau and asked for a meeting.

He was surprised, however, when she turned up with a pressure cooker.

He looked from the green metal canister to Ros, then at her companions: Nick Beckett and the Australian, Ed.

Ros put the pressure cooker down on his desk, between the gooseneck magnifying lens and the computer keyboard.

Roland stared at it, and raised his eyebrows as far as they could go.

Ros grinned, took the lid off the pressure cooker.

There was a tea cosy inside it.

Roland leaned forward, swung the gooseneck lens over it, and looked.

Ros removed the tea cosy and revealed a bomb. It wasn't obvious at first, because it had coloured itself the same ceramic white as the interior of the pressure cooker.

But Roland recognised it.

'Cyberscope?' he said.

'Be careful what you say,' said Ros. 'If Beckett speaks, we all get blown to bits.'

Roland nodded, rather sadly. 'Voice activated. So they targeted you?' He looked at Beckett, who nodded.

'And me,' said Ros. 'There's currently a rather large

hole in my living room floor.' She put the tea cosy back over the bomb, then carefully replaced the lid on the pressure cooker.

'We hoped you might have some suggestions,' said Beckett, speaking very quietly.

Roland stood up, turned and looked out of the window. The view was dull, no more than a redbrick wall across the street, neat white squares of windows spaced evenly across it. He'd been warned it might come to this, and he had his instructions. He wasn't sure he liked them, but he had no choice but to obey.

'As a matter of fact, I can help you,' he said. 'Come with me.'

Marasco led the Managing Director in to the lab. It wasn't often that she came down here. She looked uneasy in her surgical mask and white coat, as if the real business of the company was somehow repugnant to her.

Marasco knew that the uneasiness was only another mask.

Her words gave it away. 'Two down, one to go. So what's your plan?' She sounded almost cheerful.

But then, as usual, she hadn't been the one taking the risks.

Marasco led her past the workbenches, the steel microscopes, the sealed flasks in their protective cages. He leaned down and looked into an isolation cabinet, pointed through the clear glass at a tiny piece of blue cloth.

'One piece of torn trouser, harvested on the run. We found it near the main entrance.'

'You're sure it's his and not Beckett's?'

Marasco glanced at her. 'Blood type matches hospital records.'

'And there's –' A pause. '– enough for a sample?'

'Oh, yes,' said Marasco. 'Do you want to proceed?' He waited, amused, to see how far the Managing Director would go towards giving him a direct instruction.

'You'd better separate out the dog saliva,' she said after a while. 'We don't want to be targeting the wrong organism.'

Marasco smiled.

He was beginning to really enjoy this operation.

The storage room was almost too small for the four of them. The low ceiling, the blue lighting, reminded Ros uncomfortably of the Hive. She glanced at Beckett, who was looking around anxiously, as if someone had put him in a cage.

Obviously, he'd noticed the similarity too.

Roland Blatty was peering into another of the large gooseneck magnifying lenses that seemed to be standard issue at the Bureau of Weapons Technology. He beckoned Ros forward.

'Take a look.'

Ros looked. She saw several pieces of twisted metal. One looked like part of a miniature turbofan. Another might have been a wing. A smudge of shattered glass had probably been the camera lens. A tiny computer chip appeared to have survived intact.

Separate from the other items was a long, fine, metal needle. It had traces of dried blood on it.

Ros swallowed. 'Yes, that's definitely what I saw.'

Blatty nodded. 'It matches Cyberscope patent applications made by Irene Campbell last May. We reckon she had them on international sale in December.'

Ed snorted. 'Quite a Christmas present.'

'They're very fragile,' Blatty went on. 'It's rare to find any trace of one at all. The poison that this one delivered to the Regent was a particularly nasty neurotoxin.' He paused. 'It killed him in less than five seconds.'

Ros remembered the toxin that she'd been exposed to, and felt a chill in her stomach. She hoped the stuff didn't have any after-effects.

Realised that, sooner or later, she would have to try and find out.

She moved away from the lens, looked up at Roland. 'How does it know who to bite?'

'It's pheromone specific. They feed it any kind of sample and it will sniff you out like a bloodhound. As a weapon of terror it's close to perfect.'

'Like the bullet with your name on it.'

'Bullets sometimes hit the wrong people. These never miss and there's nowhere to hide.'

'You could try the broom closet,' offered Ed.

No one laughed.

'You know, no entrances, no exits.'

'Shut up, Ed.' Beckett.

Ros grinned. 'Any other delights, Roland?'

Roland opened a paper folder on the desk by the lens. 'This is another one of Irene's Cyberscope devices.'

Ros looked, saw a complex diagram of something that looked like an electronic ladybird, segmented and separated out into individual layers of circuitry and armour. After a moment, she recognised it.

'It's the thing we found in Beckett's flat,' she said. 'The voice-activated bomb.'

Roland nodded. 'That's without its camouflage cover on, of course. Inside the casing there's a computer more powerful than the average desktop item, and some very sophisticated voice-recognition software. It's pretty well guaranteed to explode only by its chosen target – and it leaves no trace.'

'A computer, hmm?' said Ros. She was beginning to get an idea. 'I don't suppose we could hold on to this?'

Beckett glanced at her sharply, waggled his eyebrows,

then said quickly, 'Where are you getting your information from? Ex-employees?'

'With stuff like this around,' said Roland, 'an ex-employee would have to be mad to talk to us.' He glanced around the three of them. 'Fortunately for us, one of them has gone mad.' A pause. 'He's in the Oxley Garden Psychiatric Hospital. Ward G2.'

'And you want us to go and see him,' Ros guessed.

Blatty looked around the three of them again. His expression had become exceptionally vague, something Ros immediately realised was a bad sign. 'I think one of you might want to go and see him. The other two – well, I think we should hold them in reserve.'

Ros raised an eyebrow.

'Now hold on,' said Beckett.

'I know. We're involving you in a covert operation. But we'll pay you on your usual terms, if you accept. And you'll have the satisfaction of putting Irene out of business.'

Ros looked at Beckett. Beckett looked at Ros.

'I'm game,' said Ed.

'That's good,' said Roland solemnly. 'Because you're going to be the target.'

« Twenty-eight »

'This is a remote answering service. Please leave your name and message after the tone.'

'Er – Ros, this is Ed. Look, I've got a lead on this Cyberscope business. An ex-employee, name of Ralph Bloch. He's in Oxley Gardens Hospital, ward G2. I'm going over there now to see if I can get any information out of him.' A pause. 'You'd better meet me there if you get back in time.'

Click.

Peter Marasco watched the connection indicator on his line tap go down, and smiled.

She won't be back, he thought. Not in time to meet you there. In fact, she won't ever be back.

And neither will you.

Oxley hospital looked nice in the sunlight. Red brick, green painted wooden beams, red tile-pointed roof. A sleepy car park, only three or four cars. An open green space, a cedar tree, a patch of shrubbery. A gardener, even, raking over the flowerbeds.

If I ever go mad, thought Ed, I'll ask to come here. It looks good.

He walked in through the dull red door marked RECEPTION. A guard nodded at him.

Another man, in doctor's whites, but with suspiciously military shoes, also nodded at him, though the movement was almost imperceptible.

Ed didn't nod back.

Grey and white signposts on the walls directed him to ward G2. Down a corridor tiled with white lino, up two flights of stairs. Along another corridor, more white lino.

A staff nurse, male, greeted him at the entrance.

'I'm here to see Ralph Bloch.'

The man nodded. 'Yes, I'm Keith,' he said. 'I – er – hope you have a pleasant visit.'

I wonder if he knows what's going on, thought Ed. Probably. But better not to mention it. If Roland's people do their stuff, Marasco won't even get into the building.

So let's just hope they do their stuff.

But Ed had to admit that he wasn't too confident about it. He remembered Ballantyne shooting from the helicopter, missing. He remembered something Beckett had said: 'Civil Servants with guns.' It wasn't a very reassuring image.

Keith led him across more white lino, towards the sound of a piano. Simple chords, crashing, repeating again and again behind a closed door.

'Ralph?' called Keith. 'A visitor for you.'

A final, even louder, chord, then a sigh. The door opened, and a young man stepped out. Wild blond hair, wraparound sunglasses, a battered blue felt jacket and a white pullover.

The sunglasses were raised, and pale blue eyes stared into Ed's.

'You're that man,' he said. 'Ed. Blatty from the Bureau –' He made it sound like the name of a children's

TV programme. '– he told me all about you.' A pause. 'I'm Ralph, but then you know that.'

Ed nodded.

'Come on, we'd better talk in here.' He went back into the room. Ed glanced at Keith, who nodded approval.

'He's quite OK. Reactive depression – prone to suicidal despair. We just have to watch his medication.'

Ed nodded, went in.

Ralph was standing by a window, the sunglasses back across his eyes. He was looking out across the lawns, the cedar tree, the village beyond. 'What do you need to know?' he asked.

Ed paused. He hadn't actually thought much about that. The setup was to catch Marasco. But there was no harm in gathering information. Anything this man said might be useful.

'Tell me about Irene Campbell,' he said.

Ralph stared out of the window without speaking, for so long that Ed thought perhaps he hadn't heard the question, or didn't want to hear. But, at last, he said dreamily: 'She hires you when you're young and bright. We didn't have girlfriends but we all had Porsches. After two or three years you're all burned out but you never have to work again.'

Ralph turned away from the window, looked at Ed, raised his sunglasses. 'I looked around one day and realised the real price of all that. I realised exactly what it was we were doing. We were designing this stuff like it was for a TV cartoon. You know, wouldn't this be great, wouldn't that be a great way to kill someone. But no one ever gave a thought to the real people who'd be dying.' He flipped the glasses down again, walked past Ed towards the piano.

'I suddenly did. I thought about it. I even talked about it. And she had me out of the door like I was poison.' He

sat down at the piano stool, played a crashing, dis-
cordant chord. Looked up at Ed one more time.

'Did lightning strike her dead yet?'

Ed pursed his lips, shook his head.

'Never an act of God when you need one.'

Marasco left the village supermarket with a shopping
bag in each hand. One contained potatoes.

The other had more important contents.

He walked down the narrow High Street, weaving
between the other shoppers, until he came to the
entrance to the hospital.

The guards were still there.

To someone else, they might have been just two
workmen lounging about, newspapers in hand, waiting for a job to start.

But Marasco wasn't that stupid.

He walked on until he came to the park that
adjoined the hospital grounds. Empty flowerbeds, neat
lawns, a few straggling autumn crocuses around the
base of the willow trees. Marasco found a bench and
sat down.

He propped the bag of potatoes up next to him,
propped the other bag on the other side, and sat back
as if having a rest.

He counted to sixty.

Then he frowned, began rummaging in one of the
bags. His hand touched cold metal. He peered into
the bag, pulled out a small medicine bottle with a
dropper.

Only someone standing very close to him could have
seen the slight frosting on the bottle, implying cold
storage, implying a bag that wasn't full of eye drops
and shopping. And Marasco had made sure that there
was no one standing that close to him.

He rummaged in the bag again, opened a hatch on

the launching device inside. Using the dropper, he put a couple of cold drops from the medicine bottle into the hatch.

Then he found the trigger, squeezed gently.

The sound of a shutter opening. The faint whirr of mechanisms pumping fuel and payload into the tiny missile.

Both were drowned out by the bouncing of a football, a boy crying out.

Marasco jumped back. The football landed on his bag of potatoes, then rolled onto the floor. He saw the boy, purple tracksuit and trainers.

He smiled at him and kicked the ball back.

The boy grinned and ran off.

Marasco glanced into his shopping bag, as if to check that everything was OK.

A green light showed on the launching device.

Marasco pulled the trigger.

'Ralph, did you guys ever talk about – some kind of invisible killing machine?' asked Ed.

Ralph Bloch waved his sunglasses in the air. 'What do you mean by invisible?'

'A missile. Very small. Specific to one target.'

Ralph smiled. 'How would that work?'

'You tell me.'

Ralph put his sunglasses on, turned to the window. 'I've told the Bureau everything I know.'

There was a distant slamming of doors, the sound of running footsteps. Ed looked sidelong at the door, heard someone shouting.

It sounded like time was running out.

'Come on,' he said to Ralph. 'You've got to know something. People are being killed –'

The commotion outside was suddenly nearer. The door burst open.

Ed looked up sharply, saw Beckett and Ros.

'Ed, there's a problem –' began Beckett.

Behind him, Ed was aware of Ralph shrinking back, trying to hide behind the bulk of the piano. He reached out, clapped the man on the shoulder.

'It's OK, Ralph. They're on our side.'

Ros was speaking now: 'They've spotted Marasco's car leaving the area.'

'Leaving?' Ed was confused. 'Surely that's good news?'

'They stopped him, but he wasn't carrying anything he shouldn't have been. They think he might have already –'

From the corner of his eye, Ed noticed Ralph staring through the open door, his sunglasses off, an expression of alarm on his face. Suddenly he shouted, 'Close the door! Now! Move!'

Ed didn't hesitate. He ran forward, slammed the door shut.

'It's one of hers,' said Ralph. 'I designed the eyes. It's got the scent of someone in here.'

'She thinks we're dead already,' said Ros. She looked at Ed. 'It must be after you.'

'Or me,' said Ralph. Suddenly he jumped up at a ventilation grille above the door. 'Block that! If it can't get in it'll look for some other way.'

Ed looked around wildly, saw a booklet of sheet music on top of the piano. He grabbed it, jumped up to the grille and tried to force the booklet over it.

It wouldn't fit.

'Get on my shoulders!' yelled Beckett.

At the same time Ralph shouted, 'Look out!'

A buzzing, whining sound filled the room. Ed saw something small and fast moving straight towards him. He dodged back, flapped at the thing with the sheet music in his hand. Ros had found a pillow from the camp bed in the corner of the room and was flapping that at the machine, perhaps trying to knock it off course.

Ed did what Ralph had done earlier: he dived behind the piano.

The buzzing sound came closer.

Then there was the hiss of an aerosol spray, and a smell of furniture polish.

'What good's that going to do?' Ros's voice.

'Confuse the scent for a while.' Ralph appeared, holding the can of polish. He sprayed some on Ed's jacket, grabbed his arm.

'You! Out! Run!'

The door was open. Beckett was shouting too: 'Get out, Ed!'

Ed ran, heard the door slam behind him, then Ros's shout, 'The grille!'

And Ralph: 'Too late! It's after you, Ed! It'll smell you for two miles!'

Just what I need to know, thought Ed. He accelerated into a flat out run, passing an astonished Keith.

'What –?'

No time to find out what Keith wanted to know. Just run.

The corridors, which had seemed so empty and quiet on the way in, were now full of people. People staring in astonishment, people getting in the way. Perhaps some of them were on Blatty's security team.

No time to worry about that either.

Downstairs – outside. He had a chance if he could get outside.

He slipped and skidded on the polished lino of the stairs, almost fell. At the bottom, off balance, he collided with a male nurse.

The man grabbed hold of him. 'Hey! Calm down! What's the matter?'

He thinks I'm one of the patients, Ed realised.

And there was no time to explain. He could hear the buzzing of the bug behind him.

He chopped at the nurse's arm, hard. The man shouted, but let go. Ed ran flat out down the corridor.

Wrong way, he realised suddenly. This wasn't an exit. This was a dead end.

He turned, heard the buzzing getting closer again.

He pushed open the nearest door, saw a female nurse in a green uniform emptying something into a narrow waste disposal chute. He dived into the room, slammed the door behind him.

The woman turned to him, astonishment and some fear on her face.

He grabbed hold of her, shook her, shouted at her. 'Is there any other way out of here?'

'What? No! Let me –'

The door opened: Ed saw the male nurse he'd hit, and a colleague.

'Close the door!' he yelled.

They didn't. They stepped forward and grabbed him instead.

He could hear the bug.

He could hear it loud and clear, surely no more than a foot from his ear.

He struggled, shouted, but the nurses were prepared this time. He couldn't get away.

They pushed him against a wall.

Ed heard the bug, and something else.

A fan.

A fan expelling air from the room.

He looked up and saw the bug quite clearly, a tiny, deadly fragment of metal, its eyes on him.

But it was slipping back. Back towards the fan.

Suddenly Ed felt a current of pure relief. The painful grip the nurses had on his arms, the shouts in the corridor behind them, none of that mattered.

The bug was getting sucked into the fan.

He saw it go, heard the clatter as it broke apart between the blades. There was a bang, and the fan stopped. The air filled with smoke.

Ed coughed.

'Look out!' Ros's voice. She was running up to him, pushing the male nurses aside.

And Beckett: 'Let him go! Right away!'

The grip on Ed's arms slackened, was replaced by a powerful grip on his jacket.

Ralph. Pulling him upright, shouting.

'Hey!' shouted Ed. 'I'm all right, it's just smoke from the fan!'

'It's not smoke and you're not all right!'

Ed stared.

Ralph released his jacket slowly, pointed behind them.

Then Ed saw it, realised that the others were staring too.

There was no smoke.

Instead a white vapour crawled around the floor, almost like a liquid, almost as if it had a life of its own.

Ed swallowed, looked back at Ralph. 'What's that?'

'It must be something new,' said Ralph. 'But be assured there definitely is a problem. And it lies in that vapour!'

The Managing Director wasn't feeling as comfortable as she would have liked. Things didn't feel as if they were under her control any more. Marasco from one side, and her clients from the other, seemed to have somehow put her in a box, a box smaller than her office with its glass chair and glass desk and shark-decorated wall screen.

A box where she had no choices about her actions any more.

A box where people died, and she knew it was happening, and she knew it was her fault.

She didn't want to think about that.

She looked at the other box, the box that sat on her glass desk. It was ready, tested. The final weapon.

For her customers, the final solution.

She lifted the lid, looked at the golden vials inside, the spider-like dissipation pods, the keypad lock with the time release. All so ordinary. It could be a high class pesticide.

But it wasn't.

She picked up the phone and dialled a number.

The call was answered almost immediately. 'Ms Campbell?'

'Yes. I've started the test.'

'Is the subject dead yet?' The voice was cold, remote, clinical.

'No.'

'We will take delivery this afternoon. Half the money in cash. The other half when we have proof that the subject is dead.'

'Yes.' The Managing Director swallowed, looked out through her glass screens. For the first time in many years, she almost wished that they weren't there, that she was outside, free of all this.

'Of course,' she said to the man on the other end of the phone. 'Everything's in hand. He'll be dead before morning.'

« Twenty-nine »

'Hey – do you know how a porcupine makes love?'

Ros had to smile. Here was Ed, covered with electrodes, virtually strapped to the bed, in a containment unit surrounded by medical staff so thickly swathed in white plastic and masks and filters that they looked like zombies – and he still managed to work out that one of the staff was female and make what he thought was the appropriate response.

She tapped on the double thickness window, waved through the half-closed shutters.

Ed waved back.

'Ros, this is ridiculous.' His voice was made into a parrot-like squawk by the tiny intercom speaker attached to the thick glass. 'I feel a hundred per cent.'

Ros tapped the TALK button. 'It's just a precaution, Ed.'

Ed nodded. 'Sure, sure.'

He knows, thought Ros. He's got to know there's something up. The can't-be-bothered act is just a front.

She became aware of Beckett standing behind her.

'There's something you should see,' he said quietly.

She turned, followed him along a corridor to a small lab. A red notice was taped to the door – VIRAL CONTAINMENT SAMPLES – AUTHORISED PERSONNEL ONLY. Inside, a woman in doctor's whites was looking into a microscope. Roland Blatty, looking solemn, stood behind her.

He looked up when they came in. So did the doctor. She glanced at Roland, then left the room.

Roland gestured at the microscope. 'This is Ed's blood. Take a look at this.'

Ros looked. She saw red blood cells – individual platelets drifting around in yellowish plasma.

Drifting. With a shock, Ros realised that most of the cells were dead.

She looked up at Roland. 'How recent is this sample?'

'Five minutes ago. The virus is targeting red blood cells at the moment, but there's evidence to suggest it's moving on to the central nervous system. They're saying it's much faster than any such organism they've ever seen. And it's only attacking Ed's cells. It wouldn't touch yours or mine, or anyone else's.'

'Target specific,' said Beckett, who was taking a look at the sample.

'Exactly,' said Roland. 'Irene has made a programmable virus. It can be tailored to the exact genetic characteristics of an individual.'

Beckett looked up. 'Or any group of individuals with common genetic features. I mean, never mind the royal bloodline. With this thing you could wipe out the population of the country next door and then just stroll across the border. Right?'

Roland nodded.

'An ethnic cleanser,' he said solemnly. 'A genocide device.'

Beckett took another look through the microscope. 'An invisible assassin.'

Ros looked from one to the other of them. A cold feeling was forming in her stomach.

'What are Ed's chances?' she said quietly.

Roland swallowed, looked at his shoes. 'Now that he's infected, they just don't know.'

'How do you stop something like that?' She pointed at the microscope.

Roland shook his head. 'These are target specific viruses. Either you burn them off the face of the earth before they're released, or –' he broke off. 'I'm sorry, Ros.'

The cold feeling in Ros's stomach intensified. 'You mean he's going to die, don't you?'

Roland and Beckett looked at each other.

Eventually Roland said, 'Very probably, I'm afraid.'

Something inside Ros snapped. 'You messed it up, didn't you, Roland? You just assumed that they'd use a voice-activated bomb. Even after what happened to the Regent, you didn't think that they might –'

'Hold on, Ros.' Beckett. 'He didn't know that Ed got bitten by that dog. He didn't know that he'd left a possible tissue sample on Cyberscope's premises. That was down to me. I should have told him. Anyway, the question isn't whose fault it is, it's what we're going to do about it now.'

'Rest assured he'll receive the best possible medical treatment,' said Roland. 'If –'

He was interrupted by the sound of an alarm from the corridor outside. Ros and Beckett looked at each other, then rushed out of the door.

In the containment unit, Ed was slumped forward on the bed. Two of the medical staff were rolling him over onto his back, a third lifted his legs. He was as limp as a puppet.

As they laid him flat on the bed, the bipping of the alarm became a continuous tone.

Ros closed her eyes. She heard the clatter of machinery, the thud of resuscitation equipment, the hiss of breathing apparatus.

Suddenly, the alarm was silent.

Ros crossed her fingers, opened her eyes. She saw Ed breathing through a tube in his nose, his chest rising and falling. One of the nurses came to the wall and spoke through the intercom.

'We've got him stabilised,' she said. 'But I can't say for how long.'

Ros nodded. She saw Beckett standing beside her, his hands pressed against the glass, the knuckles white.

'We've got to do something,' she said. 'We can't just stand here – waiting.'

Beckett nodded.

'There must be some way of stopping it.'

Beckett shrugged. 'The only person I can think of who would know anything about that is Irene Campbell. And she isn't exactly going to be willing to help.'

He stopped, met Ros's eyes.

'Unless we make her,' supplied Ros.

Beckett nodded. 'Right. I'll keep watch on the factory – you see if you can get into their system the way you did with the Hive.'

Ros grinned. 'I think I can do better than that,' she said. Then she glanced back at Ed and the grin fell away. 'I only hope that it's going to be enough.'

Wind blew across the Cyberscope car park. Thin saplings rattled the last of their leaves, and grey clouds raced overhead.

Shame it's not getting dark yet, thought Beckett. I'm supposed to be dead – and this is a great setting for a ghost story. All it needs is a few gravestones.

234

He drew the hood of his old parka coat tighter around his face, and walked towards Irene's red Ferrari.

If I'd been a villain, he thought, I'd be driving something a whole lot less easy to spot.

But then Irene didn't think of herself as a villain. That was the whole point. Beckett approached the car cautiously. It was bound to be alarmed. Casually, he took a small *Nature Watcher's Book of Birds* from his pocket and leafed through the pages. To complete the effect he raised the field binoculars he was carrying to his eyes, and pointed them in the direction of one of the scrawny trees.

After a few seconds he lowered them again and flicked through the book. Page 63. Goldeneye duck, male. Identification: forty to fifty centimetres long. Striking black and white plumage. Neck and underparts white.

And there was an illustration.

This particular goldeneye duck had a *very* golden eye. Or, more accurately, a copper-plated eye. For good electrical connection.

Beckett detached the eye from the illustration, took the thin metal disc between his finger and thumb, then dropped the book. It landed about ten centimetres from the front wheel of Irene's Ferrari.

He bent down to pick it up, let his finger and thumb brush one of the projecting balancing weights on the hub cover.

The bug stuck first time.

Beckett retrieved the book, took another look at a couple of trees for good measure, then shook his head sadly, as if his mission had been unsuccessful.

He marched back to the rough ground that bordered the car park, bird book and binoculars in hand.

* * *

235

City of tiny lights, thought Ros, gazing at the display on the screen. She should have guessed it.

Images of LEDs, captured by Beckett's camera on the night of the Cyberscope raid, flickered red and green. Slower and slower.

Next to the window containing the digital video picture, a flickering schematic of interpretative software was at work, looking like a family tree on its side. It was identifying fragments of code, tying them to probable compression routines, then unzipping what was left and seeing if any of it passed one of several standard parity tests.

And something was coming out. Ros could see it, text slowly filling a dialogue box on the left of the screen.

'PpeoHunms c rtd5tdps s eyyeea –'

It was gibberish, but Ros knew at once that it was a certain type of gibberish. There were no computer control characters, apart from the occasional end of line marker. This was ordinary text, with some of the letters missing. Scanning the slowly scrolling column, she checked the frequency of certain letters: e, a, y, d, h.

Yes. English. Not even encrypted.

Then she checked the percentage recovery figure at the bottom of the screen and winced.

The program indicated that it was recovering 85% of available information. But what was on screen was a lot less than 85% of intelligible English. Ros guessed it was about 30%.

Which meant that more than half the information simply wasn't there at source: the LEDs had been flickering too fast for the camera to capture all of the data.

She took a gulp of coffee, turned to the other computer. It still showed the information dump from the phone system on the receptionist's desk at Cyberscope, which was as far as Ros had been able to get into their well-protected systems. The computer was still running a password interrogation, but the password was more than a hundred characters long. Ros reckoned it could easily be all night before she got in.

Ed could be in the morgue by then.

Ros decided it was time to take a chance. She aborted the password interrogator, asked instead for the receptionist's computer to send a dump of the contents of its C and U drives. It meant the system would go off line for a few minutes.

She would just have to hope the receptionist was having a tea break.

The dump quickly filled the screen, then scrolled upwards: lists of directories, files, mostly to do with telephone numbers, answering machine messages, communications operating programs.

Then: Assassins.

Ros hit the HOLD SCREEN key so hard she nearly broke it.

When she brought up the file, she got the message 'File incomplete' – but she'd expected that. This was obviously a recycled disc, that had once been part of the main operating system: the files from that system had been partly overwritten.

But not erased.

That was an oversight.

Ros smiled, told the computer to display what it could of the file.

There was a pause, then the data began to appear: '%%e[:A**&! tt tt @?//op –'

Of course. Encrypted. She ran the decrypter. It ran through a dozen of Dave Young's standard keys. Within a few seconds the decrypted information began to appear.

'in=sel/transact/*get#"INFOS-E" –'

'Damn,' said Ros aloud. It was the operating program. A set of instructions for the machine. On its own, it didn't prove anything. It was the data she needed – and it wasn't there.

She swung her chair back to the other machine, which was still reeling off all the data she wanted, but with too many pieces missing to make it any use.

She put her head in her hands. There had to be another source of data somewhere. There just had to be.

Then she thought of something.

« Thirty »

Beckett drove fast but carefully, glancing from time to time at the white blip that marked the position of Irene's Ferrari as it moved across the map superimposed on the screen of the RaSearch.

He kept a safe distance behind, staying out of sight. No need to take any unnecessary risks.

Low winter sunlight shone through the windscreen, almost blinding him. The river was ahead. He could see a bridge, people crossing it, hurrying, their bobbing heads silhouetted against the bright sky.

Beckett glanced back at the RaSearch, but couldn't see the dim screen after the glare. He pulled in, suddenly, attracting an irritated beep from the car behind.

After a moment, his eyes adjusted. He saw that Irene had pulled off the main road into one of the riverside developments.

She was slowing down.

Stopping.

Beckett pushed the car into gear, pulled out as suddenly as he'd pulled in, attracting another irritated beep.

He followed the trail as far as the entrance to the development. Three-storey redbrick flats surrounded him, flat blue windows with blue frames, a few balconies with geraniums. Beckett saw a walled off area marked PRIVATE CAR PARK, pulled in there.

Looking over the top of the wall, he could see Irene, standing by the low red roof of her car, which was parked in the central square. She was smiling.

Keeping his head low, Beckett wound down the window. He took the pen mike from his pocket and aimed it at Irene, who had now been joined by Marasco.

Her voice came through the headset at once, but he couldn't make out the words. He turned up the volume.

Marasco's voice said: 'Here they are.'

A gun-grey limousine with blacked out windows briefly blocked the way. Beckett watched as it pulled up next to Irene's car and the familiar figure of the military attaché got out.

Beckett touched the RECORD key on the DAT attached to the pen mike.

Irene spoke. 'How will you get it out of the country?'

'That's not your problem.' The attaché's voice was coming through clearly as well.

'The virus won't attack you,' Irene was explaining, 'or anyone other than the ethnic group that it's meant for.'

'The complete eradication of the royal bloodline, at last,' said the embassy man. 'How do I release it?'

'Just enter the time-release code into the keypad, and wait.'

Beckett risked a glance up, saw Irene handing a metallic briefcase to the embassy man, and a small manilla envelope. The code, he supposed, was in the envelope.

'Or, if all else fails,' Irene went on, 'just smash the glass. The virus will still work. You can start the chain of infection from anywhere in the world. Of course the closer you are to your targets the faster they'll fall.' A pause. 'If you – change your mind, for any reason, find a furnace and burn it.'

Beckett heard the slam of the Ferrari door, a muffled goodbye from the attaché. He saw Irene drive off, saw the gun-grey limousine start in the opposite direction.

Time to take a short cut, Beckett decided. No point in worrying about Irene now, when the evidence was about to leave the country.

He started the car, drove forwards out of the car park, straight through a flimsy ornamental evergreen, across some pebbledash and the pavement and out into the main road.

The limo was using the proper exit a hundred metres away. As he watched, it accelerated smoothly into the lane that led to the docks.

Beckett set off in pursuit.

Ros surveyed the smoke-blackened interior of the warehouse. It was hard to see anything very much. The roof was still intact, but there were no working lights. The result was a landscape of shadowy grime, broken by the long stripe of sunlight entering through the burned-out door frame. Even when Ros shone a flashlight into the gloom, all she could see were shades of dark grey and black.

The air still smelled of burning.

She glanced over her shoulder, but Roland was nowhere in sight.

'I don't know this is happening, remember,' was all he'd said when he'd got her past the security cordon.

She began to make her way across the floor, towards a tower of warped shelving where she could see the ash-blackened image of the Cyberscope logo. Pieces of broken glass and burnt plastic crunched under her feet. Her boots stirred up the dust: she coughed.

Ros was ploughing her way through a pile of half-burned packing materials towards the shelving when her foot hit something solid. She pulled away the twisted, charred wreck of a plastic crate, pointed the beam of her flashlight down, saw the gleam of metal. She pulled at the metal object, grunting with effort. There was a splitting sound as it came free.

But as soon as she saw what she was holding, she knew she'd hit the jackpot. It was a disk drive, smoke-blackened but otherwise intact.

Ros looked at it, rubbed the soot off the label, and smiled.

As soon as he saw the docks approaching, the white and yellow hydrowing freighter tied up by the sheds, Beckett knew how the attaché intended to smuggle the virus out of the country.

The question was how to stop him.

Beckett pulled up his car at a safe distance from the ship. The embassy limo was pulling away. The attaché had already climbed the tubular gangplank and was on deck. Beckett watched as the attaché spoke briefly to a tall, dark-skinned man wearing a captain's cap, then disappeared inside.

The hydrowing's main engines were already running: Beckett could feel the vibration through the body of the car. He didn't imagine that they would waste much time getting under way.

He got out of the car and trotted along the quayside. The boat was one of the newest of its type. The broad curves of its hull and superstructure blended into one another seamlessly. Lights flickered above the bridge, a radar scanner whirled.

Beckett bent over the quayside, saw water churning under the smooth shape of the underwater wings.

They were going any minute, he realised. Any second. He had to do something now.

He glanced up at the sailors standing on the deck, who were watching him without curiosity.

But that would soon change if he made a run for the gangplank.

Beckett looked around, noticed three bulldozers in an open shed level with the stern of the ship. The machines appeared to be brand new, awaiting shipment. A red label on each machine attracted Beckett's attention. FITTED WITH NEW MAGNO-LOX ALARM SYSTEM!

He wondered what a MAGNO-LOX alarm would do.

Well, there was a way of finding out.

He searched the quayside, found some loose pieces of concrete. Then, feeling quite a lot like a naughty schoolboy, he retreated to the cover of the shed and threw them.

'Are you sure you want to do this?'

Roland would ask that, thought Ros. Always the gentleman. She sat forward in her seat and stared through the windscreen at the approaching Cyberscope building.

'How else are we going to save Ed?' she asked simply.

Roland didn't seem to have an answer to that. He showed his Government pass to the guard in the car park. The man waved them in.

Glancing over her shoulder, Ros saw him talking rapidly into a phone handset.

'I don't think we're going to be welcome,' she said.

'In my job I don't expect to be welcome. I regard it as a good sign if I'm not.'

They glanced at each other.

'I only hope this idea of yours works, Ros,' he said quietly, as he manœuvred the car into a parking space. 'For your sake.'

They got out of the car. Ros unloaded her holdall from the boot, heard the satisfying sound of bits of electronics and cabling shifting around inside.

She set off towards the building, leaving Roland to follow her.

It's going to work, she thought. It has to.

For Ed's sake.

The bulldozers were still blaring their hooters and flashing their lights when Beckett reached the far side of the shed. As he'd hoped, the sailors on the ship were all standing at the stern rail, staring at the things.

He heard someone shouting, 'Can't someone shut them up?'

Beckett crouched down, sprinted for the tubular gangway.

He made it to the deck before the shouts started behind him. He looked over his shoulder, saw the sailors starting towards him at a run.

So much for diversionary tactics.

He sprinted up a curving metal stairway to the second level of the deck, around the bridge, where he'd seen the attaché talking to the captain. He came to a yellow and white door with a large plate glass inset.

Through it, he could see the attaché, sitting behind the captain, and a crewman peering over the radar screen. The metal case containing the virus was on the seat beside the attaché.

Now, thought Beckett.

He slammed the door open, dived across the narrow bridge and grabbed the case before anyone could react.

He turned back towards the door, only to find his

way blocked by the captain. He pushed the man off balance. He fell, sprawling across the controls of the ship. Its hooter blared. The engines roared.

Beckett was out of the door before the sounds had stopped. The sailors were at the bottom of the stairway, stalled, apparently confused, but blocking the way to the quayside.

Beckett could hear shouts from the bridge, the accented voice of the attaché among them. There wasn't time to decide: he just had to jump.

He ran to the front of the bridge and swung himself over the rail, bracing his legs for the three metre drop to the lower deck.

He made it, then tripped and fell over a stanchion. The briefcase flew across the deck.

Beckett heard the sound of a gunshot, saw the attaché leaning over the rail, a large-calibre pistol in his hand. Without thinking, Beckett raised the metal case as a shield.

Something punched into it, flinging him to the deck. He didn't hear the shot.

He scrambled to his feet again, yelled, 'I think your diplomatic status just came into question.'

The attaché smiled. 'Probably so. But as you may have noticed, we will not be in your territorial waters very much longer.'

Beckett stared around him. He realised that the ship's engines were still roaring, that the sailors were casting off ropes. As he looked at the quay, it began to recede.

The ship was under way.

He looked back at the attaché. The gun was aimed at his head.

'Drop the case,' said the man.

Beckett hesitated, looking over the rail. If he could just . . .

The man followed his gaze, and his lips twitched in the ghost of a smile. 'As you say, it would not be diplomatic to kill you whilst we are still guests in your country. But in these circumstances I am prepared to be – undiplomatic. Drop the case.'

Beckett dropped it.

The man shouted orders in his own language to two of the sailors, who ran across the deck and took Beckett's arms. A third came and picked up the case.

The men took Beckett to a door in the lower deck, bundled him into a small, dark cabin.

The attaché appeared in the doorway. 'Tie him up,' he said, then addressed Beckett.

'We will be taking you on a short voyage. Until we are in deep water. Then you have an appointment.' That ghost of a smile again. 'An appointment with the sea.'

« Thirty-one »

Ros crouched down in the narrow space between the connection machine stack and the wall screen and connected up the last of the cabling. She glanced up at the vast images of sharks still turning on the screen.

Time to stop, she thought.

She shoved the cable home, and the sharks froze. Ros grinned. Then she heard a voice. A familiar, authoritative, woman's voice. Shouting.

Ros could easily imagine what it was that Irene was shouting about. Her grin broadened.

She could hear the words now. 'What do you think you're doing?'

And a man's voice, presumably Marasco. 'We'll have your head for this, Blatty.'

'So?' asked Roland. 'What have I got to lose?'

Ros decided it was time to make an entrance. She scrambled to her feet, walked around the connection machine stack.

'And I'm supposed to be dead already.'

The look that Irene and Marasco exchanged was almost worth everything.

Almost.

247

She walked up to them, looked at Marasco, then at Irene.

'I want you to tell me how to save Ed.'

'That's impossible,' said Irene, with the slightest of shrugs. 'Once a –' She broke off, and for a second an expression that might actually have been regret crossed her face, but then it vanished and she went on, 'Once a target has been infected, there's no way to reverse the process. I'm sorry.'

Ros felt the chill in her stomach again. Fought to ignore it. The woman was bluffing. There had to be something. Bioengineers were just like software engineers – they always left a back door.

Didn't they?

She swallowed, made an effort to maintain her cool.

'All right,' she said. 'I'm going to break into your files and get the list of clients and weapons that Mr Blatty needs to put you away.'

Irene walked around Ros, sat down at her desk. There was a confident smile on her face.

'You're wasting your time,' she said.

'Want a bet on it?' This bit, at least, Ros knew she could deliver.

Irene was speaking to the computer. 'Voice recognition. Irene Campbell. Lock all files.'

Dave Young's voice spoke from the computer. 'The files are locked.'

'Master Key,' said Ros quickly. 'Unlock.'

'Master Key Password?'

Ros paused, glanced at Irene. Hoped she was guessing right.

'Hot rats,' she said. Arguably the best-known Frank Zappa title.

'The files are unlocked.'

Ros couldn't resist a grin of triumph.

248

But there was no time to waste. Ed could die at any moment.

She went to her holdall, reached inside and removed a large green cooking pot. Irene stared at it, raised an eyebrow.

Ros put a finger to her lips. 'Shhh!'

She took the lid off the pot, took out the tea cosy, produced the voice-activated bomb. She turned to Irene, spoke quickly. 'This is from Beckett's flat. I've reprogrammed it with your voice pattern, Irene.' She walked slowly up to the desk, put the bomb on the glass surface ten centimetres from Irene's folded hands. 'So I suggest you keep quiet and don't interfere.'

Irene opened her mouth, then closed it again and smiled. From the corner of her eye, Ros noticed that Roland was staring at her, surprised and doubtful.

Here's another thing you don't know is happening, Roland, she thought.

Marasco spoke. 'It's a bluff.'

Ros shrugged, leaned over the bomb and said, 'Test.'

The bomb spoke. 'Good attempt. But nowhere near good enough.'

Irene's voice.

Irene only raised her eyebrows.

Ros turned, saw Roland looking considerably more worried. In fact he was retreating slowly to the shelter of the connection machine.

She remembered Beckett's phrase: Civil Servants with guns.

'Er – excuse me –'

Marasco. He was running for the doors.

He bumped into them, rattled them.

They wouldn't open.

Ros smiled. 'Rats always leave the sinking ship, Mr

249

Marasco. But I'm not giving you the chance. I fixed the automatic locks.'

Marasco stared at her, his eyes cold, green, furious. For a moment Ros thought he was going to physically attack her, but slowly he seemed to regain his composure. The eyes swung away to Irene, sitting at her desk.

Ros said: 'Let me show you how I recovered your Assassins files.'

She looked at Irene, to see what effect her words were having, but there was only a faint, ironic smile on the woman's face.

Ros turned to Marasco. 'Irene thinks I can't do this. What about you, Mr Marasco? She can't tell you what to do right now. How do you deprogram Ed's virus?'

Marasco looked at Irene, looked back at Ros, said nothing.

'OK,' said Ros. 'Here's the first thing I tried. This is a video record of the break-in that you paid my colleagues to do, Irene. You can see the connection machine in the background. Now watch that "City of Tiny Lights" –'

The two sailors were still holding on to Beckett when the third man returned with the rope. The ship was at full speed by now, the roar of the engines vibrating through the hull. If they weren't already in the open sea, they soon would be.

If I'm going to do something, thought Beckett, it's got to be now. He didn't reckon that his escapologist's skills were up to Ros's standards.

As the men changed their grip to get the rope around his wrists, Beckett moved. Not towards the door – the way they might have expected – but back, hard against the blank wall.

For a moment, their grip was broken.

Beckett reached for the red fire alarm handle at the top of the wall, pulled it down with all his strength.

The effect was more than he'd hoped. Not only did a siren start to wail and a red light flash in the cabin, but the ship jolted violently, flinging Beckett and the men forward. The sound of the engines faded and died.

Safety cut-out, Beckett decided. He was already scrambling over his captors, hitting out with his feet and fists.

He made it to the door before somebody tripped him. The man landed on top of him a moment later, but he was no expert fighter: Beckett knocked him out with a couple of coordinated punches to the jaw, scrambled free and headed for the foredeck.

There were shouts behind him. He glanced over his shoulder, saw the attaché pushing his way past the sailors, gun in hand.

He ran through the door into the bridge. The captain turned from the controls, shouted, but Beckett was past him, through the double doors behind the bridge, into an open lounge area.

It was empty, and the briefcase containing the virus was lying on a seat.

Beckett didn't wait to think about his good luck. He grabbed the case, ran out of the door, along a corridor.

He ran into a crewman, struggled for a moment, hit the man with a corner of the case. Ran on, down some steps, out onto the rear deck.

He stared for a moment at the wake of the ship, at the city receding behind them, towers gleaming in the low sunlight, a thin haze of smog.

A shot rang out, thudding into the deck ahead of him. He jumped forward, ran weaving across the deck.

Another shot.

Beckett reached the rail, hung the arm holding the

251

case over it. River water churned below.

There were footsteps on the decking behind him. Beckett turned, saw the attaché, the gun.

'It's over,' he told the man.

The attaché only smiled. 'If you drop the case into the water, how long before the glass breaks? How long before the virus gets into the air above the water? How many people will breathe that air? It will take years instead of weeks, but the end result will be the same. It will find its way home.'

Without warning, he fired at the case. The bullet missed, rang off the side of the ship.

'We can use the time to build cemeteries!' shouted the man.

With a shock, Beckett realised that this man, military attaché or not, was as insane as Cottrell and Elena had been. The only difference was that this madness was officially endorsed in his country.

There was another shot, which also missed. Then a metallic click.

Beckett recognised the sound, realised at once what had happened. The gun was empty. It would take a few seconds for the attaché to reload.

In that few seconds –

He saw the red emergency kit with its flotation buoy only a couple of metres away. Keeping the case over the rail, he moved towards it, sprung open the top.

The attaché moved towards him.

Inside the kit was a large, white flare gun, already loaded, ready for use in an emergency.

Beckett took the flare gun in his free hand, then, awkwardly one handed, sprung the catches on the case containing the virus and hurled it up into the air.

'Stop him!' The attaché's voice.

Beckett ignored the approaching footsteps, aimed the flare gun at the case.

Fired.

The flare exploded as it hit the case, dissolving the virus into a white fireball that slowly descended towards the water.

Gone. No longer a threat to anyone.

Beckett felt hands grab his arms. He kicked out, heard grunts of pain, felt the hands let go.

The attaché was shouting, 'Kill him!'

Beckett didn't wait to find out if the sailors would obey. He flung himself over the rail.

The water was shockingly cold.

Shots rang out behind him. He tried to ignore them and concentrated on swimming, on getting away from the currents around the ship. His clothes were heavy, but there was no time to get rid of them. He just swam.

He became aware of the roar of engines picking up speed again. He took a breath, looked back, saw the boat accelerating away. Salty estuarine water splashed in his face, stung his eyes.

It seemed a long way back to the shore, but there wasn't much he could do about that.

He kicked off his shoes and began swimming.

Ros watched as Marasco glanced from the wall screen image of the LED display, to the disc she'd brought with the data from the receptionist's desk, to the soot-blackened object in her hand.

'You got that from –'

Ros smiled. 'The warehouse. Yes. The one you torched.'

Irene opened her mouth, then glanced at the bomb and shut it again.

Ros put the disk drive on the desk in front of her.

'So, that gives me a total of three sources, all incomplete, but – put them together, and there should be enough data to reconstruct the files. Shall we see what happens when we merge them?'

She took an optical disc from her pocket, containing the results of the merging operation she'd already carried out. Loaded it into the main computer's access drive.

'Merge and run the Assassins files,' she told the system.

The video image disappeared from the wall screen, was replaced by huge quantities of scrolling binary data on the one side and the listing of the operating program on the other.

After a few seconds, Irene's silhouette appeared on the screen.

'Wait a minute!' said Marasco. 'Irene's voice is right at the head of this file! If you let it run it'll trigger the bomb!'

'Exactly,' said Ros fiercely. She turned to face Marasco. 'So tell me how to save Ed.'

Marasco hesitated.

Irene's face was forming over the silhouette.

This is cutting it fine, thought Ros.

'Stop!' shouted Marasco. 'Pause!' He was sweating, beads of the stuff trickling down his forehead and his cheeks.

Good, thought Ros.

'It's only recognising me,' she said.

'Then tell it to stop!'

'Then you tell me what I need to know.'

Irene's face had formed. She was raising her eyes, opening her mouth to speak.

'X-rays!' cried Marasco.

'Pause!' snapped Ros.

Just in time. The picture froze.

Marasco hesitated some more, glanced at Irene, sweated some more.

Ros let him sweat.

'The virus is programmed in a field of X-rays. One high intensity dose will convert it into a tailored antibody.'

Ros nodded, patted him on the shoulder.

'Well done, Mr Marasco.' She touched the switch on the connection machine that she'd set to toggle the locks, then marched out of the room.

At the doors, she turned, smiled at Irene, then looked at Roland. 'She's all yours, Mr Blatty.'

But Roland followed her out. As soon as they were out of earshot, he said, 'That was brilliant! Especially the business with the fake bomb.'

Ros turned to him, raised her eyebrows slightly.

'Fake?' she said.

The Managing Director looked at Marasco. Just looked at him.

She knew that Blatty would be back, now that he had the evidence he needed. The woman would have made copies of those files.

It was finished.

The cocoon of wealth. Cyberscope. Everything she was.

She looked at the coloured-glass screens, at the frozen image of her own face on the wall screen.

She looked at Marasco again.

Then she looked at the bomb, resting on the glass desk in front of her folded hands.

'I thought she might be telling the truth,' said the man desperately. 'I thought we shouldn't take any chances.'

The Managing Director stood, picked up the bomb.

'What was I supposed to do?' asked Marasco.

What indeed? thought the Managing Director. And what am I supposed to do now?

Her lips opened –

And she could see that Marasco knew.

Knew what he'd done to her. Made it so that she would never be comfortable again. Never be safe again.

So that she would have time to *think* about what she'd done.

She didn't want that.

And so the Managing Director said what she knew would probably be the last words she ever spoke.

'You could have lied,' she told Marasco.

A red light appeared on the bomb on her desk, and in that instant – the last instant of her life – Irene Campbell knew that Ros Henderson hadn't been bluffing.

And she was glad.

Glass shattered around them.

Sheets of it, breaking like glaciers. Ros flung herself to the ground, felt Roland do the same.

As the roar of the explosion faded away, glass settled, tinkling. Then was silent.

Ros picked herself up, carefully. A small piece of glass fell out of her hair.

Roland sat up, brushed himself down, then looked at her. It was clear that he didn't quite know what to say.

'An industrial accident?' suggested Ros, holding out a hand to help him up.

Roland took the hand and stood, glanced back at the shattered remains of the Managing Director's office.

'An industrial accident,' he agreed. 'And you never brought that bomb to my office. I never saw it.'

He began walking away towards the entrance of the building, treading carefully over the fallen glass.

« Thirty-two »

That was the trouble with celebrations, thought Ros. There was always the morning after.

Or in this case, the afternoon after.

There'd been a lot to celebrate: Ed's successful recovery from the Cyberscope virus after the X-ray treatment, Beckett's successful avoidance of pneumonia after his thousand metre swim in the river.

But even so, there had been a *lot* of champagne.

Ros looked around the living space of Gizmos, still cluttered with the dead bottles and plates full of the remains of nibbley things. A pocket games machine thrummed and cackled beside one of the plates, running through its demo routine. The guys had found it in the warehouse somewhere. Ros hadn't even known she had it.

The guys.

Actually, where were the guys?

They'd said they were going out to get some lunch in, hadn't they? Or was it breakfast?

Anyway, they'd been gone a long time.

'Guys, where are you?' she asked aloud. Then she decided it might be a good idea to phone them and ask.

She stood up, looked around the room again, this time with a definite object in mind: the phone.

She couldn't see it. There was the base unit, right next to the mobile phone, but she couldn't see the handset anywhere. Had one of the guys taken it into another room?

She got as far as the door before she twigged. Mobile phone.

If the mobile was sitting here, there was no point in ringing the guys on it because the guys didn't have it with them.

Damn.

Then she thought of something. The RaSearch. As far as she knew it was still in Beckett's car. Which meant that she could use the search signal as a source.

She made her way to the workshop, found the audio RaSearch unit, switched it on. Through the headphones, she heard a blip, then an electronic voice giving her the frequency, direction and estimated distance of the signal.

The frequency was the mobile RaSearch unit all right. But a hundred metres? That had to be in the car park.

But they had taken the car. She remembered Ed rattling the keys, saying it was a good job someone had stayed de-alcoholised.

A cold, sober feeling crept in to Ros's brain. If they hadn't left the car park and they'd been gone for hours then –

She got up, took off the headphones, ran out into the hallway.

The front door was open.

Someone had opened it while she'd had the headphones on.

Case closed, Beckett had said, when they'd dried him out from his swim.

Obviously not.

Footsteps were approaching the front door, a slow, measured tread. Ros retreated, as quietly as she could, towards the living room.

An intake of breath. A voice: 'Careful, a little to the left here.'

Ed's voice.

What the –?

Ros ran out into the hallway again, looked down the staircase and saw Ed and Beckett. They were hunched down, carrying something in a large cardboard box. It obviously weighed a ton.

She laughed, from sheer relief.

'What have you two been doing?' she asked, when she'd recovered. 'And what's that?' They were halfway upstairs with the box now.

'It's for you,' grunted Ed.

For the first time, Ros noticed that there was a pink silk ribbon tied around the box.

'You've got me a present? Really, guys, there's no need.'

'Careful!' gasped Beckett, to Ed. 'Don't let it drop out of the box!'

Ros stared at them. It must be *heavy*. 'What is it?' she asked as they reached the hall.

'Take a look,' said Ed.

Slowly, carefully, the two men lowered the box to the floor. Ros began to undo the pink ribbon.

'It's not much of a present, really,' Beckett said. 'More a case of lost property.'

Ros saw red paint – very distinctive red paint – and a thin yellow stripe along what must have been the door of . . .

'My beautiful car.' Ros didn't know whether to laugh or cry. Of all the stupid . . .

'We don't know what it was before,' Ed was saying,

259

'but now I reckon it's a compact.'

Ros gave him an oh-shut-up look, but Beckett was sniggering too. 'Let's face it,' he said. 'The car's probably better off like this, the way you drive.'

Ros tried to stare him down, then decided there was no point. She could easily have been in there, squashed with that cube of metal. At least she was alive.

She grinned, then started to laugh helplessly.

'Tell you what,' she said. 'It'll be a doddle to park.'

The phone rang.

Ros looked at Ed, then at Beckett.

'OK,' she said. 'This time, guys, I answer it.'

She looked around, located the handset behind the television. She picked it up and said hello.

A woman's voice spoke. 'I understand that you have particular expertise in certain areas of technology.'

'Yes. We can handle anything from bugging a phone to debugging a mainframe.'

'Do any of you have any experience with aircraft?'

'Aircraft?' Ros looked at Ed. 'Sure. What sort?'

'Civil aircraft.'

Ros signalled at Ed, who nodded and said, 'I can fly anything.'

The woman must have heard Ed's remark, because she said, 'In that case, I think I might have a job for you.'

BUGS – The TV Series

This book is based on two episodes of the TV series BUGS: 'Out of the Hive' written by Duncan Gould from a story by Brian Clemens, and 'Assassins Inc.' written by Stephen Gallagher. These episodes were first broadcast on BBC1 on 1 April and 8 April 1995. They were directed by Brian Farnham and Ken Grieve respectively.

Producer – Brian Eastman
Co-Producer – Stuart Doughty
Production Designer – Rob Harris
Script Consultant – Colin Brake
Executive Producer for the BBC – Caroline Oulton

BUGS is a Carnival Films production.

Read the full story in Virgin's non-stop action novels

Available from all good book shops!